Praise for *It Might G*

What you get is a cacophony of realities. *It*
clamorous story that mixes the unmitigated p
and spirits and mysteries, into the prosaic lives of the two main characters ...
Intelligent, boundary shifting and unafraid of itself
– Karin Schimke, *Business Day*
Fierce truth-telling ... continuously exhilarating – Patrick Lenahan

Praise for *The Road of Excess*

A fascinating and meditative read, and Winterbach's narrative is exquisite,
the prose as rich and textured as a 1980s velvet painting – *Business Day*
A profoundly engaging and exhilarating read – Jane Rosenthal, *Mail & Guardian*
Winterbach's writing is delight without respite – Michael Titlestad,
The Sunday Times

Praise for *The Book of Happenstance*

Witty, allusive and beautifully crafted, this is one of
the gems of recent South African fiction – Ivan Vladislavić
An intelligent literary mystery ... Winterbach's characters are rich, her story
foreboding and tense, and her prose remarkably lean – *Publishers Weekly*, UK

Praise for *To Hell with Cronjé*

I doubt that this book could have been written in the cosy Netherlands.
You would have to go to Australia for Patrick White's *Voss*, or to the Arizona
of Cormac McCarthy's *All the Pretty Horses*. And to South Africa for *Niggie*
(*To Hell with Cronjé*) – *Brabants Dagblad*, The Netherlands
Winterbach's writing sets the mood brilliantly, and she pitches her blend
of characters perfectly to create an uneasy, occasionally frightening feel to
her narrative – *Belletrista*, USA

Praise for *The Elusive Moth*

The language of the novel is simple, but rich and suggestive – Margaret Lenta,
The Sunday Independent
Winterbach's ear for language is acute, while her sense for linguistic
irony is delicious – James Mitchell, *The Star*

Ingrid
Winterbach

THE SHALLOWS

Translated by MICHIEL HEYNS

Human & Rousseau

This translation was made possible by a generous grant from the
LW Hiemstra Trust – established by Riekie Hiemstra in memory
of Ludwig Wybren (Louis) Hiemstra.

Copyright © 2017 by Ingrid Gouws
English translation © 2017 by Michiel Heyns
First published in 2017 by Human & Rousseau,
an imprint of NB Publishers,
a division of Media24 Boeke (Pty) Ltd
40 Heerengracht, Cape Town, South Africa

First published in Afrikaans in 2015 as *Vlakwater*

Cover design and typography by Michiel Botha
Cover images by Shutterstock
Photograph of author by Brenda Veldtman
Set in 11.5 on 16 pt Caslon
Printed and bound by Creda Communications,
Eliot Avenue, Epping II, 7460

ISBN: 978-0-7981-7429-9
ISBN: 978-0-7981-7430-5 (epub)
ISBN: 978-0-7981-7431-2 (mobi)

For Lou-Marié Kruger

One

The time there was sacred. That is how I see it in retrospect. (Is sacred a word commonly occurring in my vocabulary? No.) Whatever happened before or after, that time was sacred. Sacred! I'll never forget it. It's engraved on my heart. It was cold. It was raining that day when Willem Wepener and I went to view Jacobus' body. (You didn't want to go along. You don't want to remember him like that, you said.) In the reception area of the undertakers there was a large reproduction of a lioness with her cubs, also several examples of wreaths and two receptionists with expressions of permanent piety. A man took us through the building, out by the back door, through puddles of rainwater, to a small back room (hardly designed for the viewing of bodies). A transparent dark-green chintz Mr Price curtain against one wall. A cement floor, cold. There Jacobus lies, in his coffin. God, as still as death! On Willem's face an expression of unspeakable sorrow. For a long time he stands motionlessly gazing at the body.

I spend the first night with you so that you won't have to be on your own. Willem prepares food. He comes in from outside, half-frozen, with provisions. His cheeks are pale, there are dark rings under his eyes. We sit huddled together around the dining-room table. The food and the wine console us. Late at night I shower and at last, half-drunk, crawl between the ice-cold sheets. The day breaks dismayingly soon. I'm still clinging to the night. My first thought: Nothing will ever bring him back. A sacred time, engraved on my heart for ever.

In the course of my life I've done irresponsible things. I have at times been dishonest and unfaithful. But I am loyal to those I love. Willem and I are standing in the little back room. With the back of my hand I touch Jacobus' cold cheek. The flesh does not respond. I touch my fingers lightly to his chest, just below the tip of the breastbone. The flesh feels like clay. It's as if my fingertips are still primed for the slightest indication of life – the tiniest undulation of the chest – and as if my fingers cannot comprehend the absolute immobility of the body. Next to me Willem stands motionless; I have never seen him so un-moving. For him touching is taboo, he says. He just stands gazing with the expression on his face of unspeakable sorrow.

*

I was born with a cleft palate and a harelip. I have a broad, flattish nose, a narrow forehead and hair as abundant as that of a Catholic saint. During the sixth to tenth week of pregnancy the bones and sutures of the upper jaw, nose and mouth are supposed to knit, to form the palate and upper lip. When that does not happen, the baby is born with a cleft palate and a harelip. I suspect that I was an unwanted pregnancy, and that my mother had tried to abort me during the embryonic phase. I was never told this in so many words, it is something I discerned intuitively. On account of the cleft palate and harelip I couldn't drink properly as a baby and I had trouble learning to talk. As a result I was a furious and frustrated child. Which didn't make it any easier for my mother – nineteen years old, with an unwelcome, unprepossessing baby, and a girl on top of that. I was operated upon. The cleft palate was repaired. But the scar of the corrected harelip is more prominent than it should be. People of both sexes find me sexually either irresistible or repulsive.

After Jacobus' death I packed my bags, let my house, and left for a while. I could not stand staying on in a town where mountain and tree alike are indifferent to every human vicissitude.

Two

The girl came to call him one morning.

There's a pig in the garden, she said.

Side by side they stood on the stoep contemplating the creature. A big, black pig serenely grazing. Just as well he hadn't started gardening yet.

Where did she think it came from? Where would it have found its way into the yard?

She didn't know. (Although for some reason he thought she did know, but didn't want to tell.)

Didn't she want to take a photo, for her portfolio?

No. She didn't photograph pigs. Pigs were bad luck.

Says who?

The people where she came from.

What kind of bad luck?

That she couldn't tell. Any kind.

Like what? he persisted.

She didn't want to say. It was bad luck to talk about bad luck, she said.

She believed that?

She wasn't going to take any chances.

This morning he found her pretty, this girl with the abundant hair and the soft, tea-coloured skin.

They say pigs are very intelligent, he said.

So is the devil, she said.

Oh yes, he said, and did she believe in the devil?

She said nothing, just smiled slightly. (He suspected she was pulling his leg.)

Later the pig lay down in the shade of a shrub. Perhaps a suitable subject for a painting, but he was no painter of pigs, or people. The new house still had a chaotic feel to it. The sitting room was filled with unemptied boxes. He remained conscious of the pig in the garden, in the shade. He hadn't yet tried to find the place next to the fence where it might have got in.

In the late morning someone appeared at the gate. A man. He'd come to collect his pig, he saw it lying in the garden. The man had a big, open, attractive face. Amiable. Trusting. Tanned.

He didn't know one was allowed to keep pigs in a residential area, said Nick.

He had a big plot, up there, against the mountainside, he gestured with his shoulder.

'Marthinus Scheepers,' he said, extending his hand.

'Nick Steyn.'

The man's grip was firm. Probably needed to be, to keep pigs in check.

'Come by sometime,' said Marthinus, 'come meet the other pigs.' (He uttered a short, cheerful chuckle.)

There was something about the man. The big, harmoniously sculpted head and features. A noble face. Had something gone wrong, was he feeding with the pigs now?

'Does the pig have a name?' Nick asked.

'President Burgers,' Marthinus said. 'Primus inter porcos. A true leader. A pig of destiny.'

'I see,' said Nick.

Man and pig departed. Almost near-neighbours. He'd have to go and see. Something about the man, something about the pig. Both with something distinguished about them? Both of them noble of countenance and harmonious of proportion.

*

Nick had recently bought this house in Tamboerskloof. He didn't work there, was renting a studio in Observatory for the time being. Well out of Stellenbosch, that hotbed of complacency; a fresh start, after the breakdown of the relationship with Isabel. He'd hardly moved in, when a girl knocked at his front door one morning. She'd heard that he had rooms to rent. Where had she heard that? From the woman at the gallery. He'd hardly even breathed the possibility of rental, and already there was a potential lodger on his doorstep. The girl was wearing black velvet trousers, scuffed boots, a baby-blue fleece top that looked like a pyjama top. Her hair curled and twirled wildly around her head as if she'd just hitchhiked here on dusty roads. Her eyes were alert. Her name was Charelle Koopman. She didn't look much older than twenty. She was doing a photography course at the Peninsula Academy of Art. This was her first year. She took her studies seriously. Where was she from? he asked. From the West Coast, Veldenburg. But she'd been in Cape Town since the previous year. The next day she moved into the spacious back room.

And now, suddenly, one day, there was a man with a pig in his front garden. His father and a nephew of his had bought a few pigs between them way back: Large Whites, if memory served. His father was working in Johannesburg and had the pigs looked after on his sister's farm in the Roossenekal district. Something befell the pigs. He couldn't remember what. The pigs were big and beautiful and his father had animatedly demonstrated how high they stood and how they gleamed with fat, and then something happened. Was there anybody left alive who would know what had happened? There had to be someone who knew what had befallen the pigs.

Nick's sister and his eldest brother wouldn't know, because they were, as far as he was concerned, write-offs. His sister a heart surgeon sweeping through the wards of some academic hospital, teams of white-clad underlings bearing beating hearts on ice in sterile containers hot on her heels. She wouldn't have time for pig memories. His eldest brother was a tycoon. Well, good for him. The past was not part of his frame of reference either. The only one who would have known – his other brother, five years older than he – wrote himself off big time on a motor bike in Namibia. Smuggling diamonds. (Who was to know?) His hero and tormentor. Nick was the youngest. Sickly child, everybody thought he was retarded. He led a secret life, his fantasies riding roughshod over him. Horrendous nightmares, visions of hell at a tender age; dreamt Bosch before he saw his work. Slid around on his belly in the garden like a snake or a snail, looking for something he couldn't find at eye level. What the hell, he'd eat worms if need be. His sister did have a soft spot for him; eldest brother blinkered like a horse headlong on his way to tycoon-dom. That left Nick with smuggler brother, his hero. Smoking buddies, drinking buddies, porno-mag buddies and he barely older than ten, twelve. Brother wiped his arse on the world and was irresistibly charming on top of it. He made Nick draw. All positions. Brother was the first person who recognised Nick's ability. Nick was a slow developer, and it was only when everybody else stopped growing that he shot up. Asthma, ringworm and pox could no longer hold him back. First he wanted to become a rugby player, then a bomber pilot. Become an artist, said his brother. Painters are sissies, said Nick. Brother showed him a photo of Jackson Pollock energetically at it. Does that look like sissy-work to you? (In the brother's eyes it also counted in Pollock's favour that at forty-four, drunk, he had written himself off spectacularly in a car.)

Nick found dark women most attractive, but when it came to getting down and dirty he'd always preferred blondes. Strong calves, legs slightly bandy. Gap between the front teeth. Expression somewhere between brain-dead and horny. For god's sake just not wholesome blondes. Slightly off, slightly slutty and clapped-out. The vacuous, dreamy gaze at parties after twelve. As far as sex was concerned? By his mid-thirties he'd had enough of it to last him two lifetimes. Up to and including his short-lived marriage. And after that, after his failed marriage, his relationship with Isabel for the last seven years. Her hair as white as flax and her skin honey-coloured in summer. Heavy eyelids, a languid gaze, a tentative smile. Her back and limbs long and narrow, like those of a Cycladic funerary idol.

*

One morning when he was backing out his car on his way to work, he came across Marthinus Scheepers on his morning walk. No pig at his heels.

Marthinus was wearing a kind of Peruvian woollen cap, a snazzy tracksuit bottom, strange boots and a brightly coloured windbreaker. He greeted Nick cordially. Come by this evening, he said, come and watch a video with us.

That afternoon Nick found a postcard in his postbox. It was a reproduction of El Greco's portrait of Vincenzo Anastagi. The message on the back read: *Any extra copies of* The Shallows? *V.S.*

V.S., would you believe it?! Could only be Victor Schoeman. A South African stamp. Posted here, then. This did not bode well. Did it mean that Victor was in the country? When last had they seen each other? (And that, come to think of it, went for Blinky, and Chris Kestell, and Marlena as well?!) Did he have any desire to resume contact with Victor? No. The extra copies of *The Shallows* that he'd stored for years, he'd had pulped when he heard nothing more from Victor. Why should he get stuck with the debt *and* the boxes of books?

Good choice of postcard, Victor, he thought. The El Greco was one of his favourite paintings. He'd last seen this painting in the Frick with Isabel, on their final, fatal trip together, shortly before the end of their relationship, in November the previous year. Not that he'd been all that keen to visit the Frick (had by and large had his fill of Western painting), but for her it had been a trip fraught with meaning, a kind of pilgrimage perhaps. And there in the Frick she'd suddenly pressed her hands to her ears (why not her eyes, he'd wondered), gone in great haste to claim her coat from the cloakroom, and run away (he couldn't describe it in any other way). He'd followed, into the cold streets, a freezing wind (as if from Siberia) on their cheeks and wet snow in the streets. He managed to lure her into an Oriental museum and teahouse, where he could calm her down with a delicate snow pea and shrimp soup and tea from little Japanese earthenware teapots. Some colour returned to her cheeks. (I can't any longer, he thought, I *can't* carry you any longer, it takes too much out of me.) She cheered up so much that later she was even exuberant, flirtatious, but the day had been spoiled for him. He was morose; he no longer wanted to be charmed by her. Forgive me, she said, I don't know what's wrong with me.

Three

Your lover, and my beloved friend. You were speechless with grief, your cheeks cold as alabaster. A month or so later I packed my bags and left. I should have stayed, I should have stood by you, but if I stayed, I thought, I'd perish. After Jacobus' death there was a short circuit in my head, I had to betake myself to some other environment, or perish.

We get together only at the beginning of the new year in the coffee shop, after your return from your long, extended travels. The coffee shop has a dark interior. How glad I am to see your dear face once again. I take your face in my two hands and I say: It's been such a long while that we haven't seen each other! We gaze into each other's eyes long and feelingly. We sit down at a little corner table. Outside it's been raining incessantly since the previous day. Now at last we're both back in town, I say. You have no plans to leave again? No, I don't have any such plans. And how do you find it, being back? you ask. I don't know, I say. You know how ambivalent I am about the town. I had an aversion to the place for so long. I have it still, at times very intensely. Aversion or fear? you ask. Perhaps a bit of both. While I was away, I often thought that I didn't want to come back.

The waitress brings our coffee. We are both silent for a while. How are you? I ask. You don't reply immediately, keep your gaze lowered. Move a grain of sugar around on the table with your finger. Things have never been the same again, you say softly. Everything has changed subtly but inexorably. Not quite drowning, but with the solid ground caved in under your feet. Could it ever be different again – doesn't time bring change? I ask; or so they say, in any case. Maybe, maybe not, you say, how would you know? At the moment it doesn't feel as if it could ever be different again.

Again we fall silent, and listen to the rain falling gently but persistently. And your trip, I ask, did it make any difference? It provided temporary diversion, you say, though you sometimes think you should have stayed and faced out your grief. That could perhaps have hastened the healing process.

I've started writing a monograph on the Olivier brothers, I say. You've been planning to do it for a long time, you say. Yes, but it's taken me a long time to get going, I say. There are few people in the coffee shop, the interior is dark, sound is muffled by the incessant rain outside. I hope to be granted an interview with the brothers' father, with Marcus Olivier, but it's not that easy.

We sit in silence for a while, listening to the rain. Drink our coffee. Then abruptly you look up and ask, what are you to *do*?

*

When we get up to leave, I feel slightly light-headed, whether with joy or dismay or general disorientation is not clear to me. We take our leave. I don't feel young, I don't feel old. It is high summer, in the streets the foliage is dense, the shadows sharp after the rain.

I am reading a book in which the deceased Fernando Pessoa visits one of his alter egos (and heteronyms), Ricardo Reis. Reis has recently moved into an apartment after his sojourn of more than two months in the Hotel Bragança, and this is his first night in his new abode; it's cold, he's hardly dropped off when somebody knocks. It's Pessoa. Reis invites him in, they talk for a while, then Pessoa says Reis should lie down again, he doesn't want to keep him from his sleep. Reis lies down, Pessoa tucks in the sheet over him as solicitously as a mother. Reis asks him to switch off the light. Initially the room is dark, then the light from outside seeps in through the chinks in the shutters. Reis closes his eyes and murmurs: Good night, Fernando. It seems to him as if it takes Pessoa quite a while to reply: Good night, Ricardo. Pessoa sits down on a chair in the room, crosses one leg over the other, places his hands on his knee. He is the very image of desolation. Reis wakes up in the middle of the night, the rain has stopped, the earth hurtles on through the utter silence of space. Pessoa is still sitting in the same place, in exactly the same posture, his face expressionless. Reis goes back to sleep. When he wakes up in the morning, Pessoa is no longer there. He must have left at first light.

Initially it rains incessantly in the city, Lisbon. A carnival festivity features a figure dressed in a tight black outfit with a skeleton painted on it in white. Dancing bones. At times I have a yen to dress myself in such a suit. On my bedside table is the skull of wire and white beads that I had made in the Eastern Cape by Zimbabweans. At night it keeps watch over me like Fernando Pessoa over his alter ego, Ricardo Reis.

Four

One morning a week after the pig episode Nick walked up the hill to Marthinus' place. He wanted to inspect the set-up there. The idea of pigs interested him. Perhaps he should also acquire a pig, to compensate for the loss of his father's pigs, the Large Whites.

Down the street, and then two blocks further along, towards the top of the hill (surprisingly close), he came upon the house. Whereas his house faced the sea squarely, with the mountain behind him, here the mountain was to the right and the sea to the left of Marthinus' house. The house was set fairly far back, high up, with a staircase that ran all the way from the front gate to the wide stoep. There was a sign fixed to the gate: *This property is patrolled by pigs.* Not a pig in sight. The front garden, not very big, was terraced on both sides of the staircase. These terraces were planted with flowers and vegetables. Everything here testified to the hand of a dedicated gardener.

The house had been maintained as meticulously as the garden. In its day it must have been a stately home – large, dignified, with the wide front stoep.

On the stoep a woman sat reading. A Malay beauty, dark eyes, slightly sallow complexion. In the corner of the stoep a little boy was playing. Marthinus is at the back, the woman indicated with her head. He must be working in the garden. Nick could just walk straight through the house.

The passage was wide. The ceiling was high. The house smelt of floor polish and wood. A large house; four or more rooms, two on each side of the long passage. He had to cross the sitting room to get to the kitchen. The room was tastefully furnished. Cosy. Large sofas, easy chairs, fine old fireplace. Nguni hides on the floor. On the shelf above the fireplace were a beadwork buck, a bowl of lemons, two small figurines. Earthenware pots with plants on one windowsill. A bundle of dry laundry on one of the sofas, a few glasses and mugs standing around on the coffee table. Books and newspapers. The kitchen was tidy. A woman's hand clearly in evidence here. Table scrubbed clean. No dirty dishes standing around.

From the narrow back stoep steps led down to the garden. It extended far back, it seemed to be a large plot. The garden here was equally lush and well maintained, with plants in pots, beds with herbs, a small lawn, a pergola, and half-concealed behind tall shrubs, the pigsties in the furthest back corner. Five pigs were grazing in the garden. Marthinus had in the meantime spotted Nick, and came walking up, rake and secateurs in his hands. He welcomed Nick cordially. Come, he said, he'd make them some tea.

Two little mugs were neatly set out on the tray, with doily. Sugar bowl, milk jug, rusks in a bowl. (Everything very domestic, quite different from his own set-up, Nick could see, which was empty and chaotic at the same time.) He wondered why he was surprised – what had he expected – a pigsty because Marthinus dealt with pigs?

A strong wind had come up suddenly, the little boy who'd been playing on the stoep was now watching a children's programme on the large flatscreen television set in the other corner of the sitting room, and Marthinus suggested that they might as well have their tea in his bedroom. His room was spacious and crepuscular. Wooden floors, high ceiling. Bed in one corner, wooden table under the big window facing the mountain. On the table an Apple laptop. Here, too, a Nguni hide on the floor. Two handsome Art Deco easy chairs and a leather armchair. Against one of the walls was a large built-in bookshelf, chock-a-block to the ceiling. Marthinus placed the tray on the large wooden table, pulled up the two easy chairs. Nothing scanty about this room.

'Who's living here with you?' Nick asked. (The tea was exceptionally good.)

'It's my house, but my friend Alfons rents part of it from me, he and his wife, Rosita, and his child, the little boy you saw in the sitting room.'

'Who is the gardener?' he asked.

'I am,' said Marthinus. 'I'm the chief gardener here, pig-herd, general janitor and houseboy – you could say.'

Which still did not give Nick a clear picture of Marthinus' position, or the nature of his work (there was clearly no shortage here). But, as if attracted by a magnet, his eye suddenly fell, in the over-stuffed bookshelf diagonally across from him, on a copy of *The Shallows*. Well, did you ever, so Marthinus actually had a copy of the book. The second time in a few days that he'd been reminded of Victor.

'I see you have a copy of *The Shallows*,' he said.

'Yes,' said Marthinus, 'oh Lord. That massive compendium of dissolution. Brilliant.'

'Did you ever know Victor Schoeman?' Nick asked.

'Yes,' said Marthinus. 'I knew him. Not well, but I knew him.' He rolled himself a cigarette. 'A tormented fellow, oh Lord. A man whose left hand did not know what his right hand was up to. Not a man to whom to entrust one's secrets. A destructive fellow if ever I met one.'

'I couldn't have put it better myself,' said Nick, laconically.

'And conflicted!' said Marthinus. 'Now *there* you have a psyche set up like two enemy factions against each other. Also not someone that you could – and that's an understatement – count on.'

'Did you ever know Blinky Booysen?' Nick asked.

'I *did*!' said Marthinus. 'What became of him?'

'Nobody knows,' said Nick. 'There are all sorts of stories.'

'Perhaps he and Victor went into exile together and started a business somewhere in Equatorial Africa.' He uttered his short, cheerful chuckle. 'Where they bamboozle the locals in every possible way. Mistahs Kurtz, they revived.'

'Unlikely,' said Nick. 'They couldn't stand each other.'

'Blinky,' Marthinus said meditatively. 'Made beautiful stuff. An exceptional guy.'

'Yes,' Nick said. 'Almost everything I know about painting I learned from him.'

'My goodness, really?!' said Marthinus, and regarded him for a moment with intensified interest.

'Coincidentally,' said Nick, 'I received a postcard from Victor Schoeman a few days ago in which he asks if I still have any extra copies of *The Shallows*. I stored the books for years in boxes in my garage. Schlepped them with me everywhere, truth to tell.'

'Do you still have these copies?' Marthinus asked.

'I got rid of the lot a few years ago, after hearing nothing from Victor for a very long time.'

'How long has Victor been out of the country?'

'For a long time, as far as I know,' said Nick. 'Late nineties. A while after the publication of *The Shallows*.'

'Where was the card posted?'

'It's not clear, but it's got a South African stamp.'

'Well, what do you know,' said Marthinus, 'that probably means that he's back in the country. So here he turns up again. That does not surprise me one bit. Putting out his feelers. Spadework. Count on it, he's got something up his sleeve. It wouldn't be Victor if he didn't have something up his sleeve.'

This was not what Nick wanted to hear at that moment. He did not want to hear that Victor was back in the country with something up his sleeve. When Victor left, he'd hoped never to see him again. And in the years of Victor's absence, Nick's judgement of him had not become more charitable. On the contrary.

Shortly afterwards he got up to leave. 'Keep me informed of Victor's moves, and come and watch DVDs some evening,' Marthinus called after Nick as he saw him off at the garden gate.

Victor Schoeman's first novel was published in the early eighties by Dogshit, a small underground publisher. (Nick was still at art school at the time.) The book was banned. In the late eighties his much more ambitious novel, *The Depths*, was published. Highly experimental, with black pages, pages with only dialogue, interspersed with pastiches of several canonical Afrikaans texts.

In the mid-nineties Victor wrote his last great novel – *The Shallows*. According to him, the second of a projected trilogy, of which *The Depths* was the first. A dystopian, futuristic novel. An apocalyptic crossbreed of the historical South African past, a massively exaggerated present, and a science-fictional future. A piling-up of depravities, anxieties, political anarchism, corruption, maladministration, opportunism, inter-woven with elements of the Great Trek, Border Wars, miners' strikes, nuclear power disasters, religious fundamentalism, folk music, rappers, diamond diggings, imbongis, white and black tycoons, witchdoctors, muti murders. Satanism and satanic rituals. Large sections of the arbitrary action took place in a gigantic cemetery. A kind of heroes' acre, amidst the graves of heroes of the Anglo-Boer War and the Struggle. There was desecration of these graves. There were (as in *The Depths*) cannibalism and necrophilia. Eruptions of communal violence, overcrowded mortuaries, widespread mother-and-child mortality as a result of famine and poverty in the former homelands, pages with in-ventories of ministerial transgressions and abuses – among others the illicit appropriation of land, of tenders. Synodic sodomites. All of this jumbled together with astonishing technological advances: flying motor cars, robots as servants. Factions in the countryside perpetually at war, groups doggedly clinging to tradition; ancestor worship; prophets and prophecies. Communication with the dead.

No publisher would touch it. Victor was obliged to have it printed and distributed at his own expense. Nick invested a hefty sum in the project. And could he, while he was about it, store the boxes of books with Nick, please, from where he, Victor, would then dispatch them to people on order.

When, after a year and a half, sales were still not up to expectations (few people could stomach that inventory of debaucheries) and the feedback was less rapturous than Victor had anticipated, he cleared out. From one day to the next Victor had vanished.

*

Nick's friend Blinky Booysen was short, chunky, permanently per-spiring, slit eyes, slit mouth, flared nostrils. A rat-face – sly, pointed and smirking at the same time. Outrageous work – shocking, scandalous. Fantastic. Blinky's studio was also a large loft in an industrial building, near a railway track, in one of the grimy Dickensian buildings near Nick's in the vicinity of Cape Town station. In his studio everything was filthy – years of accumulated soot and dust. There he painted his large canvases and they were, Lord knows, miracles. Blinky was a neo-expressionist and a disciple of Trotsky's.

When Nick returned to the Cape after his army training Blinky was dead, or had disappeared. Nobody could inform Nick definitely on this point, and he was no longer in touch with Marlena Mendelsohn, Blinky's constant companion.

*

Blinky had organised Nick's working space for him. Like Blinky's studio, it was cold and soot-bemired, full of birdshit (pigeons in the open rafters), but it was big. Blinky's companion, Marlena Mendelsohn (platonic companion, as far as Nick could make out), was embarked on a master's degree in psychology, or history of art, or both at the same time, he never knew exactly. Because Blinky's studio was close to Nick's, she sometimes came to sit with him in his studio. She was a source of abstruse information. In the twentieth century, she said, monochromatic work was originally associated with the dawning of the radically reductive painting of the Russian avant-garde. (Nick at that stage had a preference for tonalities of grey.) She sat on the only chair (plastic) in his studio and drank her tea. In summer she wore short dresses and in winter a jersey full of holes, of which the sleeves were too long. She had high insteps, narrow feet, and bony, boyish knees. The delicate bones of her ankle (the lower parts of the tibia and fibula, where they join the little bones of the foot) were perfectly proportioned.

She said: Don't look only at contemporary art. Look at the older stuff. Look at Matthias Grünewald's Isenheim altarpiece. See if there's anything in contemporary art to equal the intensity of it. The demon in *The Temptation of St Anthony*. St Anthony himself, with his suppurating sores and hideous abscesses. The afflicted demon suffering from St Anthony's fire in the lower left-hand corner of the *Temptation*. Nick's use of grey interested her. She pointed out the greys in the work of Goya and Manet. She was blonde. Her apparent dissipation was just a defence. Her eyes were an indeterminate grey-green, dreamy, and eternally fixed on something just behind him. She pointed out to him how he held himself back in his work. She showed him how grey was the colour of denial and resistance.

Grey, Marlena said, is inert, it's neutral. Black and white have too much baggage. Black has too many mystical associations. White has too many modernist associations of purity and transcendence. Grey is the only anonymous, the least personal colour. Juan Gris, she said, changed his name to John Gray, to be as anonymous as possible. Grey didn't stimulate, it was perceptually motionless. Giacometti almost went mad, she said, with a mug of tea in her hand, her legs crossed (in itself something to drive you mad), and grey was an escape. Already so tormented by anxiety, Giacometti nearly went off his head while painting the portrait of Isaku Yanaihara. He had not succeeded in capturing the image of his sitter, compulsively reworked the areas, until larger and larger undefined areas of grey appeared in the work. Sartre said about the six variations of these Yanahaira portraits that they represented the existential conflict between being and nothingness. The colours had fallen away one after the other, Giacometti said, and all that had remained was grey, grey, grey. Nothing envelops the figure, said Sartre, nothing contains him, he is isolated in the immense boundlessness of the void.

When Nick returned after his army training, Blinky was gone – he'd either committed suicide or simply vanished. Nobody could inform Nick definitely on this point, and he was no longer in touch with Marlena Mendelsohn. There was some talk that she'd begun a relationship with Victor Schoeman.

*

The girl renting the room from him was a hard worker. She was mysterious about what she was working on. He didn't want to enquire too closely. They did not see each other often. She was the ideal lodger. Quiet, tidy in the kitchen, she had her own bathroom. They sometimes bumped into each other in the kitchen in the late afternoon, when she made herself a cup of coffee. All that he knew about her was that she'd come to Cape Town to do a photography course at the Peninsula Academy of Art. He hadn't asked to see her portfolio. Kept his distance. Other things on his mind at the moment.

Is her room large enough for her to work in? he asked.

Oh yes, she said. She'd never had so much space to herself.

Five

Late one afternoon, a few days after receiving the postcard, Nick was returning from his studio, where he'd been working all day. As he pulled up at his gate, a car with tinted windows drove by slowly, stopped next to him, a window was wound down, and a string of obscenities was hurled at him. Then the car accelerated and drove off.

Nick hurried into his house. It was unpleasant. He had no idea why he should have been targeted in just this fashion. The house was eerily silent. He had a sudden feeling of foreboding. His lodger had said she was going away for the weekend, perhaps she'd returned by now. She'd said she was going to take photos somewhere. She'd left here with a woman, a Desirée somebody, a tall, thin woman with a turban round her head. Not very friendly. In the kitchen there were a cup and a side plate in the drying rack (always considerate – she never left a crumb anywhere, washed up everything the moment she'd used it). That meant she was back.

He lingered indecisively in the passage leading to her room. Her weekend bag was standing in the passage and her door was ajar. He wouldn't do it normally, but he went up to the half-open door. He knocked gently, called her name. No reply. He knocked again, more loudly. No reply. He pushed the door open further and peered into the room.

The curtains were drawn. Charelle was lying on the floor, on her stomach, her head turned awry, her cheek to the floor. 'My God, Charelle,' he exclaimed, and went on his haunches next to her, 'what happened?!' She opened her eyes slightly. A smear of bloody spittle dribbled from her mouth. She groaned. No blood on the floor or on her clothes, as far as he could see. She was wearing pyjamas, one leg had shifted up to her knee (delicate ankle and calf). No sign of any external injury. He didn't know what to do. He cautiously touched her upper arm. 'Charelle,' he said. She opened her eyes a bit wider this time. She didn't seem to recognise him. Should he phone an ambulance? She seemed to be breathing normally.

Very cautiously he tried at least to turn her on her back. He placed a pillow under her head. Apart from the blood-flecked foam in the corners of her mouth she seemed unharmed. She tried to sit up. He helped her up carefully, so that she could sit on the chair. Her hair frizzed up wild and dusty around her head. The wooden floor had left an imprint on her cheek. She still seemed not to recognise him.

'What happened?' he asked. 'Did somebody hurt you?' She licked her dry lips. 'Wait,' he said, 'I'll fetch you some water.' His hands trembled as he held the glass to her mouth. Her gaze was slow, as if she could not register him. She frowned slightly, her eyes oddly sleepy and unfocused, and then apparently all at once she recognised him.

'What happened, Charelle?' he asked, once she'd taken a sip of water. 'Are you okay?'

'A fit,' she said. 'I suffer from epilepsy.'

'Good Lord,' he said. 'And you were at home alone.'

'It's okay,' she said. She spoke slowly, as if her tongue were an encumbrance in her mouth.

'Should I take you to the doctor?'

She shook her head. 'It's okay.'

'I'll make us some tea,' he said, 'for the shock.'

She nodded.

His hands were still trembling as he made the tea. Tea with lots of sugar for both of them. He'd had a fright. He knew nothing about epilepsy. Should she sleep, should he try to keep her awake? What if she went into a coma?

He sat by her. They drank their tea. When she'd finished, she said she was tired, she was going to bed. She always slept after a seizure. He wanted to help her to lie down on the bed, but she said it was okay, she was used to it, she'd manage.

He went and lay on his bed. Uncertain what to do. Perhaps she shouldn't be left on her own after a fit.

That evening he heard her in the kitchen. She was wearing a dressing gown, she was moving slowly, a bit unsteadily, as if not quite trusting the ground under her feet. He forestalled her; I'm making us some tea, he said, sit down. She obeyed. They sat together at the kitchen table having their tea. For the second time today, he thought. At first they'd hardly seen each other, now they were taking tea together for the second time in a day. Her face was sleepy, her eyes still slightly unfocused, she looked as if she hadn't entirely recovered her wits. There was a bruise on her right cheekbone and her lower lip was swollen. Her hair was still curling wildly around her head.

'Is there anything in particular that causes such a fit?' he asked.

At first she just shrugged; anything, she said. Then she said, stress. Then she said: 'There's somebody after me. I think he was here this afternoon.'

'Who is it?' he exclaimed, shocked.

'Somebody,' she said. 'Somebody who can't take no for an answer. He was here with his friends.'

'In a black car with tinted windows?!' he asked.

She shook her head. She didn't know. She hadn't really noticed. He'd been at the gate. She didn't want to let them in. She'd had enough of his nonsense. Then he'd threatened her. Then they'd cleared out.

What time was that?

She didn't know. She hadn't noticed. Round about four o'clock. She'd only just arrived home. Desirée had dropped her here. She'd just dumped her stuff. Seen Nick wasn't here.

And when did she have the fit?

A while later. Five o'clock or thereabouts.

Chances were good, he thought, that the same fuckers who'd

pestered her had sworn at him. They might think she was living with him, that they were lovers or something.

She'd started feeling odd on Saturday already, she said, but she hadn't really taken any notice of it, because she hadn't had a fit for a long time, and she was enjoying the weekend.

Who is Desirée? he asked.

She was a friend of her older sister. She'd known her all her life. They came from the same town. She was teaching at the university, gender studies.

And the man who was after her?

Oh, he was just a nuisance guy. It was someone who'd fancied her for ever, from schooldays. But she'd never wanted to have anything to do with him.

He wasn't part of a gang or something, was he?

Maybe. She didn't know. She thought his friends might be skollies. Tik-heads, some of them.

Skollies, gangsters, tik-heads, what's the difference, he thought. All of them spelt trouble. For her, and perhaps for him as well.

'You must be careful,' he said.

She nodded.

At first she'd been just a girl renting a room from him, and now he felt – against his will – responsible for her safety.

Six

Two days a week Nick taught at a small private art school just outside Stellenbosch. He was substituting for one of the lecturers, a woman who'd suddenly had to take sick leave. He could have stayed on in the Stellenbosch house after he and Isabel split up, but he'd found the house and the town claustrophobic. There was nothing to keep him there any longer. The house had been sold. He'd bought the house in Cape Town; Isabel had gone her way. They were childless.

The students were mainly children of well-to-do parents. He didn't expect much of them; it was rare for a student to surprise him. This was just a temporary job he was doing. His heart was hardly in it.

The day was oppressive. It was hot. The heat had persisted without a break for four days now. In the last few days there'd been fierce mountain fires around Stellenbosch and in the Franschhoek valley. No wonder that tempers were getting frayed: the terrible heat, the wind, the strikes everywhere, bloody confrontations with the police, public unrest.

Today he had to discuss his students' projects with them. His first appointment was with one of the few students whose work interested him. The young man sat hunched up in his chair facing him, gazing fixedly at a point on the carpet. Spoke in a monotone. Long silences. He didn't like talking about his past, he said. Spent a lot of time on the streets. What he wanted to evoke was his happy childhood. He wanted to work in a variety of media: painting, drawing, sculpting, text and film. He slowly edged a file across the desk to Nick. Nick paged through it: images of headless seagulls, hotels with broken windows, a deserted sanatorium. A photo of a small wax figurine of a child, his eyes sealed with pins. (If these were memories of a happy childhood, he didn't want to know what the contrary would look like.)

All day long he was edgy with his students. The heat was torrid. The surrounding mountains were still burning. He thought he could smell smoke. The remote sound of helicopters, of sirens some distance away in town – fire engines or ambulances. He wanted to get away, he wanted to go and work in his cool studio. He'd had enough of students for a while. Most of them didn't belong here, they had too little talent and their parents too much money. They didn't know what they wanted to do, they weren't really interested, they were on their laptops and mobiles all day long and they talked like barbarians. He knew he was prejudiced, but he thought they looked stupid.

The last student he saw had hair piled on top of her head in a blonde nest and she was wearing black shorts so tiny that he thought he could see the fold of one of her hairless (waxed) labia. Shameless. But no, of shame and shameless she knew, to look at her, equally little – her countenance was as uninscribed, as unfilled-in, as if no experience had ever left its mark on it. Neither good nor bad. Ever been penetrated, he wondered, that little plucked pussy? She was like something that had just crawled out of an egg, of which the carapace was still soft. Although you never could tell with these kids. Behind that shallow gaze could lurk a lifetime of experience of which he had not the faintest inkling.

How old could she be, he wondered, eighteen, nineteen? And what was she planning to do for her semester project? he asked. She wasn't quite sure yet herself, actually. Her features were regular, her hair blonde, her limbs slender and well proportioned. Physically perfect, without the slightest visible flaw or defect. Was there perhaps a theme, a cause, that she took to heart (he asked wearily). He had to caution himself to be patient, not snide, not sarcastic, *patient* (the parents were paying a packet, the kid's emotions were tender and budding, vulnerable). He should try to nurture the meagre talent that there was; who knows, under the right – encouraging – tutelage something might blossom forth after all.

Yes, perhaps she'd like to do something on her doggies. What kind of doggies did she have? he asked. As in miniature poodles, she said. Poodles, he asked, or *as in* poodles? As in *poodles*, she said, with a little frown. (As in, what's his *case*? he thought.) What was she thinking of? he asked. (A scrapbook, perhaps? He had to restrain himself, be patient.) Was she thinking in terms of an installation, he asked, perhaps a video, a photo series, and from what theoretical perspective did she want to approach it – eco-criticism, the analysis of animal discourse that was so fashionable at the moment? (He knew he had to stop this. It was unfair, he could see a vague intimation of distress in her eyes, like a panic-stricken dog in water paddling to reach the opposite bank. Have compassion! he urged himself. She was a child, she wasn't responsible for the gaps in her education.)

No, she didn't actually know. Changed position uncomfortably on her chair, crossed one tanned, shaved leg over the other. She didn't think so. But there *was* something else that she actually felt quite strongly about.

And what was that?

Satanism.

Satanism, he said.

Yes, she said, she wanted to do something on satanism.

What aspect of satanism, Karlien? he asked. (Or was it Karla? He glanced surreptitiously at the register in front of him.)

She'd seen a photo in *You*, as in a place that they'd discovered in Joburg, you know? (Sing-song rhythm, where did the kids learn to *talk* like that?)

He'd have liked to send her on her way with the brief to go and look into the life and work of Ilya Kabakov, into his life under Soviet rule. See if you can understand any of it, he'd have liked to say. But that would have been pointless, the child had been brainwashed, her head was full of clichéd phrases, her imagination formed by Facebook images. He wanted to give her the brief to go and look at all the representations of devils in the Middle Ages, but the kids no longer knew what the Middle Ages were.

Bring photos, he said, bring any information, any pictorial matter and think of a format.

*

After terminating the conversation with the girl, he decided to go and drink something in town until the traffic had subsided somewhat. The town was bustling, he struggled to find parking; it was hot, he was irritated.

He ordered coffee, scanned the newspaper. An article on the misdemeanours of some cardinal. Of course the portrait of Cardinal Niño de Guevara is beautiful, Isabel had said, a miracle, and also the two Vermeers, and the Halses, especially the Halses, they were among the few paintings that she could still look at with pleasure, but would it have made any difference if she hadn't seen them? *He* could still delight in what the day had to offer, she'd said, whereas *she* could only think that at the end of this day she'd be a day closer to the end of their trip. Delight, he'd said bitterly, delight in what the day had to offer, what made her think that? She's sorry, she'd said, sorry sorry sorry.

Someone touched his shoulder lightly. He got such a fright that he actually spilled coffee in his saucer, because for a moment he thought: Chris – Chris Kestell! (Chris, of whom by chance he'd dreamt the night before. Chris Bitterbile, a friend of Victor Schoeman's.) The man had the same longish, greasy hair, the same large black-framed glasses and owlish gaze. The confusion lasted for only a moment.

Was the seat opposite him taken? the man wanted to know. The coffee shop was crowded, Nick was sitting at the single long table. Did he mind, the man asked, if he took the seat opposite him? Refusal was not an option, Nick was tired and tetchy, he didn't feel like chitchatting with a stranger, especially not now after briefly taking the man for Chris Kestell.

The man sat down opposite him. Nick carried on reading the paper. From the corner of his eye he could see the man's hands trembling while holding his cup of coffee. He got another fright, because Chris's hands had trembled just like that. Especially when he'd drunk more than usual the night before, or was embarking on some vehement diatribe (as was often the case). And even more than usual towards the end. Just before he topped himself. Trust Chris Kestell for a dramatic exit. Swallowed pills and a whole lot of alcohol, tied a stone to his leg, and drowned himself in the town dam. Ironic, because Chris had never wanted to set foot in water. Always sat on the edge with a bottle of liquor, nursing his foot fungus, hurling insults at the swimmers. Vigorously calling down obscenities upon their heads.

The man was watching him, noting when he turned a page. He clearly wanted to chat; Nick not. He hid behind the paper, but his peace of mind had been shattered. He couldn't have his coffee in peace when he knew somebody was watching him. He got up, greeted the man with a nod, paid, and went out into the glaring sun. It was still too early to drive home, the traffic was still too heavy. He went and sat in the bar around the corner, even though he didn't like the place. At least it was cool in there. As long as the man didn't follow him, and why would he?

But would you believe it, it wasn't long before the man came into the bar. This time he took a seat a little way along. Nick turned his back on him, but nevertheless got the creepy feeling that the man was watching him. This he did not like at all.

As he paid and left the bar, he found the man next to him. For a moment Nick was blinded by the bright sun. The man took him by the arm and said: 'Are you *sure* we haven't come across each other somewhere?' From close by the resemblance to Chris Kestell was considerably less marked than he'd thought at first glance. For a start, the man did not have Chris's mocking, ironic gaze. He seemed bewildered and one of his eyes strayed sideways as if on a mission. More than just a slight squint.

A bit repugnant. 'No,' said Nick, 'I'm sure we've never come across each other.' He curtly wished the man goodbye and started walking briskly to where he'd parked his car. The man kept up with him at a trot. 'Do you live in town?' he asked. 'No,' said Nick, by now convinced that the man had a screw loose somewhere. If not even a trifle retarded. Whereupon he quickened his pace and left the man behind, he hoped.

*

Marthinus had invited him for a beer after work. When he arrived, Marthinus was sitting on the stoep. He came to meet Nick with a mug of tea in one hand and a cigarette in the other. Beautiful view over the city from here.

He told Marthinus that his lodger had had an epileptic fit the day before.

'When I got home last night,' he said, 'I found her on the floor in her room.'

'Oh no!' Marthinus exclaimed. 'You should talk to her, people go into altered states before such a seizure.'

'The point is,' said Nick, 'that someone had threatened her just before. Someone who's been targeting her for a long time and that she doesn't want anything to do with. By chance a car stopped next to me when I got home and someone wound down the window and swore at me most foully.'

'That doesn't sound like chance,' said Marthinus. 'You have to be on the lookout. Keep your eyes and ears open. I have contacts. People who know what's happening in the neighbourhood. I can find out from them.'

'Did you know Chris Kestell?' asked Nick.

'I did!' said Marthinus. 'Weren't he and Victor hand in glove?'

'They were friends, yes,' said Nick. 'By the way,' he said, 'a man accosted me in Stellenbosch today – actually followed me at first. When

I saw him for the first time, I thought he was Chris's double. But from close up not that much like him after all. Still, it was creepy.'

Marthinus got up. 'Let me show you something,' he said. He returned with a small book. 'See what I came across by chance in a second-hand bookshop yesterday. Look!' he said, and lit a cigarette, 'check what's written in the front.'

Nick looked. The title was *A Biblical-sociological Justification for Racial Segregation in South Africa*, by Professor J.G. Kestell, Professor in Old Testament Exegesis, also Moderator of the Dutch Reformed Church in South Africa. In the front was written, in Afrikaans: *For Christiaan Gerhardus Kestell, from his grandfather, J.G. Kestell. Honour your God, your father, your leaders and your nation, and you will always walk in the light of righteousness.* Below that, in a large rounded childish hand: *This book belongs to Christiaan Kestell*, and the date: *15 July 1966.*

'What does this tell you about the childhood of Chris?' said Marthinus.

'The childhood of Chris,' said Nick in wonderment.

'Can you imagine what such a patriarchal injunction would do to the spirit of an intelligent, sensitive child, somebody who off his own bat had started questioning the status quo? Then to be confronted with this lunacy? His grandfather was a minister, his father was a minister. Both of them foursquare behind apartheid.'

'I did think that Chris had taken a bad knock somewhere,' said Nick faintly.

'But exactly!' said Marthinus. 'Here you have a possible key to Chris's deep psychic wounding. Not to mention his great undefined anger.'

'I suppose one could call it that,' said Nick, not sure whether the whole Chris-business interested him that much at the moment. He looked at the table of contents, paged through the little book. One of the chapters was 'Apartheid as vocation, the responsibility of the Stronger for the Weaker'. There were subsections such as 'Intra- and Extramarital miscegenation', and 'The infiltration of non-European blood'. In the conclusion racial apartheid was seen as the task of the European race, failing which, racial interbreeding would result.

'You must be right,' he said to Marthinus, 'that kind of thing could warp a sensitive child for life.'

*

When he turned into his street, Nick saw a black car slowly driving past his house. It seemed suspiciously like the car from which he'd been sworn at. Although he couldn't say for sure. He hurried into the house. He found Charelle in the kitchen. She was making tea.

'Was there somebody here?' he asked.

No, she said, surprised. She'd come home a while ago and there was nobody here. Could she make him a cup of tea as well? He collapsed into a chair, relieved. He suddenly felt surprisingly moved by this gesture of hers.

He watched her while she made tea. He found her pretty. She had dark eyes and dark eyebrows, and a largish nose and a resolute mouth and her teeth were irregular. (Money for orthodontic work there had probably not been.) And then, the soft, abundant, dense head of curly hair. Delicately built. He generally preferred more robust women, but he found her attractive. Amazing that an adult (he assumed she was older than eighteen) could have such slender childish wrists. He was grateful, touched that they could sit together at the kitchen table like this.

He did not want to bombard her with questions, but there was a good deal that he didn't know about her. He'd hardly had a proper conversation with her since she'd moved in. He didn't want to be pushy, he didn't want to spoil the new conviviality of their sitting there. She was shy, first of all he wanted to set her at ease.

How did she find her course?

She liked it. It was exciting.

Did she have any work to show him? (Immediately regretting that he'd asked it. Actually he wanted to be as little as possible involved with her life. With anybody's life.)

She'd be happy to show him. (Her face changed colour slightly. A dark blush.) She'd get her portfolio together. He could see that she wasn't entirely at her ease. He had just got up to make more tea, when the doorbell rang. At first he considered ignoring it. He didn't want to disturb their companionable togetherness. But the bell rang again. Twice. Emphatically. But when he opened the front door, there was nobody outside at the gate. He switched on the stoep light. Closed the front door again. How had the person who'd rung the bell managed to make such a quick getaway? He did not like this.

He went back into the house. 'Nobody,' he said. She said nothing. Looked down at her hands.

'This man who's stalking you,' he said, 'is he capable … do you have reason to be afraid of him?'

She shrugged. She didn't know. She thought his friends were a bad influence. And he was also thoroughly mixed-up in his head. But she didn't know. It depended on who he was hanging out with.

In what way was he mixed-up in his head? he asked.

He'd had this thing about her ever since schooldays, but she'd never been interested in him. He'd come to Cape Town to look for a job. But she didn't think he'd found one yet. She thought he was hanging out with tik-heads now.

Had she talked to him yet?

Not really since coming here. Just that once before she had the fit.

What had he said then?

He'd threatened her. (She looked down. Unwilling to talk.)

With what?

He'd said she wouldn't get away. He'd come after her until she went with him. If she didn't want to, he'd make her pay.

'You can't report him to the police?' he asked.

She shook her head. 'He's done nothing yet,' she said softly.

'So do you have to wait until he does do something?!' he asked.

She shrugged again.

The companionable atmosphere had been disrupted. Shortly afterwards she went to her room. He remained behind on his own at the kitchen table. Restless and disgruntled. That was how he'd sat at the table in their apartment in New York as well. Isabel had cried every morning. In the afternoon she hadn't talked at all. Later he'd been afraid for her, she was so doggedly desperate in her blue dressing gown. They'd had moments of silent closeness on the subway, in streets on their way to museums, but the thrill of New York had largely passed them by. A sullenness had come over him. Nevertheless he'd still desired her at times. Desired her intensely. He'd wanted to blast open her blue dressing gown and stoke her like a furnace. Until she spontaneously burst into flame and they were consumed by it. In the museums only Oriental art had retained its appeal for him. The delicate hand of Jizō's *Bodhisattva Ksitigarbha* from the twelfth or thirteenth century. The eleventh-century Bodhisattva from the Northern Song dynasty with its erect back and proud, enlightened-ecstatic facial expression. Western art, with very few exceptions, no longer did it for him. El Greco's *View of Toledo* and the portrait of the cardinal; the work of Jeff Koons (Ilona's trim little butt-hole).

Latish the next afternoon he shopped – for the first time in weeks – extensively for ingredients. Tonight he was going to cook. He wanted to ask Charelle if she wanted to join him for dinner. He hadn't cooked properly for a long time and he was a good cook. He made a green Thai curry. The kitchen was filled with enticing aromas. The windowpanes steamed over. The unusual heat had broken. It had started raining suddenly. A good day for curry. He didn't want to invite her officially, he was afraid it might scare her off. He'd take the chance. Perhaps she wasn't even coming home, or had other plans, although thus far she'd not often gone out during the week. Not that he'd really taken note all that carefully before.

She came home in the early evening. Alert eyes, observant. How had she got home? Took a taxi, she said, then walked a few blocks. On her cheeks again the dark-red blush (from the brisk walk, with excitement?), and fine droplets of water in her dense hair. He invited her to have supper with him, he'd made food, he said, she might as well. At first she seemed a bit undecided. But she let herself be persuaded. Together they sat in the steamed-up kitchen. He and the child with the slender brown wrists like Tamar in the Bible. (Child?) Cut off from the world, and secure, while sitting here. She ate. She was evidently hungry. He hadn't given much thought before to what she actually lived on, because in the fridge there was hardly anything: now and again a tub of yoghurt, a little block of cheese, a container with cheap margarine. He asked her about her family on the West Coast. When she'd started taking photos. They drank wine and she talked more freely than before. She'd started taking photos at high school, university students had handed out small cameras to the kids as part of a project. She'd been crazy about it from the start. She'd photographed everything in sight. Mainly the people of the town. The cemetery. The landscape. Gradually she'd become more daring. Before leaving the town she'd made a series of self-portraits in weird contexts. She had lots of new ideas – the ideas just came. She was enjoying her course at the art school – it was challenging, and the little job she was doing on the side wasn't too bad. She helped out two afternoons a week in a friend's hairdressing salon. Did the clients' nails and so on. (To his shame he'd never even asked what she did.) She'd been in the city for two years now, but this was her first year at art school. She'd worked hard to save up for it. Her skin was remarkably soft, flawless like that of a prepubescent girl. They didn't talk about the guy who was threatening her, but it was there, as a given between them. He was sure that she also sensed it.

The next day he experienced a strange excitement. He was going to cook again that evening. Perhaps they could now have supper together more often. At least she'd be having a decent, nutritious meal every day.

He planned the menu in detail. He was stepping with a lighter tread; the students were less irksome than usual. Even the girl who wanted to work on satanism seemed less ridiculous. He was patient with her, even though she didn't seem to be making much headway. Perhaps she could do something with the installation project after all. He was supportive. To such an extent that in an unguarded moment he found her staring at him fixedly, something she hadn't done before. Perhaps she thought he was trying to seduce her – how could he know what was happening in that head. Perhaps she thought he was planning to tumble her on the leopard-skin rug that she wanted to use in her installation (based on a *You* photo of a 'satanic pit' that had been discovered in an abandoned mineshaft), commit indecent acts with her. Kids nowadays were probably warned at length against paedophiles.

That evening he made an aromatic chicken dish. Top drawer, he thought. Charelle joined him more readily. They drank wine and she talked even more freely than the previous evening. Was Charelle a family name? he enquired cautiously. No, she said, coloured people were fond of fancy names. It was a bit of a fashion, names like Lisché and Shinique and Izona. What kind of people were her parents? he asked. She shrugged. Simple small-town people. Conservative. Religious. And she? She just shrugged again. But she did believe in the devil? She just laughed, shook her head in denial. They talked about the art they liked. She was clearly eager to get to know as much as possible about contemporary art. (Unlike his blasé, torpid students at the art school.) She had a habit of lifting her eyebrows when talking animatedly about something. (Towards the end Isabel's eyebrows were like two crossed swords – pale, like her hair.) He told her about Ilya Kabakov, whose work he was studying with renewed interest of late. (To his regret there had been none of it to be seen in New York.) She listened with interest; lively eyes. He asked her about her youth. Her father had at first worked at a crayfish factory in Klippiesbaai, she was born there, but later they moved to Veldenburg, where he was now working for a timber firm. She'd gone to school there, in the town. But she'd known from an early age that she wanted more from life. She wanted to be an art photographer. That was her purpose with her training. Had she made many friends in the city? No, she was a bit of a loner. And the man, the guy who was pestering her? He'd only arrived in Cape Town at the beginning of the year.

He cautioned himself not to get too familiar with her, to keep an appropriate distance. The next two evenings they ate together again. She showed him her portfolio. He was impressed. Surprising, that this girl, who'd grown up in a small West Coast village, with probably no proper high school education and very limited exposure to international art, could produce work that was so fresh. Like Cindy Sherman, she posed and photographed herself in all kinds of artificial situations. One of these self-portraits had been taken in a butchery, with metres of sausage wound round her naked body. (It shocked him, he had to admit.) He shouldn't underestimate her – delicate wrists or not, she was daring, focused and ambitious. If she could persevere, she could, with her natural talent and ingenuity, go far.

Seven

Late summer turned to autumn. It rained. It gradually got cooler. Two days a week he was at the art school. The rest of the time he spent in his studio. It was not a space that he much liked, he was renting it temporarily, he'd have to start looking out for something else. He was working on figures that he carved from wood – simple, stylised figures, with strange heads: sometimes of animals, sometimes of humans. Sometimes standing, sometimes kneeling, with exaggerated genitals. Sometimes even with tails, grinning, with grimaces. It had been quite a few years since he'd last painted, only carving, and drawing. He was booked at his gallery for an exhibition the following year.

In the weeks after Charelle's epileptic seizure Nick got into the habit of cooking supper for the two of them at least twice a week and often also over weekends. He quizzed her about the guy who'd threatened her. No, she said, he wasn't stalking her any more. She hadn't seen him for a long time. She didn't know where he was hanging out nowadays. But with him she could never be sure – he had a weak character. What did she mean? he asked. No, it wouldn't surprise her if he had criminal tendencies as well. She'd seen it coming from far away. Ever since school. Nick didn't notice any more suspect motor cars in front of or in the vicinity of the house, and there was no repetition of the swearing incident.

It was quite a bit cooler by now, and he found the evenings with Charelle cosy in the warm, steamed-up kitchen. He started to look forward to these occasions. He took trouble over the food. He thought she was gradually getting to feel more at ease with him. He found her sharp, witty; the more comfortable she got with him, the more she dared – he teased her about the devil, and she teased back. He found her pretty. Uncommon, with the slender wrists and the dense, warm hair. Although she wasn't his type, he found her sexy. She started cautiously questioning him about his life, about his work. He didn't reveal much. A bit about Isabel. About the trip to New York. He told her what he was working on, but didn't take her to his studio. Perhaps later. He was cautious. When she needed a book, he sometimes brought it from the art school for her. She told him about her childhood and about her schooldays. When she was ten, they'd moved to Veldenburg, her father had found a better job there. When she started taking photos at the age of fifteen, she wanted to document everything around her. She photographed the young people in the township, outside the town. She photographed things at random, like people's back yards, and the food on their tables, everything that caught her eye. She liked taking photos in the cemetery of all the new graves being added every day. And of the pregnant girls standing with their arms around their friends (never a father in sight). And of the young mothers with their babies – the girls that she felt sorry for, because once they had a child on the hip, that was the end of their lives. She was twenty-three. (Older than she looked.) She'd worked in the town for a few years to earn money before coming to Cape Town. They often talked about art. It was going well for her at the art school. She was glad she was doing the course. It had been a good decision. She also liked her room very much. She'd never had so much space to herself, she said again. Sometimes she felt guilty about that, but she wasn't complaining. She'd thought she'd outgrown her epilepsy – she'd stopped taking medication for it a long time ago. She'd been so ashamed, she said, after he'd come across her that day. No, he said, no, that she should never feel. He hesitated to ask her whether she'd ever been in a serious relationship. He was scared she'd take it the wrong way. But she did once volunteer the information that when she'd had a relationship with someone after school the guy who was stalking her now had been bitterly jealous.

She told him how miserable she'd been the first few weeks in Cape

Town. How she'd missed her parents and the familiar surroundings of the village. Obs had felt dangerous, the little streets were so narrow. She'd never known from which direction she could expect danger. In Main Road and everywhere the non-stop hooting of taxis had rattled her. The mountain she'd only later started to find beautiful. But she still preferred the West Coast and surroundings.

Isabel was always present, when he and Charelle were having supper in the kitchen. Naggingly, under the surface – always just outside his field of vision, just beyond his sphere of consciousness. He considered making a statue, a kind of harpy-like figure, with the body of a bird and the head of a woman, balancing on the edge of a bowl, or a dish, in which his head, the size of a hen's egg, was displayed.

Apart from his sketchbooks, in which he drew every day, he started working again on large sheets of paper of 150 x 110 cm each. In his drawing books he drew little elongated figures, figures on fire, figures with chopped-off limbs, with pig's snouts, skull-like heads, comic-eyed heads and bulging cheeks, sideburns – all distorted in some way or other. He drew skulls and crosses, coffins, glowing coals, flames and demons – all the props and paraphernalia of hell – inspired by their medieval depictions. But on the large sheets of paper he did not distort the figures. On a large, barren plane he drew a multitude of male figures doing violence to one another in various ways: shooting, beating with sticks, burying, suffocating, torturing, hanging and sometimes even executing. Not a tree, shrub, plant or blade of grass on this vast plane, only the men violently harming one another, in every conceivable manner.

Sometimes in the late afternoon, after working in his studio all day, he had a beer with Marthinus. Marthinus often invited him to watch DVDs at his place in the evening, but Nick accepted only on those evenings he wasn't cooking for himself and Charelle. He and Marthinus watched, among others, *Aguirre, the Wrath of God* (with crazy Klaus Kinski – evidently one of Marthinus' heroes). They watched a few classic masterpieces of Japanese cinema. *Woman in the Dunes* and *Ran* made a great impression on him. The first of these he had seen before, but for some reason he found it painful to watch it now. It was something to do with the texture of the woman's skin. For days he was still under the spell of the atmosphere of the two films. Afterwards Marthinus usually had a fair amount to say about the DVDs. An intense man, who reacted enthusiastically to everything that interested him.

The parents of Karlien, the student doing the satanism project, came to see him one morning. The mother was small, blonde, sexy, tanned, dressed in riding gear. Luxuriant eyelashes, lavish mascara. A trophy wife? The father looked familiar to Nick, some big-shot businessman. He was wearing a sports jacket and smelled of liquor, at eleven o'clock in the morning. The mother did the talking. The father looked bored, checked his watch every so often. They were concerned about Karlien. They did not like the idea that she was meddling with satanism for her project. They didn't think it was a healthy interest. They thought it might lead her astray. Art was her life, it was her dream, the great interest in her life, apart from horse riding. And her little dogs. She was determined to make it in the world of art. (This was news to Nick.) They were concerned about her, because at home they could still keep an eye on her, but she'd moved into a flat in town with a friend a while ago. Nick didn't know how to respond. The mother looked pleasant enough, but the father looked like a real bastard. The sort who thought art was a waste of time.

*

Charelle told him one evening about the first day she arrived in Cape Town two years ago. She'd got a lift from Veldenburg with somebody, it was cold in the early morning when he dropped her in Cape Town. She'd had bad period pain (Nick was wrong-footed by this intimate disclosure), and she was scared of the mountain. She didn't want to look at it. The mountain was everywhere. She'd be staying temporarily in a friend's room in a house, until she found her own place, while the friend was overseas. The domestic had let her in. She'd told her to wait in the kitchen. Later she'd heard someone come in. The person went into one of the front rooms, closed the door, and started crying bitterly. She'd remained sitting aghast at the kitchen table. Later the girl had come out and joined her in the kitchen. Her parents' dog was dying, she said, and made them both tea.

Nick was cautious at all times. Not a word, not a gesture that could possibly give her the wrong impression. He was careful never to say too much about himself. He kept his distance. It was only in the kitchen that they were ever together – never in any other place in the house. The single exception was the day she had the epileptic seizure, when he'd gone into her room. Sometimes the woman with the turban came to pick her up for the weekend, and once or twice she visited her parents in Veldenburg. She always informed him when she was going away for the weekend.

*

One Saturday morning in mid-April Marthinus knocked at his door at the crack of dawn. He was wearing a woollen cap and an army overcoat. He blew on his hands and stamped his feet. It was a cold morning. Nick glanced over his shoulder, half expecting to see a pig at Marthinus' heels. Nick invited him in. They sat at the kitchen table. Nick made them some tea.

'Did you see?' asked Marthinus.

'What?'

'The news.'

'No, what?' He hadn't watched television for a long time. (Of late too busy preparing food in the evenings.)

'A failed assassination attempt on a businessman in the Moorreesburg vicinity. An unknown man and three other people are under suspicion. The police are searching for them.'

'So? Nothing out of the ordinary there.'

Could he smoke?

Sure.

'No, not at first sight!' said Marthinus and blew out the match. (What an animated guy this was. He reminded Nick of a cousin of his, the son of his father's eldest brother. Always full of bright ideas.) 'No, but wait for it – the other three people are psychiatric patients on the run!'

'So?' said Nick.

'I have a hunch Victor Schoeman has a hand in this – mark my words!'

'How can you say that?' asked Nick, astonished.

'Not your common or garden businessman – he's also an art collector. The plot thickens!' exclaimed Marthinus.

'In what way, Marthinus? I don't see any plot here. I see only a couple of coincidences.' (Would Charelle be up by now? He'd not heard anything. She might be shy to come into the kitchen if she heard there was somebody there. He'd not heard her come in the night before. But he'd also been out for a while.)

'Victor left England under suspicious circumstances. An issue with a creditor or something of the kind. He's in financial straits,' said Marthinus, 'and he has an art background.'

Nick wondered whether Marthinus hadn't perhaps been watching too many DVDs. 'How do you know all this?' he asked. 'Besides, Victor has always been in financial straits, ever since I've known him. That's nothing new either.'

'A friend of Alfons' is in touch with someone who is in touch with Victor.'

'That still doesn't prove anything.'

'Look,' said Marthinus, 'do you remember the part in *The Shallows*,' and he moved closer confidentially, 'where a group of escaped psychiatric patients roam around running amok? Exactly that – escaped psychiatric patients! Can it be coincidence?! They're a kind of marauding band wreaking destruction as far as they go. Their headquarters are in a room behind a mortuary. The leader spends the nights lying behind a green plastic curtain separating his bed from the stockpiled coffins, and he schemes. He schemes till the cows come home. Brilliant! Internal monologue upon internal monologue! Brilliant! A portrait of a paranoid schizophrenic Dostoevsky would have been proud of! I've always thought that was one of the most astonishing parts of the novel.'

(Nick remembered the scene vaguely. He'd never read *The Shallows* all the way to the end, he'd been too pissed off with Victor at the time.)

'Doesn't the man shoot the others and then himself?' he asked. (He was impatient, he didn't really want to be having this conversation. Kept his ears pricked up for any sound in the passage.)

'Yes. Oh Lord. A scene that sort of reminded me of *Salammbô* by Gustave Flaubert. Static. Almost slow motion. But magisterial. Horrendously barbaric, the violence of it.'

'Victor never shied away from the depiction of violence,' said Nick drily.

'No! He didn't! Violence is his medium. It's his natural language!'

'You'd never say it, to look at him,' said Nick. 'However. I don't suppose it's a coincidence that he looks like Willem Dafoe in some villainous role.'

'Too true,' said Marthinus. 'David Lynch and Tarantino are also right up his alley.'

'Blinky couldn't stand him.'

'Not?! Well, I never.'

'He thought he was a poseur.'

'A poseur, eh? Yes, he did have rather a penchant for the affected flourish. And do you know who his heroes were?'

'No,' said Nick.

'Brigadier Theunis "Red Russian" Swanepoel, and the Dalai Lama.' He lit another cigarette. His tea must have been ice cold by now, but he drank it with undiminished relish.

'Be that as it may,' said Marthinus, 'I'm prepared to bet my bottom dollar that Victor is behind both the escape *and* the assassination attempt. It's *there*, it's all in his novels!'

'So?!' Nick exclaimed. 'Surely his novels can't form a basis for such an assumption!' He was impatient. He was no longer in a mood for Marthinus' far-fetched suspicions. It was ten o'clock already. Charelle never slept this late. Should he go and tell her it's okay, she can come to the kitchen at any time, she must be wanting a cup of tea by now?

'Wait and see,' said Marthinus. 'It's one hundred per cent Victor's kind of scenario.'

'From where did the patients escape?' asked Nick.

'Some high-security psychiatric hospital in the Moorreesburg vicinity. Only the most extreme cases are to be found there. The really severely disturbed cases. Oh Lord, it's right up Victor's alley. The more deviant, the better.'

Marthinus drank the last of his tea. Smoked another cigarette. Then (fortunately) he had to go and do something at home, attend to the pigs or whatever.

What should he do? Nick wondered. To go and knock at Charelle's door now might be taking it a bit far. She might emerge of her own accord as soon as she no longer heard voices in the kitchen.

At eleven o'clock he knocked at her door gently. No response. He called her name and knocked louder. No response. Against his better judgement he opened the door gingerly. She wasn't there. Her bathroom door was open. Nobody there. Her toothbrush was still there. Her room was tidy, as always, the bed made. Her weekend bag was on top of the wardrobe. He hadn't heard her come in the previous night nor leave in the morning. Why should he be upset – she didn't owe him an explanation of her comings and goings.

He had an appointment in Woodstock to view a prospective different studio space. He'd shortly have to vacate the studio that he rented in Observatory. He'd put it off for too long. He hadn't wanted to face the disruption. He had no all-consuming desire to go and have a look this morning. But good studio space was hard to come by.

Reluctantly he went to inspect the place. (Where could Charelle have gone to so suddenly? She seldom went out.) The space looked fair enough. He'd take it. Today it didn't matter that much to him where he worked. The work he was embarked upon was not yet substantial enough for his exhibition the following year. He'd have to work faster, produce faster. The move to Cape Town had been disruptive, had made him lose momentum. The pressure on any artist to remain on the radar was great. (He was substituting temporarily for somebody at the art school because the move had left him in financial difficulties.) In the meantime the art world was moving on. There were hundreds of young artists every day doing interesting and innovative stuff. All of them were driven and ambitious. Like Charelle. Perhaps not all of them as talented as she, but talent was no prerequisite nowadays. He would not be able to bank for very much longer on his name and his prior success.

He read the newspaper while having coffee in a small coffee shop. He saw no report on either the assassination attempt or the fugitive psychiatric patients. Could the whole thing have been a figment of Marthinus' lively imagination? He had at times suspected the chap went overboard with things (very much like his unrealistic cousin) – as with the talk about Chris Kestell.

Late in the afternoon he arrived home. Once again there was no response at Charelle's door.

By Saturday evening she'd still not returned. Eventually it turned nine o'clock, ten o'clock. She hadn't said she was going away for the weekend. She usually did so. Not of course that she *had* to do it. She'd gone away the previous weekend with the woman in the turban. Desirée, not a particularly friendly woman. He didn't want to phone

Charelle. She'd think he was checking on her. Unforgivable. At eleven he went to bed. At first he dozed off lightly, listening for her footsteps. Somewhere in the early hours he half woke up, imagining he could hear voices on the pavement in front of the house, hoped, half-asleep, that it was Charelle, but didn't hear her come in, and slept on restlessly.

He woke up the next morning in a grumpy mood. He should have known he would scare her off sooner or later. A middle-aged white man suddenly starting to cook for her. Her landlord to boot. Much too close for comfort. He felt embarrassed and humiliated. What had he been thinking? Then he reconsidered: apart from their eating together regularly over the last few weeks, he'd done nothing that could in any way have given her the idea that he was in the least making up to her or intent upon a mission of seduction.

By Sunday evening she had still not returned.

Eight

The trees are being stripped of their leaves. Every day it gets light a little later. In the mornings I have my tea in bed and look at the mountains. My gaze, I see in the mirror, is laconic. My spirit is refractory and troubled. The negotiations with Professor Marcus Olivier – professor emeritus in history – are not making headway. He is the father of the Olivier brothers, twins, on whom I'm writing the monograph. That such a father could beget such sons! I want to talk to him, though I'm still not sure what I'm hoping to learn from him. The more obstacles he places in my way, the more determined I am to gain access to him. I don't negotiate directly with him – all communications (telephonic or by email) are channelled through his secretary-cum-housekeeper. I have no idea what she looks like, but I picture a curtly competent woman, dressed in a uniform, with sensible leather shoes with thick rubber soles.

On cards I enter everything relating to the brothers and their work. Biographical information (the father, the absent mother, their youth in South Africa), their training (undergraduate as well as postgraduate), puppetry, literary influences (Franz Kafka, Bruno Schulz, etc.), surrealism (a vital component of their work), music, the technique of stop-action filming (their technique of choice and a field in which they are regarded as modern masters), the critical reception of their work (a lot has been written about them). Meanwhile I'm negotiating with the secretary-housekeeper. I intend to persist until I manage to secure an interview with the old father.

The town is pretty, but also repugnant.

I avoid people. This is a time of isolation. In the foreground: the mountains and I and the brothers. At times there is a zooming in the air. The mountains vibrate. In the background: the absent but urgent presence of the pig-headed old father and his sidekick-cum-house-keeper. Sometimes I meet up with you in town. Always we talk about him, because his death is still fresh in our minds. At times it's better, at times it's worse, you say, but the emptiness remains.

When I'm not occupied with the cards, I follow links on the internet. I read that Philip Roth says in an interview that he's done with writing. He's devoted the largest and best part of his life to the novel, but now he no longer feels the compulsion. There's a photo of him: he looks like a disillusioned old man, but his gaze remains piercing. Done, presumably, with characters like Mickey Sabbath: panty-sniffing, outrageous Sabbath, singing a paean to the clitoris, masturbating on the grave of his lover with the short legs (or am I confusing her with another character – Winnie Verloc, perhaps, in *The Secret Agent*? Winnie, for whom life did not bear much looking into).

Then, one fine day, the secretary, a Miss De Jongh, phones. Professor Olivier is prepared to grant me an interview. But the interview is subject to strict conditions. It can't be longer than half an hour, perhaps even shorter if the professor finds that it exhausts him too much. I will have to submit my questions in advance for the professor's approval.

We make an appointment for the end of the week, at four o'clock in the afternoon.

Nine

When by Monday afternoon Charelle had still not returned, Nick called her on her cellphone. The subscriber you have dialled is not available, was the only message he got repeatedly. He went to check her bedroom again. Spacious, almost the size of two rooms. She'd said more than once that she'd never in her life had so much space to herself. Everything arranged in a very orderly fashion on the large work-table (which she'd been very pleased with). There were few of her own possessions in the room, apart from her crocheted spread on the bed. Everything painfully tidy. Not a frilly, girlish room. He looked in the wardrobe. All her clothes were still there, as far as he could tell. He'd so often been fascinated with her attire – everything seemed second-hand to him – not fashionably second-hand, poor second-hand. The worn boots and the home-knitted jerseys. He'd wondered whether he should take her to buy clothes – but that would probably have been outrageous and presumptuous on his part. He looked in the bathroom again. Toothpaste and toothbrush. Skin products (not very expensive, by his estimate). In a small make-up bag (soft material with an embroidered Chinese dragon motif on it, probably bought at some Chinese store) – mascara and lip gloss. Two flagons of nail polish. (Slender fingers, slender nails.) Nail scissors, nail file. Tampax in the cabinet under the washbasin. Toilet paper. Shampoo and conditioner in the shower, a shower cap. He couldn't remember what she normally took with her in the morning. He vaguely recalled that she sometimes carried a ruck-sack. It was not there.

He sat down on her bed. He recalled that she'd told him she hadn't known the girl very well in whose room she'd stayed when she first came to Cape Town. The room had been terribly untidy, and terribly cluttered.

She couldn't believe that anybody could have so many things – so many useless things. She'd tried to tidy up, but she hadn't known where to put everything, and then she'd become discouraged. She'd felt completely alienated in that room. And she'd always been cold there. But she'd really liked the other girl who lived in the house. The one who'd cried so much that day about her parents' dog.

On Tuesday he phoned again in the course of the day. Still the same message. He didn't know where to get hold of the Desirée woman, he didn't know her surname.

By Wednesday morning Charelle had still not returned. He reluctantly went to work. The students were back from their three-week-long Easter break. Thank God he didn't have an appointment with the Karlien girl that day. At the end of the previous term she'd started dragging her feet on her satanism project (stillborn, Nick was starting to suspect). Possibly because her parents disapproved. (The father had looked like a bully. A brutal fellow, used to having his way.) He didn't think he'd be able to be tactful with her today. He went home early. He phoned Marthinus and asked if he could drop in. There was something he urgently needed to discuss with him. Marthinus awaited him at the top of the stairs, mug of tea and cigarette in hand. Come in, come in, he said. A cordial kind of guy. Nick was grateful to see him.

He explained the situation to Marthinus. How long had she been gone? Marthinus asked. Ever since Saturday morning. That was to say four days. Should he go to the police? No, said Marthinus, forget the police. They weren't interested. There were too many missing persons. He had a better idea. He'd take Nick to a place where the people had a very shrewd notion of everything that happened in the neighbourhood and down in the city – everywhere: under bridges, in tunnels and culverts, in every conceivable hideout. These guys had their fingers on the underground pulse of the city. Underground and above ground. He'd take him there this very afternoon.

'Where does she work, who are her friends?' asked Marthinus later that afternoon as they walked, first a few blocks towards the mountain, then turned right and walked another few blocks up a slope.

'I don't know. She has a friend, Desirée, a woman with a turban.'

'That's a start,' said Marthinus, 'there aren't many women with turbans.'

'Her name is Charelle Koopman,' said Nick. 'She's studying at the Peninsula Academy of Art. She's very serious about photography. She helps a friend twice a week at a hairdressing salon. She's quiet, she doesn't go out very often. She's never really received friends at the house. I sometimes cook for us in the evening.' (He feels a bit shit having to say this.)

'Where does she come from?' asked Marthinus. From Veldenburg, said Nick. And he was scared that the people who'd sworn at him, and the chap who'd threatened her a while ago, might have something to do with her disappearance.

What made Nick think that? (Any intrigue, and the man was all ears. The matter of Victor Schoeman and the escaped psychiatric patients a case in point.) A black car that he'd seen driving past his house once or twice after the swearing episode, he said, and if memory served, he'd also been sworn at from a black car, although he couldn't say that with any certainty. She had, however, recently said that for a long time she hadn't had grief from the man who'd threatened her. Apparently he hung out with bad company – tik-heads and the like.

'Doesn't sound good,' said Marthinus. 'There probably is something to your hunch.'

'Where are we going?' asked Nick.

'To a settlement here up against the mountainside,' said Marthinus.

'A settlement?' asked Nick.

'A friend of Alfons' started it as a refuge for outcasts and rejects. You could say the man was a kind of founding father. He managed the place for years in a very unorthodox style. Then he handed it over recently to a younger chap – very idealistic – who's in the process of as it were reforming the whole bunch,' said Marthinus, uttering his abrupt little chuckle. 'Oh Lord,' he said.

'Oh,' said Nick, not entirely buying into Marthinus' plan, but relieved that he was at least *doing* something, not just sitting around fretting and fiddling.

At the top of the steep hill they turned right again. A short distance along they came to a gate. There was a guard here. The gate was locked. Marthinus evidently knew him, he talked to him in Xhosa. The man let them in. As they followed the road up, Marthinus explained.

The first building on the right was the kitchen and recreation area. Here once a day a nutritious meal was prepared, sponsored by the Department of Welfare. On the left there were a few prefab buildings, where the permanent residents lived. It was still early, most of the people had probably not returned from work, said Marthinus.

Behind the kitchen was the vegetable garden. It covered a large area, everything here was planted in neat rows and clearly well maintained. The people worked in the gardens themselves in exchange for accommodation, said Marthinus. He'd helped here with the new layout and plantings – the original garden had been so neglected, there was hardly anything left of it. Now they were growing enough fruit and vegetables to be self-sustaining. Man, woman and child were expected to work here.

To the right of the vegetable garden was where the animals were kept: pigs, chickens and two milk cows. Eggs and milk were plentiful, said Marthinus. His pigs were the descendants of these pigs.

Behind the vegetable garden was the orchard.

'Everything here used to be much more chaotic,' said Marthinus. 'Less regulated. The founder had previously taken in more or less anybody in need – although mainly orphans and homeless people. He laid out the original vegetable garden and planted the trees. It was an admirable project but it started getting out of hand eventually. Hygienically it left a lot to be desired. The kitchen was apparently so dirty that the Department of Health was scared the plague would break out here. The inhabitants started fighting amongst each other. The dogs proliferated. The pigs wandered about in the neighbourhood. Nobody cared for the gardens any more. The orphans formed roaming gangs. They shat on suburban sidewalks. The Department of Welfare received complaints from all over.'

At the very top of the hill the road swerved to the right. (Nick was struggling up the hill, he was unfit, he hadn't exercised for a long time.) For the last few days it had been good and hot again during the day. In front of them were five bunker-like buildings.

'Arms depots during the British military occupation of the Cape,' said Marthinus. 'The man was an artist. An artist and a founding father! He used the bunkers as installation spaces. Now *that* sure as hell was something to witness,' he said, shaking his head and whistling softly through his teeth. 'Oh Lord. It was ground-breaking, it was way out. Five separate spaces and each with a different theme. But *dark*, make no mistake. A merciless onslaught on established Afrikaner cultural values.'

'What became of him?' asked Nick.

'I'm not sure. Look, that man was a pioneer, and restless. He got bored with the whole project. He got fed-up with battling the Department. The whole neighbourhood. He had every department and body and bourgeois interest group constantly at his throat. The logistics demanded too much of his time and energy. The animals and the people started irritating him. He was most definitely humanitarian and philanthropic, but he also knew how to look after his own interests. He may have started feeling that all the demands on him were driving him into a corner. So he left this place. From one day to the next. Handed over the whole project just like that to someone else. Who knows – perhaps he founded something else somewhere else. A man with vision. Needed a new challenge. A complex fellow, all in all, even though I didn't know him very well.'

Nick was listening with half an ear, worried about where Marthinus was taking him.

'The man who took over from him,' said Marthinus, 'has a totally different approach. Good organiser, orderly mind-set. Possibly too orderly, but good. A kind of reformer – one of your missionary types. I suspect he's planning a kind of utopia here – his idea of an ideal society. But it's one thing planning something like that, and another making it work. Oh Lord, you'll see. The man has no idea as yet of what he's up against. There are forces at work here that won't be thwarted by any utopian visions. Perhaps we'll come across the man. A kind of Albert Schweitzer incarnation.' And he laughed pleasantly.

Nick was no longer quite sure what all this had to do with Charelle's disappearance.

'Come,' said Marthinus, 'I'll show you inside the spaces.' From one of them came the sound of a little children's choir. What they were singing sounded like something between 'This old man' and 'Shosholoza'.

'Preschool children are now being looked after while their parents are at work,' he said. 'Previously they roamed around here and in the neighbourhood like stray dogs. Now they start each day with a balanced breakfast.'

Nick was tired and impatient. He didn't want to see the spaces either from the inside or the outside. He now wanted to make contact with whoever might be able to provide information about Charelle.

'The new man,' said Marthinus, 'got rid of an almighty pile of rubbish. Do you feel like meeting him? He may be somewhere around here. Otherwise we can arrange something. As I've said, he's also a friend of Alfons'. We'll invite him for a beer. Although he may well not even drink beer!' And he laughed. How unquenchably the man exuded enthusiasm and a sense of fun. Godaloneknows. The last thing on earth Nick wanted now was to meet this reformer – not now and not in the foreseeable future – whatever the scope and nature of his utopian dream or project.

'Let's move on,' he said. 'Some other time perhaps.'

'For sure, for sure,' said Marthinus. 'We'll make an appointment with the man sometime so he can show us around personally.'

'Good idea,' said Nick.

'Come,' said Marthinus. And he struck out along a small footpath to the left of the bunkers, until they reached a sturdy wire fence some distance along. They had by now climbed one of the slopes. He whistled. Shouted something in Xhosa. A man appeared from behind one of the low slopes and came up to them. They walked along the fence for a distance, up to a gap in the fence, artfully concealed with branches, which the man moved aside so that they could climb through.

'Do you come here often?' asked Nick.

'Yes,' said Marthinus. 'A while ago I had my eye on someone here.'

'Okay,' said Nick.

'A woman from the Democratic Republic of the Congo. Suffered terrible hardships to get as far as this. On foot through war-torn regions.'

'Where is she now?' asked Nick.

'She's gone to Johannesburg to be trained as a lawyer's clerk. She'd had to interrupt her studies when she fled here. She'd considered her options carefully. She's a principled woman of sound judgement.'

'I see,' said Nick.

They'd in the meantime trudged a good distance up the slope, and when they were halfway to the top they looked down on what looked suspiciously like a small informal settlement, in a basin between two slopes. Not visible from further down. A laager of shelters. A variety of materials had been used to cobble together these tent-like structures – thick sheets of cardboard, planks, fibreboard, canvas, although mainly plastic and branches, which the people had probably scavenged from all over. Higher up, against the slope, it even looked as if shelters had been dug out, the entrances covered with plastic bags. Discreet wisps of smoke. A subdued atmosphere prevailed here.

'These are the people, you understand,' said Marthinus, 'who live with their ear to the ground. They know everything that happens down there in the city. They're in touch with people living like rats in cement tunnels under the city. In culverts under roads and bridges. This place gets bigger by the day. But the people are careful. They keep a low profile. Some of them only emerge at night. Supervigilant. If they're caught, they're deported. Back to former homelands and internment camps.' He laughed. 'Oh Lord,' he said. 'But who's going to stem the flow?!'

'I get the picture,' said Nick.

They walked towards a relatively solid little corrugated iron structure. Outside, seated in the sun on an old car seat, were two men.

'Nick, meet Messrs Tarquin Molteno and Junius X,' Marthinus said.

Nick considered going forward to shake hands, then thought better of it. Tarquin was picking his teeth with a match. His forearms were tattooed, he was wearing a thick gold chain around his neck and a signet ring on his little finger. His hair was short and gelled up straight. Small chin tucked deep into the folds of the neck. Fleshy gills. Neat pair of jeans. Dark glasses. Fancy sneakers. Cool customers, thought Nick. Perhaps drug lords. Fuck knew.

Tarquin gestured towards two plastic garden chairs. Marthinus dragged them up. He and Nick sat down. An audience, Nick thought. He could smell himself, he was sweating like a pig, from the walking and the tension. He hoped the two of them couldn't smell him. It could make a bad impression. Marthinus, by contrast, seemed not fazed in the least. He lit a cigarette, exhaled the smoke at his leisure, admired the view, which indeed was quite something from this height. In front of them all of Table Bay lay stretched out. Under different circumstances one could have admired the breathtaking view.

For a short while they sat in companionable silence. There was an uncomfortable prickling under Nick's armpits. Not his idea of an afternoon's entertainment. Alfresco with the mafia. Convivial. He took a deep breath, tried unsuccessfully to enjoy the view, and hoped for the fucking best.

Tarquin called over his shoulder and a girl came out. She didn't look much older than fifteen. Tight jeans and big earrings. Tarquin signalled something with his head. She went back inside and re-emerged shortly afterwards with a tray, a bottle and four glasses. Pour, Tarquin indicated. Johnnie Walker Blue Label. Nick was on the point of suggesting that it was too early in the day for whisky, but he caught Marthinus' eye and something in his glance told him you don't turn down this drink. The girl poured briskly. Tarquin and Junius X knocked back theirs virtually in one gulp. Nick was scared that if he tried it he'd throw up. Not a good start to any negotiations.

'What's your problem?' asked Tarquin.

Marthinus said, 'My friend Nick's lodger has been missing for several days now. We want to know if you know of any missing or abducted girls in the area.'

'Stacks of 'em,' said Tarquin. 'So what's so special 'bout this one?'

They all looked at Nick, who was sitting with the half a glass of whisky in his hand, and the sun blazing down on his head, and a fucking blank as big as a house suddenly hitting him.

'She's an epileptic,' he said.

'So?' said Tarquin. 'Stacks of 'em too. Ep'leptics and worse.'

'She's renting a room from me and I feel responsible for her safety,' said Nick. (All of a sudden he felt like a big white bourgeois cunt. Ridiculous.)

'What's her name?' asked Tarquin. 'Anything to ID her with?'

What was she wearing the last time he saw her? What should he say: soft skin, slender brown wrists? They'd shit themselves laughing at him.

He cleared his throat: 'Her name is Charelle Koopman,' he said, 'she's a student at the art school in town,' and he gestured in an indeterminate direction with his head. 'She takes photos. She's smallish with . . .'

he indicated with his hands, 'dark hair, curly.' (Prick, he thought, couldn't he think – what coloured girl is going to have straight blonde hair?)

Tarquin's face was expressionless behind the dark glasses. Over his shoulder he summoned the girl again. 'You!' he ordered. 'You go call Blackie.' Away she went, weaving fleet as a gazelle through the shelters.

Tarquin checked his cellphone. They sat. Nick drained his whisky. Jesus, the stuff scorched his stomach and had already gone to his head. Soon afterwards the girl emerged from among the tents with someone. An albino with snow-white dreadlocks.

Tarquin hardly looked up from his cellphone. 'Any casualties this weekend,' he said, 'rapes and mutilations and abductions and so?'

A girl was raped down in Strand Street – first strangled with the hands and then with a wire hanger and thrown on a rubbish dump, the albino said in a flat, expressionless voice. The rest of his inventory was also delivered with no show of emotion. A girl's decomposed body was found in the Liesbeek there where the road makes a bend near the highway. At Bellville station a girl was raped and robbed and left for dead. A student from the university was ambushed and robbed and raped and kicked. Two children were abducted there by the flats in Clarke Estate. The cops haven't found anything yet. A man shot his girlfriend dead in Riverlea. A girl was gang-raped in Bishop Lavis. Two children were murdered in Lansdowne. Two high school girls have gone missing in Khayelitsha, the cops reckon it's the satanists sitting behind it. One child was raped in Delft South and set on fire and another child was raped when she used the communal toilets nearby her house. A child was shot dead when he landed in the crossfire of two gangs. Three other laities from the one gang were shot dead by the other gang and one car was set on fire in Bishops and two houses in Delft South when some of the gang went to hide out there.

Nick wanted to hear no more. The fucking sun, the fucking whisky, and now this gruesome fucking list. Marthinus was regarding him sympathetically. A reply was probably expected from him. He didn't know, he said, he couldn't tell.

Audience over. Tarquin and associates would keep an eye open. Down again went Nick and Marthinus. Down the steep mountainside. Through the settlement or whatever it was called. Utopian experimental farm. Back to the coolness of Marthinus' house.

'Come watch a few DVDs with us tomorrow evening,' Marthinus invited him. 'It will distract you.'

Nick didn't want to. He did not want to be distracted.

Ten

At four o'clock in the afternoon I report to the retirement village. (A luxury resort, it must cost a tidy sum to live here.) The iron gates swing open, I am admitted. The resort is on the edge of town, the surroundings are beautiful. The housekeeper-cum-secretary receives me. If, like most people, she is slightly wrong-footed by my appearance, she hides it well. I do, though, note that her gaze (like most people's) lingers a fraction too long on my unsightly lip scar. She introduces herself as Miss De Jongh. So no first names. By no means a uniform and sensible shoes – a full-blown décolletage, with imposing breasts. Little low-necked black top, tight black jeans. (Would that meet with the professor's approval – wouldn't he prefer her in a demure uniform?) And a raving bottle blonde. Did you ever. If she's a mite taken aback, so am I.

She conducts me to the stoep overlooking a lush fynbos garden. Professor Emeritus Olivier is seated in a wheelchair, with a rug over his knees. His back is turned to us. When he greets me, he shows no sign of recognition. And why would he, it was almost thirty years ago. His cranium is bonier than ever, without the softening effect of hair, of which he never had an abundance. I don't want to stare too much and too unguardedly. He indicates with a broad, yellow-pale hand (affliction of the liver?) he wants to be wheeled down to the garden. It's a fine day, bright, not too hot. The woman rearranges the rug. She pushes the wheelchair, I walk behind them. No chance now of any conversation. Down the winding pathway, through beds of fynbos and fragrant shrubs, up to a large pond. He indicates that he wants to stop here. We are standing on the paved edge of the pond, actually more of a dam. Big koi immediately come swimming up. One in particular remains floating near the edge, fairly close to the surface. Standing there, gazing at the fish, the professor and Miss De Jongh and I. What a bizarre apparition, seen at close quarters. Bright red, with two protrusions on either side of the mouth and something, I notice, like a blue membrane over the eyes. Could the fish be blind? The mouth, as it opens and shuts, has something obscenely sexual about it. Is it a coded message from the old father? An oblique reference to our sexual escapade almost thirty years ago?

'Did the twins ever keep fish?' I ask (to start somewhere).

'No,' says the old father (without turning his head in my direction), 'no fish. Dogs, yes.'

'What did they like playing with as children?'

Olivier waits a while before replying. He's obviously not going to make it easy for me. Miss De Jongh kicks the brake firmly into place, sits down on a bench a short distance away, thrusts out her legs in front of her and lights a cigarette. Very cool and casual, and old father does not object.

'Just what healthy, normal boys usually occupy themselves with,' he says.

'And that is?' I ask.

'They read, cycled around, climbed trees, played ball,' he says (irritated?), 'took part in sport. In fact, they were very gifted in that direction.'

'Did they like reading comic strips?'

'Within limits,' he says. (These limits, I suspect, were of his paternal edict.)

'I assume they were fond of drawing?'

'Naturally.'

(Should I lean forward, my mouth to his ear, and whisper: I know what you're capable of. I haven't forgotten. Quickly and nonchalantly, before the blonde notices a thing?)

'What did they draw?' I ask.

He makes an impatient gesture. 'Anything. Animals. Aeroplanes. What do you call them – superheroes.'

67

'As children, did they attend puppet shows?'

'I took them once or twice.'

'Do you have any idea where their fascination with puppetry came from?' I ask.

'That you'll have to ask them,' he says.

'And do you still have regular contact with them?' I ask.

The man hesitates a moment before saying: 'They are busy. They have a high international profile. But they faithfully send me catalogues of each of their exhibitions.'

Then he extends his hand wordlessly in Miss De Jongh's direction, who gets to her feet, produces a small plastic dish from somewhere in his wheelchair and hands it to him. Now he starts feeding the koi. The obscene mouth of the fish appears above the surface at rapid intervals, gobbling at the food. I stand watching in fascination and revulsion. The interview hasn't exactly got off to a flying start. The old father could hardly have been less cooperative. I ask another question or two, but they're not really to my purpose. Before long he makes another hand gesture in the woman's direction. She steps on her cigarette end, gets up, kick-releases the brake, and I get the impression the interview is over. Not once did the old man look at me. Or give any sign of recognition.

*

I carry on working at the monograph. When I try to make another appointment, Miss De Jongh alleges that Professor Olivier is in bed with a severe flu. I don't believe a word of it, but I don't give up that easily. I still have quite a few questions I want to ask him. Why should I let him off the hook so easily?

Eleven

Thursday morning, and Charelle had still not returned. It had now been five days since her disappearance. That is to say, if she had really disappeared, and hadn't just left to live elsewhere without notifying him. But all her stuff was still in her room. He'd checked and rechecked. All her clothes and underwear and shoes were still there, as far as he could judge. He phoned the academy of art, but at first they refused to provide any information about their students. Even to him, her landlord, as he patiently explained to them. Even if she were his lodger, they stuck to their guns. Her parents' address, then. Nothing, no information. When he phoned again (he'd persist until they capitulated), the secretary said – half unwillingly – that one of the lecturers had said the student in question had not been to class since the beginning of the week. This made Nick sick with worry. Perhaps he should go to the police after all.

On Thursdays he didn't have to go in to work, and he had to vacate his temporary studio urgently. He asked Marthinus to help him move. No problem, said Marthinus, he'd bring a bakkie and helpers. Amazing how many contacts the man had. The move was hard labour, because Nick's work had to be handled with care, but Marthinus was the soul of vigour and good cheer, and he took charge of everything – just as well, since Nick had little enthusiasm for the whole undertaking, he felt anxious and distracted.

The new studio was in Woodstock, on Main Road, on the first floor, in an old but well-maintained building. At street level there were a few small shops: a little supermarket (Best Price Superette), a video store (Vezi's Home Videos), a take-away joint (Bismillah's Fast Foods), a small second-hand store, and on the corner, above the Battery Centre, the House of Glories Ministries. Over the road, glimpses of the mountain between the buildings. The area was noisy, with hooting taxis, and heavy traffic at peak times, but Nick did not find that a problem. He preferred it to the area where he was living now (he should have known when he bought there), and definitely to Stellenbosch, where he and Isabel had lived for a few years in middle-class isolation. He'd hated it, that area, where the renovations and the aesthetic choices of their neighbour, poor unsuspecting Mr Burger, had driven Isabel to distraction. The last few months, before the final termination of their relationship, had been insufferable – Isabel at times at the end of her tether and just about berserk, some days almost incapable of going to work. He'd felt like a prisoner in his studio (the converted former servant's quarters), in the house, in the affluent neighbourhood, and in the relationship.

In the late afternoon after the move they sat in the new studio having a beer. Marthinus was impressed with the space; he was enthusiastic about Nick's work – what he'd been able to see of it thus far. The person who'd rented the studio before Nick – a painter who was making it big time internationally and who'd moved to a more upmarket area – had left behind a few pieces of furniture. A bed, a sofa, a bookshelf, some plastic chairs. The room, with bathroom and storeroom, was big, actually much more acceptable than Nick had realised when he'd rented it so precipitately. He was grateful for this new, neutral space. He preferred it to his house – which he was in no hurry to return to today.

Later they bought rotis from Bismillah's Fast Foods and they drank some of the whisky that Nick always had to hand in his studio. The large room was cool – it was going to be cold in winter, the single heater wouldn't be of much use. But this evening, with Marthinus here with him, it was cosy. They sat on the plastic chairs, their food and drinks on a crate because Nick's big table was full of not-yet-unpacked-and-unwrapped objects. Marthinus with his large, august head, his tanned face. His hair a bit like the mane of a lion. Large features, his expression full of confidence, his eyes sympathetic. A good-natured man, radiating magnanimity. Big heart. Generous with his time and attention. Apparently so unguarded, and open to the world at large. And tactful. Nick wondered about all the roads Marthinus must have travelled, because he could surely not have spent all of his time tending pigs.

But a talker! A talker par excellence. Now he had warmed to the subject of pigs. 'Look,' he said, 'you get your Large Whites. A hardy and robust breed, that thrives in any climate, but I prefer the black pig' (he laughed), 'or even the speckled. The original Large Blacks came from America, but my pigs – the descendants of the farm pigs – have been bastardised to such an extent that you can hardly tell what the original line was. I like dealing with pigs. They're clever. They're sly. They have character. You even find your pig with integrity. President Burgers is such a pig. A natural leader. Inspires confidence in humans and fellow animals.'

Nick told Marthinus that long before he was born his father had kept Large Whites on a relative's farm. Marthinus quizzed him extensively on this, but Nick was uncertain about many of the facts.

When they'd exhausted the subject of pigs, the conversation moved on to Zen, prompted by the small Japanese teabowls that Nick had unpacked and from which they were now drinking their whisky. (He'd brought the bowls and a small teapot from New York.)

'I ask myself,' said Marthinus, 'should one have a teacher? And if you should, who should it be? The Buddha, Jesus, Mr Mandela, Noam Chomsky, Jiddu Krishnamurti? It's a difficult choice. Each has his merits. I like the smile with which the Buddha is always depicted. Siddhartha Gautama. Also known as Shakyamuni Buddha, the sage of the Shakyas. On the night of his conception his mother dreamed that a white elephant entered her womb. The dream signified that the child would be special. He received tuition in astrology, mathematics, languages, archery, wrestling and horsemanship. He was an educated, cultured man. He ran away, life at the palace had become tedious. He tried several options. He starved himself, mortified the flesh. Finally, sat down under the tree. Resolved not to get up until he'd reached enlightenment. Afterwards, saw everything with fresh eyes. Very attractive as a teacher. I like the way he sits – comfortable, rooted. When he sits, he sits. When he walks, he walks. Somewhat rotund, compassionate smile. Attachment as the root of all suffering. Food for thought. Jesus, on the other hand. Intelligent, charismatic, but difficult to think him off the cross, as it were. By the way, have you seen Pasolini's *The Gospel According to St Matthew*? We must make a plan to watch it. Very convincing. Read Saramago, *The Gospel According to Jesus Christ*. "Why save the lamb and slaughter the sheep?" Good question. Mr Mandela – he was probably our only chance for a great man in this country. Sense of vocation. Benign. A good dose of the Buddha nature. Powerful, in combination with the aristocratic Xhosa birth. An indigenous prince. Chomsky, if his kind of political activism is your thing. Personally I nowadays incline towards old Jiddu, Mr K.' (Nick had never heard of him.) 'Now there's a man for all seasons, and a tough teacher. Uncompromising.'

Marthinus took a sip of whisky from the delicate teabowl. 'Look, I saw this wonderful documentary about a Chinese weightlifter.'

Nick liked listening while Marthinus was talking. Then there was no need to think; then he thought less often of Charelle. A part of him felt that was enough, he needed nothing more (as he'd felt with Charelle at the kitchen table), the effortless camaraderie had the same warming effect on him as the whisky. Another part of him felt desolate, beyond the reach of warmth or comfort.

Marthinus told him about the documentary. 'Look,' he said later. 'Enough of this idle chatter. We're watching Bergman's *Cries and Whispers* this evening. Do you feel like joining us?'

'If I have to watch *Cries and Whispers* this evening,' said Nick, 'I'll blow my brains out afterwards.'

'Oh Lord,' said Marthinus, 'do you have a gun?'

'No,' said Nick, 'but if I had one.'

'You gave me a fright,' said Marthinus. 'But perhaps Bergman is a bit heavy. We can always watch something else. Buster Keaton, Laurel and Hardy?'

'No, thanks,' said Nick, 'then rather Bergman.' He was not in the mood for Bergman's dark drama, but Godknows also not for slapstick of any kind. He wanted to be at home if Charelle should perhaps return. He didn't say it, but he knew that Marthinus suspected it.

*

Early on Saturday morning – a week after Charelle's disappearance – he went to his studio. When he was at home, he tended to listen out for Charelle all the time. Rather get down to work, organise his studio, everything was still right where it had been dumped. Today he would draw. He used a special large-sized sketchbook in which he also wrote down his ideas and made preliminary sketches of the figures that he carved. He filled pages with drawings of little figures with exaggerated heads and sexual organs. The heads had stubbly beards and starkly staring eyes. Some of them had something of the bulging cheeks of the comic strip character Popeye or something of Robert Crumb – but in both cases considerably more malign – thugs and killers the bunch of them. These little figures assailed each other with all kinds of objects: cudgels, sticks, cat-o'-nine-tails, horsewhips. Simplified, almost childish-naïvely drawn little figures stood with hands raised or on their knees in pools of blood. Women with conspicuous breasts and curves in bikinis – pinup-ish – stood armed with knives, or in combat posture like Barbarella.

Isabel had not liked the way he portrayed women. What is this male obsession with sexy sluts, she'd asked. Take Alban Berg – a composer she really liked; his ambivalence struck a chord with her, his fascination

73

unto death with negativity – but the operas, *Wozzeck* and *Lulu*, no, sorry, she'd have no truck with that fixation on stereotyped sexy sluts who get murdered.

At first she'd had no problem with his work in general (even though it could hardly be accused of being uplifting). But later she'd said that she found his fascination with violence abhorrent. The fucking male obsession with violence and its constant representation, she'd said – as if the prick were the eye through which the world was surveyed.

When he'd done enough work and his studio was more or less organised, he washed his hands in the small bathroom. He regarded himself in the mirror. Today he could discern his mother's lineaments in his own. This alarmed him. A man of early middle age, slightly thickset (physically unfit), his hair not as abundant as previously, the expression in his eyes guarded. Was Charelle safe? Why hadn't she told him she was going away? He checked his cellphone for messages, it had been switched off while he was working.

There was a message from Marthinus: *Tarquin has reported there's a possible link in Blue Downs. We can go there tomorrow.* He'd never been to Blue Downs. He didn't think he wanted to go there. It sounded dreadful, what one could come across there.

*

In the last months Isabel had seldom looked at him straight-on (which had not done his already shaky self-regard any good), but she had still told him her dreams. He'd resented this. She wasn't talking to him, he felt, she was just using him as a sounding board. When she was walking in the front garden and saw a fresh turd left by the neighbour's dog, she had the strange compulsion that the neighbour was forcing her to eat it, she said one morning. (Nick was shocked.) Her therapist, she said, would probably say that she felt that the neighbour was forcing her to eat shit. (Nick could just imagine what the poor upright, innocent, well-meaning but limited Mr Burger, who just couldn't see that his choice of bricks might offend against Isabel's aesthetic sense, would make of this.) Her dreams did not bode well, he'd thought. And how right he'd been.

What had been supposed to be a shared voyage of reconciliation (a trip she'd long wanted to take), was for the most part a punishment and a tribulation for both of them. So often she sat across from him in museum restaurants and cafés, her face pale, her blanched eyebrows like two crossed swords. So here she was now, she said once (in a Chinese eatery – City Lights of China; pretty dismal lights, as far as he was concerned), and she was fucked good and proper. What did she mean? he asked (reluctantly). She looked down. (Her food just about untouched, whereas he was half-drunk with all the rice wine.) To think that she was compelled to feel that the neighbour was forcing her to eat his dog's shit every day – not as an abstract metaphor, but as something that she imagined graphically – while all her life she'd had an intense loathing for the exaggerated optimism surrounding her. So she was being fucked over, she said, as a champion of negativity.

Can't you see, she said – I yearn for disambiguation, I yearn to be free for a day, for a single hour, of the murkiness. Every minute I'm trudging through a swamp, each movement of mine feels as if it requires superhuman effort. (I can't move freely any more, he thought, I feel as if I'm chained to you, we move together like two manacled convicts.)

He said nothing. He started looking forward to the end of the trip. What a horrendous waste of an expensive trip to New York. He should have read the signs in advance. He'd hoped that the journey would lift her out of morbidity, shared pleasures would bring them closer together. He'd been fucking naïve. Pallid as a nun she sat opposite him, tortured by her need, her food untouched. In the evenings she folded the blue dressing gown around her rebarbatively, like a knight's cuirass, like the Japanese battle garb he'd looked at for a long time in the Met. It had reminded him of something, but he hadn't known what. That

Japanese battledress had touched something deep within him. He'd felt a weird affinity with it. In the last few weeks of their travels, in fact, he'd visited nothing but the Oriental rooms. It was all that he was still receptive to. He had increasingly developed an aversion, something so potent that it verged on the physical, to the whole bang shoot of Western art. Strangely enough, only the work of Jeff Koons – him, of all damn artists, whose work he'd never before taken seriously – still spoke to him to an extent. As if Ilona's clean-shaven little butt-hole were somehow inexplicably uncontaminated, as if it, at least, wasn't carrying any baggage. What you see is what you get: Ilona's ass. And then the two paintings by El Greco – the portrait of the cardinal, and the *View of Toledo*. For the rest, only the endless rooms of Oriental art. That was all that still spoke to him.

He'd bought a few books: among others *How to Read Chinese Paintings*, and had found some support in it. About one of the scrolls of the artist Ni Zan from the twelfth century (ink on paper) it was said: Distant mountains often symbolise a refuge or paradise, but in this scroll Ni Zan clearly sees such a refuge as beyond his reach. The distant mountains are cut off from the foreground by trees and a wide body of water.

And then one more thing that had excited him: in MoMA there was an exhibition of the Olivier brothers' most recent work. They'd come a long way, the twins. Near-contemporaries of his at art school, slightly younger than he. Two shy and likeable chaps, sons of the celebrated historian Marcus Olivier. Two gifted youngsters, identical, difficult to tell apart. Attractive in appearance – indeed almost angelic: blond, blue-eyed, slender as adolescents, light-footed and graceful (good tennis players as well, apparently), but from the outset something exceptional about their work. Something much more rounded and sophisticated than the work of their fellow students. And even then, something enig-matic. The father was a different kettle of fish, according to reports a difficult customer – controversial, confrontational, even unscrupulous, if there was any truth to the stories in circulation about him. Nick couldn't remember these in detail, but he did recall the air of notoriety that hovered about the man.

Twelve

Charelle was gone and there was no getting away from that fact. He shuddered to think what could conceivably have happened to her. The visit with Marthinus to Tarquin and company on the mountainside had not been reassuring in the least. The albino guy with the snow-white dreadlocks reciting a whole litany of murder and rape, as if he'd rehearsed it. Marthinus was convinced that those people had their fingers on the pulse of whatever happened in the city and surrounds – from Blue Downs to Bishop Lavis. If they didn't know where somebody was, Marthinus argued, that person was as good as untraceable.

Nick wanted Charelle back in his kitchen; he wanted to know that she was safe. He did not want to have to go to strange people in strange settlements to find out whether they had any idea of her whereabouts. He wanted her back at his table unharmed. It was probably presumptuous, even ridiculous, to want such a thing. Perhaps she'd left exactly because she'd found his attentions improper. A white man, her landlord, cooking for her. She'd not shown any signs of awkwardness with the situation, but perhaps she'd sensed something, and had wanted to spare him the embarrassment of taking him up on it.

*

Normally he did not work on a Monday, but this Monday he had to go in specially at the behest of the principal of the art school, Albrecht Bester. A visiting artist was coming to give a talk, and Albrecht wanted the full staff complement to be present. Nine days since Charelle's disappearance. Cold and dry, but windy. Nick did not feel like going in. He knew who the woman was, Liesa Appelgryn; she was quite a noted artist these days; her work had suddenly become massively popular, he wasn't quite sure exactly with whom, but it was now all the rage and she was exhibiting at leading galleries, according to Albrecht. Nick found her stuff hideous. Albrecht could hardly contain his enthusiasm about the prospective visit. He was camp to a fault and he enunciated impeccably. Old school, though not much older than Nick.

Nick was late. The proceedings had started. Albrecht acknowledged his presence with a curt nod and an icy glare. The school's rooms were state of the art. (No lack of funding here.) The talk this morning was being held in the main exhibition area, a large, circular space. The students sat on the floor, the lecturers stood against the wall at the back. In front, at the lectern, stood Liesa Appelgryn and a blushing, bubbling Albrecht Bester. A few of the woman's paintings were hanging against the wall. For the rest they were fated to be treated to a Powerpoint presentation, without a doubt.

Liesa Appelgryn was younger than Nick, she'd been at art school with the Olivier brothers, if his memory served. He had a vague recollection of her as mousy and put-upon, but she had manifestly put that behind her. She'd gone blonde in the meantime, with opulent curves and an imposing cleavage – she was dressed in a form-fitting dress with a neckline plummeting almost all the way to her navel. So this was the drab, untalented Liesa Appelgryn reincarnated. In the flesh her stuff was even more horrendous that he'd imagined it. Female nudes – a hybrid of sentimental Cardies mush and porno-mag drools. Nudes with enormous tits, bums, forests of pubic hair, on flower-strewn hills, on swings in gardens, on beds in boudoirs with the wind coyly tweaking the transparent curtains, in pious attitudes: the hands clasped, the eyes cast heavenward. Saccharine pastel colours. Very obviously a Statement. 'It's about allowing the work to embarrass you,' he read in the small photocopied leaflet in circulation. The otherwise apathetic students were humming like tops. The light in the room was too hot. It caromed off the large sunflower-yellow and baby-pink and apple-green canvases.

Albrecht Bester introduced her. He was toupeed and moustached and pomaded for the occasion and wearing a satin-shimmering three-piece suit with a chevron motif. (Ordered on eBay, or bought from De Jager's Men's Outfitters on the corner of Andringa and Crozier Streets?) A red handkerchief roguishly peeping from the top pocket of the jacket. The toupee styled at a rakish angle. Effervescent with excitement. A grotesque travesty of godaloneknowswhat.

He would like to say a few words before yielding the floor to the artist herself, said Albrecht. He would like to impress upon all those present here what an enormous privilege it is to host an artist of her calibre here today. (The proceedings would conclude with somebody emerging from the wings with a bunch of flowers, Nick guessed, or a basket with fruit and nuts and a bottle of choice wine.) He would like now to call upon his colleague, Rick Toerine, to say a few words about Liesa's work, before savouring the privilege of listening to the artist herself.

Nick took to Rick Toerine as little as to Albrecht. No, even less, because Albrecht at least had a kind of old-world vocation for the teaching and appreciation of art, but Rick was young, ambitious, unbearably pretentious, lacking in intellectual integrity, a player of the first rank who knew exactly which modish discourse to zoom in on. A narcissistic operator, very much taken with his own learning, his appearance, his position. He was wearing a pair of hip-hugging green trousers, dark-blue open-necked shirt (both impeccably cut), a belt of plaited leather. His hair was short on the sides, longish and gelled erect on top of his head. Strutting his stuff. To Nick he came across as the kind of man who would have self-designed Art Deco chairs in his home, gilded ornaments like rabbits and pineapples, and a small collection of expensive vases in old gold and turquoise. Nick felt like shit; he was over the hill, past his sell-by date. (The vases of old gold and turquoise displayed on top of a lacquered black cabinet.)

Liesa Appelgryn's work was a celebration of sexual politics, said

Rick Toerine. This was the woman artist claiming for herself the right to reappropriate and upend the female nude. (His discourse spiked with just enough modish terms to resonate with the students.) It also channelled the politics of class, he said. The artist potentialised her own working-class background – her father drove a truck between PE and Johannesburg – to activate and problematise the detritus of a white-trash imagination. At art school she had for the first time engaged with official canonical art when, as a young student, she had operated the slide projector during lectures to earn extra pocket money. At that stage she had not yet engaged with contemporary art. Her early student output she herself characterised as small second-hand imitations of German Expressionism. (If only she had never deviated from it, thought Nick.) But then she had suffered a major depressive episode – she was not ashamed of this (the woman nodded, laughing, in confirmation – Oh hell, let it all hang out, the dirty washing, the personal detail, it was all part of the right to be embarrassed) – reinvented herself and started channelling the work of Jeff Koons and Mike Kelley. (Her stuff alas nowhere comparable with Koons's outrageousness and Kelley's dark delirium, thought Nick.) That was when she gradually started to apprehend that the tasteless, the vulgar, the sexual – that it all had to be embraced. (A clever move, thought Nick.)

Liesa Appelgryn's work was all about edge, said Rick Toerine. Her work was about the edge between provocative and disgusting, between good and bad painting, between psychological entrapment and psychological liberation. She succeeded in keeping the surface of each work stretched to breaking point by her intelligence; with her fine apprehension of dark and light she kept company with the great tradition of Vermeer and Rembrandt; with her undermining of this tradition she claimed kinship with masters like Jeff Koons and Takashi Murakami.

This couldn't be true, thought Nick. The man could surely not be serious. This stuff had less than fuck-all connection with the tradition of Vermeer and Rembrandt. He had no idea what the kids were making of this, whether they could make head or tail of it, since they knew as little about Vermeer as about Murakami. He should stop thinking of them as kids, they were students – young adults. A few, he noted, were on their cellphones. They all had attention deficit disorder, they couldn't listen for more than ten minutes to a lecture or talk. But he should stop underestimating them like that. There were bound to be a few among them who were talented as well as critical. Not that he'd ever come across one.

Now Liesa was given the floor. She'd come a long way. Shy this woman was not, she had definitively appropriated the right to embarrass herself in public. She kicked off with a personal confession that wouldn't have been out of place at an AA meeting.

'My work is like heavy personal and heavy psychological,' said the woman. 'Way back I was, like ordinary, you know? I had such low self-esteem I could hardly talk I panicked so about myself. Then my breakdown happened, you know? So then I was in therapy for a long time, so now I'm cool with self-exposure. Now I can handle it all, every facet of my personality, now my work is feisty, now it's, hey, a celebration of my repressed sexual fantasies, you know?! And I think I'm speaking for all the girls here.' (Wink-wink; minimal response from the girls in the audience.) 'People ask me when I'm going to paint, like, men, then I say: When they grab hold of my imagination. I'm not a political artist, but I am practising the politics of class. I deal in images of women, in case you hadn't noticed' – she gestured at the work behind her; a few students laughed. 'I'm not scared of painting saggy-breasted, blowsy bottle blondes. I give the middle class the middle finger sort of. All those well-kept girls with their trim bodies and unwrinkled skins.' (The majority of the audience were in the first flush of youth, all of them clones of Karlien – trim, blonde, unwrinkled, unblemished, untouched, clothed in expensive designer-label gear.) 'It's the detritus of my white-trash imagination and I cherish it, where I used to be ashamed of it. I didn't always have as much self-confidence as I have now. I had a breakdown, it made me think and think – perhaps I was ashamed of something, you know? I couldn't paint. Therapy taught me to channel my anger and my insecurities in my work. That toxic soil of "it's not good enough". Nothing grows in it. So I thought: I'm going to utilise that poison as fertiliser, and not try to see painting as an exalted, sacred place in which only beautiful and elevated things happen. So then I started painting straight from the imagination, the subconscious, a huge nude, and stuffed flowers into her mouth to stop her gob hole and schemed: Hell, this is fun.' (A stirring in the audience. A few cellphones are raised on high.) 'Then there was no stopping me. So then I started painting these huge, overweight girls with bums and tits and these enormous bushes.' (A tittering at the mention of tits and bushes.) 'I was liberated, I realised it was part of me: This loudness is my strength. My message to you all – we all *know* that toxic poison. Utilise it as fertiliser, don't be scared to challenge everything. Break loose. Challenge. Challenge your own preconceptions. Challenge society's preconceptions. Challenge art, challenge the whole of art history!'

And sure enough, when she'd finished, and Albrecht had thanked her ecstatically, a thin blonde kid came up (Nick at first thought it was Karlien), and presented Liesa with a giant bunch of flowers – an over-the-top bouquet of arum lilies and flaming red-hot pokers. After this several girls leapt up and mobbed the artist, so that their friends could take photos with their cellphones of them with Liesa Appelgryn. There was an excited giggling and huddling around the woman. Somewhere they had after all registered that they were in the presence of a celebrity, even though they did not care a fig or a fuck what had been said about her work.

He'd done something to offend Charelle. Or else the guy who'd been stalking her had instructed her not to have anything to do with him. Despair and desolation. After the photo opportunity Liesa Appelgryn bore down upon him, embraced him, all steaming bosom and profuse, perfumed female flesh. She was so glad to see him, she'd always so much adored his work! What did she want of him, for heaven's sake – he was unkempt, bothered, emotionally strung out. He ventured some feeble comment on her work, but fortunately did not have to say much more, because Albrecht, arms flung wide and broadly smiling, bore down upon them. Ready to spirit Liesa away to the next phase of the proceedings – a meal somewhere on a wine farm. All the colleagues had been invited. (Nick had neglected to reply.) Was Nick coming along? asked Albrecht, a mite icily. But Nick declined the invitation, mumbled a feeble excuse. He went home, still hopeful of finding Charelle in the kitchen, making herself a cup of tea.

*

When he got home, after the woman's shameless performance, there was someone waiting for him outside the gate. The person was sitting on the pavement, swaddled in a big military overcoat, his back against the wire fence.

He jumped up when Nick arrived. 'Help,' he said, 'we come in peace.' He did not look at Nick, made no eye contact. He hadn't shaved recently and his close-cropped hair was also starting to sprout stubble. Convict, was Nick's first thought. 'We come in peace,' he said again. 'Somebody sent us. We are not allowed to say who. It's just our hand.' (He held up his left hand – it was wrapped in a dirty bandage through which blood was seeping.) His leg as well (he pulled up one pants leg, a wound that did not look too good.) 'We were sent. We're not allowed to say by who. The devil will get us if we say. We have promised. Water, we are thirsty. We are hungry.'

'Come in,' said Nick. Against his better judgement he let the man in at the gate with him. He made him sit down on one of the stoep chairs. 'What is your name?' he asked. The man was sitting on the edge of the chair. He now started obsessively tapping his index finger against his upper lip. Rapidly and incessantly. 'Our name,' said the man. He still did not make eye contact. 'Our name is our pride.' The man was clearly not all there. 'Where do you stay?' asked Nick. 'We stay put,' said the man. Something weird about him. Nick couldn't put his finger on it. The man was unkempt, and he clearly had a screw loose upstairs, but he wasn't retarded. Something noble about his (convict's) countenance, and his features were aristocratic. His eyes pale as a seagull's. Nick's first thought was that the man must have escaped from some institution. He didn't even want to think of the implications of this. Perhaps he should summon Marthinus.

'We are thirsty,' said the man. 'We are hungry.' Now Nick had no choice. He couldn't now refuse the man food and drink. He had no other option – he had to take him along to the kitchen.

When he opened the door to the kitchen, Charelle was standing in front of the sink. Her back turned to him.

'Charelle!' he exclaimed, surprised, 'where have you *been*?'

Something had changed. She was uncommunicative. When he went to stand next to her, he noticed blood-red chafe marks on her (slender) wrists. On her left cheek a large bruise was still visible.

He gestured at her wrist. 'Where did that come from?' he asked.

'That's my business,' she said, without looking at him.

'No, it isn't!' he said. 'I have a right to know! I was worried. I was afraid something might have happened to you.'

'I'm moving out,' she said. 'I've come to give notice.'

He took her by the shoulders, turned her to face him. 'Charelle, look at me!' he said. She tugged herself free. But not before he'd seen a large scab on her brow.

'Somebody hit you,' he said.

She said nothing.

He ordered the man, who had remained frozen stiff in one place, to sit down at the kitchen table. (Why had he let the fucking guy in?)

'Charelle,' he said, 'who hurt you like that? Have you had another fit?' (Though he knew that it took much more than an epileptic fit to leave somebody looking like that.)

She said nothing. Rinsed the cup. Put it on the drying rack.

'Was it the man, the guy who threatened you?'

She shrugged.

Behind him the man started tapping his fingers lightly but urgently on the kitchen table, making a strange high nasal humming sound like a singing telephone pole.

'Just shut up for a moment,' he told the man. Who all of a sudden lowered his head in his arms and started wailing softly. For crying in a fucking bucket.

'Charelle,' he said, 'please, let's sit down. Let's talk. I'll make you a cup of tea.'

'There's nothing to say,' she said. 'I'm going to pack my stuff. Desirée is coming to pick me up.' He did not recognise her. This was not the same girl who had sat with him at the table eating and laughing and talking.

She dried her hands on the dishcloth. Hung it up neatly. When she turned around, he involuntarily moved closer to her, but she stepped back so violently that he thought he was getting the message: Don't touch me, stay away from me.

He stayed behind alone with the man. He now had no choice but to make him some tea and bread, which the man devoured hungrily. Clearly famished. He sent Marthinus an SMS. He had a problem, please could he come over. No problem, he was coming right away, Marthinus replied. Nick was at his wits' end. What should he do – try to talk to Charelle in any case? Follow her to her room? He lingered in the kitchen indecisively. He made the man some more tea and bread. At least it gave him something to do while waiting for Charelle to leave. He couldn't *believe* it.

After a while she came to stand in the door. She held out the key to him. He followed her down the passage. 'Have I done something wrong?' he asked. She shook her head. Opening the front door for her, he said: 'I'll go with you to the police. You must get protection.' She laughed, derisively. Her reaction was so unexpected, and so obviously with the intent to hurt, that he felt deeply mortified. He walked with her to the gate. He buzzed her out. Further down the street a car was parked, must have been the turban-woman. Charelle walked up to the car, didn't even look back once, got in. The car pulled off. She was still gazing straight ahead of her. He turned round, flabbergasted. He went into the house. His scalp felt tight and cold. And now there was a deranged stranger installed in his kitchen.

The man was still sitting gazing in front of him fixedly.

Shortly afterwards Marthinus buzzed. Nick was glad to see him. The man remained motionlessly gazing in front of him. Nick informed Marthinus briefly of the situation. He made tea for them. The three of them sat at the kitchen table. (Where he and Charelle had so recently still shared such convivial meals.)

'Charelle was here,' he said. 'She's gone. She only came to give notice.'

Marthinus was shocked. 'No,' he said.

'She's been assaulted,' said Nick. 'She didn't want to say by whom, she doesn't want to stay here any longer. I have no idea if it has anything to do with me. Whether she's been targeted because she was living here.'

'Let's go and hear what Tarquin and company can tell us,' said Marthinus. 'Perhaps they'll have information.'

'Information of what kind?!' Nick exclaimed. 'It's too late now!'

All of a sudden the man started talking. Rapidly and totally expressionlessly he gabbled the words, like something he'd learnt by heart, while staring fixedly in front of him. 'A thing came down from the sky – a round thing – a shiny disc – it shone like gold – spun like a wheel – it was a great wheel – it had almost like wings – we were afraid – the heavens grew dark – we tried to run away – then there was a voice – do not be afraid, it said – a man emerged – he was garbed in

87

fire – his countenance radiated a glow – he was like a mighty ruler – he extended his hand to us – then there was a terrible noise – like unto the wings of thousands and thousands of locusts – there was a great cloud of dust – we shouted – then the sky was dark with the sound – we could see nothing for the dust – we called out again, but it was too late – we lay flat on the earth – there was blood everywhere – there was much pain, and great darkness.'

As suddenly as he'd started, the man stopped talking.

'Oh Lord,' said Marthinus, leaning forward across the table to Nick. 'Do you remember the part in *The Shallows* where this huge thing – something between a flying saucer and a home-made spaceship – lands in a maize field? An ambush. A helluva shooting match ensues between the occupants and the locals – a real bloodbath. At one point the bullets are compared to locusts.'

'So?' said Nick, but he knew without any doubt what Marthinus was getting at.

'So,' said Marthinus. 'It would not surprise me one bit if Victor Schoeman were behind this little lot. Read *The Shallows* – it's all there! It's ominous. Unheimlich.'

Nick was tired. He was upset. He did not want the man in his kitchen. He had to leave, *now*. He didn't want to listen to Marthinus' theories. He wanted to go and lie on his bed in his room. He wanted time to get over the shock of Charelle's sudden reappearance and departure.

'What do you mean, Marthinus?' he asked wearily. Across from him the man still sat staring fixedly in front of him.

'My suspicion is that Victor sent him. This man is a calling card from Victor.'

'Why would he want to do that?' Nick asked, aghast.

'From an excess of unchannelled ingenuity and malice,' said Marthinus.

'Which means *what*?' Nick exclaimed. Impatient, irate.

'Victor is a restless schemer,' said Marthinus. 'He thrives on intrigue.

He's paranoid. As blackguards often are. He's manipulative, he's a schemer. He's inventive. He wouldn't be such a good writer if he weren't. But unfortunately he doesn't confine himself to writing. He's devious and unscrupulous. In short, he has an excess of imagination, but no form or medium can contain his destructive energy. And he's his own greatest enemy. I don't know. Does he have some issue or other with you?'

'No,' said Nick. 'Apart from owing me money. Which I don't expect he'll pay back after all these years. So how do *you* know him?'

'I had the dubious privilege of seeing him in action when we were on the same committee in the late eighties. We collaborated for a while with the trade unions. Just before I packed my bags for foreign shores.'

'So what now,' said Nick, 'I'm not up to keeping the man here.'

'I'll take him to our place,' said Marthinus. 'No problem. There's an extra room. Rosita can check out his injuries. Tomorrow we can find out where he's from.'

'Or whether perhaps he's escaped from some high-security psychiatric institution,' said Nick. Wryly.

'Indeed,' said Marthinus, 'oh Lord.'

The man let himself be led away by Marthinus without demur. Nick was profoundly grateful. He had neither the patience nor the empathy to concern himself any further with an injured nutcase. He shouldn't have let him in in the first place. Whatever would have happened to the wretched guy in that case, it was none of his business. And of Victor he didn't even want to think this evening.

It was nine o'clock when Marthinus at last cleared out with the man. Nick remained behind dumbfounded and exhausted. He went and sat on the bed in Charelle's room. The room was as empty as if she'd never lived there. If he had to accept that anything whatsoever that he'd done had contributed to what happened to Charelle, he'd go round the bend.

He would sell this house. He'd put it on the market the very next day. He'd live in his studio for the time being. This space had lost any appeal it once had. It had been spoilt for him for ever. He wanted to put it behind him. And he didn't want Victor to find him here. Calling card or not, he had no yen to see him again. He didn't like him and he didn't want to see him again.

He had trouble falling asleep and his sleep was disturbed. Half-asleep, in the early hours, he turned to Isabel next to him in bed and called her name. He reached for her sleeping form, but woke up with a shock when he realised next to him the bed was empty; Isabel was gone from his life. In the months since they'd separated, she'd not once got in touch with him again.

Thirteen

The following morning Nick contacted the agent who'd sold him the house, and by the afternoon she phoned to say that she had a buyer. The person had made a cash offer and was interested in immediate occupation. Nick was alarmed. And who was this prospective (over-eager) buyer?

His name was Buks Verhoef, said the agent, perhaps Nick knew about him, he was a Stellenbosch artist. He wanted to convert the house into a small private gallery.

Buks Verhoef?! Enormously successful artist. He'd achieved fame through his heart-warming daubs: cheerful, gaudy street and country scenes. A few years earlier he'd moved on to three-dimensional work – bronze sculptures of wild animals – leopards, hyenas, lions, warthogs, and nowadays even elephants, which were bought at gigantic prices by foreign visitors. It was unlikely that he was personally responsible for these sculptures – he presumably had a team who executed his concepts in his enormous workshop behind his gallery. Buks was a big man, with a melancholy vibe. He looked like a pushover, but rumour had it that he was an astute businessman.

Marthinus reported that afternoon that he'd contacted all psychiatric institutions in all of Cape Town and surrounds. Nowhere was there a patient missing. The three chaps who'd escaped from the high-security institution near Moorreesburg were safely back under lock and key after their little escapade. And none of them had been injured. Rosita had dressed the man's wounds and Marthinus had taken him to the police station that morning, where he'd been reported as missing. He hadn't reacted to Victor's name, said Marthinus (ever so slightly disappointed?).

Nick was relieved. The less Victor featured (loomed ominously on the horizon) in his life, the better it suited him.

'I put my house on the market this morning,' he said. 'The agent's already let me know that the Stellenbosch artist Buks Verhoef wants to buy it. Cash.'

'Buks Verhoef!' Marthinus exclaimed. 'You can't sell your house to Buks Verhoef!'

'And why not?!' asked Nick.

'Bad energy!' said Marthinus. 'You don't want to soil your hands with his money – he's a crook and a swindler! And besides, his work's an abomination; an insult even to the man in the street. Like me,' he added, and laughed. 'No, oh Lord. Just for that you must avoid him.'

So that solved the matter for Nick. He phoned the agent and said he no longer wanted to sell. He was thinking of letting sometime in the future.

*

At the Metropolitan Museum in New York Nick had more than once gone to see the Astor Court. The design of this courtyard was based on the Garden of the Master of the Fishing Nets, from the Ming dynasty. This garden was in Suzhou, near Shanghai, and was celebrated as one of the most beautiful gardens in China. The courtyard consisted of three typical garden structures: a covered walkway, a small reception area, and a half-pavilion against the west wall. The small reception room also served as a terrace from which the moon could be viewed. Here the master of the house had gathered with friends to write poetry, taste a new tea, and to enjoy the full moon. The courtyard was designed in such a way that at full moon it was wholly illuminated. The plaque above the entrance to the courtyard as a whole read: 'In Search of Quietude', and the one above the entrance to the Ming Room: 'Elegant Repose'. Gardeners chose poetic names for their structures to evoke a specific emotion or literary association. Every rock in the Astor Court was a piece of weathered limestone from Lake T'ai near Suzhou. The Chinese word for landscape (Shanshui) literally meant mountains and water. In Chinese gardens rocks represented high mountains, swathed in mist, or floating islands. In particular, rocks with freakish forms, top-heavy, with many perforations, were highly prized. These holes in the rocks represented caves and grottos – symbolic portals to other worlds; a refuge from times of unrest and confusion. In one corner was a small pond between a group of rocks, with koi fish and purling water, evoking a waterfall in a distant landscape between mountains.

Nick recalled this moon-viewing terrace when Marthinus asked him the following day (Wednesday) whether he didn't want to come round that evening for a drink. Nick accepted. Perhaps the evening with the full moon and unfamiliar friends might prove interesting.

When he arrived, there were two men sitting on the stoep, a big man with an egg-shaped head and a small man with a peaked cap. The man with the egg-shaped head was called Anselmo Balla and the smaller man's name was Selwyn Levitan. Anselmo growled something and Selwyn jumped up and shook Nick's hand. They gazed out over the bay. They drank beer. The sun set. Anselmo from time to time broke wind. He glowered grimly straight ahead of him. He was restless, he fidgeted, he snorted, he produced strange sounds through his nose. A cool breeze came up from the sea. Nick thought: if only he could have a proper conversation with Charelle.

Later the full moon rose over the mountain, diagonally behind them. They drank more beer. No tea tonight as on the Chinese pavilion from which the moon could be viewed. The moon climbed higher. No poetry either. Anselmo snorted and harrumphed and wriggled about while talking (passionately, emphatically). His foot tapped up and down and his hands were never still. Selwyn Levitan, on the other hand, sat virtually motionless all evening, marvelling at the moon.

*

When Nick got home late on Thursday afternoon who should be waiting for him in front of his house in his motor car but Buks Verhoef. (A Jaguar, in case Nick needed further proof of Verhoef's prosperity.) Not only was he corpulent (descending from his car with difficulty), but apparently also asthmatic. He wheezed his way up the stoep steps. Wiped his forehead with a handkerchief. Wouldn't Nick consider selling after all, he asked when they had sat down. He could offer more than the asking price. Cash. Why was he so keen on buying this particular house? Nick asked. He'd had his eye on a house in this area for a long time, but there weren't all that many available. He wanted to convert the house into a small private art gallery. What did he mean by private? Well (Verhoef seemed uncomfortable), an exclusive gallery that was not accessible to the general public. Nick got a notion that Verhoef was not telling the whole truth. An exclusive gallery for exclusive buyers? That could mean anything. Buks plied his asthma pump, wiped his forehead once more, shifted about uncomfortably. Enormous thighs. Something disarming about him. Something of the shy, fat, awkward schoolboy. Nick found him engaging, in spite of not trusting him.

For the time being no, said Nick, but he would give it some thought.

Fourteen

A month or so after Jacobus' death I flee to the Eastern Cape. I know I'm leaving you in the lurch, but I can't stay here any longer. If I stayed, I would perish, that I know. I stay with friends on the outskirts of an Eastern Cape town. A beautiful view of the quarry and the surrounding hills. A clump of bluegums in front of the house. They put a spacious outside room at my disposal. That suits me well. I can still do my freelance work here. It is bitterly cold. The end of winter, often the coldest time of year. Sometimes I accompany my friends to town when they go to work. Once I go to look at the coelacanth in the museum. The big fish is yellowish-pale, so different from what I had imagined. In its natural habitat, apparently, it glimmers like mother-of-pearl, in iridescent greens and blue-greens. At times I simply walk through the town, or have coffee somewhere. In the main street, once, I see goats eating from the refuse bags put out in the streets. I negotiate with Zimbabwean traders, at a stall in town, behind the cathedral, to make me a skull from wire and white beads. We agree on a price. When I'm not happy with the finished skull, they have to change it. I find that I don't want the mouth to be open (in a manic grimace). They undo the wire securing the hinges of the jaw, close the mouth; the wire teeth no longer fit snugly over one another, but it looks better already. When completed, it's too broad in the brow – it looks like a Neanderthal skull – but I like it nevertheless. I spend a considerable time in the university library. I like working there. This is where I come across a book on Nancy Spero. Her work speaks very directly to me. Also the work of Stanley Spencer – which I don't know all that well, and which is a pleasant surprise. Especially the resurrection scene, and the scenes in the British camps of the First World War. I read eyewitness accounts of five survivors recounting their experiences the day the atom bomb was dropped on Hiroshima. I read in a book on Spero that Artaud's writing is an underwater subliminal descent into a black, deadly world in which the feminine is simultaneously celebrated and stigmatised. I haven't read Artaud extensively myself, because I can barely endure his brilliant grotesquery, or his life, or his suffering, or his notebooks on pain. There in the library I also read that Nietzsche maintained that torture is a woman: the pulling of a tooth, the plucking out of an eye. The violence of the Christian idea, the idea that becomes woman. The penetration of warm female corpses presenting (offering) their orifices. In Nancy Spero's work men and dogs pollute the city, while women run, masturbate, copulate and perform acrobatics. It is bitterly cold. By now I believe that I'll never in my entire life be warm again. It's no longer just the organs in my body that are cold, the cold gradually seeps through to my bones. I imagine that I can see my frozen skeleton as if it's projected onto a screen in front of me: my bones like ice crystals. My friends stoke up a great fire in the evenings, but of what use is it to me, my core remains frozen; I am still prey to my thoughts. On the bedside table stands the Neanderthal skull of wire and white beads. Instead of hollowing out the nose, the Zimbabwean traders have let it protrude slightly.

When I don't go to town, I study my friends' medical handbooks. I examine, among others, the part on the surgical anatomy of the cleft palate in *Gray's Anatomy*.

At this time I start watching the videos of the Olivier brothers intensively. My good friend Willem Wepener put me on their track. Later he also encouraged me to write a monograph on them.

At the beginning of spring I return to Stellenbosch. It's a bracing season, the icy spring rains start to fall, millions of frail little snails hatch overnight, and the tender buds of the vineyards and the trees start to burgeon. You have in the meantime left on a long journey, to get your mind off things. You travel to far and unusual places, you peer down a crater and ascend a peak and row down a river full of green silt. You send postcards. Although you nevertheless persevere, you say, you know that all your wanderings are a futile attempt to displace your sorrow.

At the end of the year I start – hesitantly and with great circumspection – writing the monograph on the Olivier brothers. At the beginning of the new year you are back in town again and I meet you in the coffee shop, the day it rained so incessantly.

I do so like Saramago's novel *The Year of the Death of Ricardo Reis*. Reis is one of Pessoa's heteronyms. Pessoa has died and his spirit is granted another nine months on earth to set his affairs in order. During this time he sometimes appears to Reis, who has just arrived in Lisbon. Reis's life goes into a slow decline, starts subsiding more and more into passivity, and in the end he puts on his jacket and follows Pessoa to the cemetery. It is with an effort that I tear myself away from the space of the novel. Something of the sombre density of it lingers with me.

Fifteen

Once on their travels Isabel had said to him she felt like a pupa. Not something from which a moth or a butterfly was going to emerge, but as in a film being run backwards, in which the moth slips back into the pupa, the pupa changes into a worm, the worm into an egg, the egg becomes a speck, which grows smaller and smaller, until it vanishes. Until not even a molecule or an atom remains of it. She felt as if she was going to be annihilated, she said, into the most profound cosmic oblivion, into the smallest quantum unit of non-existence – and it was going to be BLISS.

They were sitting opposite each other in the cafeteria of the Metropolitan Museum. Nick didn't know what to say. He didn't let on. Keep your gaze neutral, he told himself. Don't show that you're disconcerted. She doesn't need it now.

They drank their tea in silence. Isabel watched the people intently. From her unruffled expression there was little to be read of her internal turmoil, at any rate by an outsider. When they'd finished, he asked if she wanted to go and see the Astor Court with him. She only shook her head slightly, in refusal. When he saw her sitting there like that, he had an intense desire to take her in his arms and to nestle her poor, tortured head against his shoulder. His fingers in her hair (flaxen-white like wool), his fingertips healingly on her thin, fragile skull. But he was scared of her as well – she was so completely impenetrable in her misery. He'd gone alone, and sat there for a long time on his own. The rocks represented mountains, the pond a lake or a sea. A landscape of distant mountains and rivers.

This was what Nick thought of on his way to work on Friday when he looked at the mountain range on the distant horizon. When he got home that evening he decided he would sell his house to Buks Verhoef after all. In spite of the fact that Marthinus had advised him not to do it. He no longer liked the house. It held bad associations for him. Tomorrow he would phone the agent.

*

On the day on which I can see the old father for a second time, I first have a cup of coffee in town.

Opposite me, at a long table, is Buks Verhoef, the much-loved local artist. The place doesn't really do it for me. It's pretentious, like everything in this town. I sit at a smaller table, with my back to the shelves filled with exorbitantly priced exclusive vinegars, wines, muesli, packets of biscuits and rusks. My laptop is open in front of me. I read what I've written about the Olivier brothers in preparation for my interview with the father.

A man comes into the coffee shop. I take note of him, because he's wearing a winter jacket on this hot day. A strangely old-fashioned Harris Tweed. Very ugly, very unflatteringly cut. He's wearing large black-framed glasses (also particularly unflattering), his hair is almost shoulder-length and oily, and he looks bewildered. I look at him musingly. What would he be doing here, he seems so out of place? It looks as if he wants to sit down at the little table in the centre of the shop, near the entrance, between me and Verhoef.

The next moment he suddenly snaps into action, swiftly moves to the door, aims a pistol in Buks Verhoef's direction, fires a few shots, and before I can register properly what's happened, the man is out by the door. General consternation ensues: a yelling and screaming. Deafening.

Buks Verhoef is lying head forward on the scrubbed table. Fatally wounded in the heart? No spattering of blood on the wall behind him – so the bullets didn't go through the body. In one corner a clutch of

99

screaming customers and waitresses huddle together, and in the other corner (behind the pillars) two women are yelling hysterically.

Because I have been trained in first aid, I rush to Verhoef's assistance. I try to lift him carefully from behind, my forearms under his armpits. I get him up straight, leaning back against my chest, his head lolls back against my shoulder. His face is turned towards me at an angle. My cheek just about against his. He is a big, heavy man. Too heavy for me to lay him down on the floor on my own. He's been shot in the chest. The blood is literally spurting out in a bright red arc. I try to staunch the bleeding – press a handful of serviettes to the wound – but it's difficult to keep him upright at the same time with just one arm. But it's certainly too late already. Blood is burbling out of his mouth. He must have been hit in the lungs as well. He is dying. His face is half turned towards me. At first, for a few moments, there is shock and disbelief in his gaze, then bewilderment, then despair, and then he casts up his eyes to me in a last look of resignation as he surrenders himself to the inevitability of his own death. With my rapidly fading image as accompaniment, the soul of Buks Verhoef takes flight from his mouth. Poor Buks. His body goes limp in my arms. His head drops forward again, his arms droop limply by his sides when I remove my arms from his armpits. That's how I leave him. I've never been scared of blood, but I'd forgotten how vividly it pumps. So as a result I am beset by an enormous sorrow.

There is blood everywhere. It's already formed a puddle on the table in front of him. Customers are ushered out of the shop. I leave the man with his head on the table, and quickly slip away to the bathroom at the back of the shop, before it can be cordoned off. Just as well the bullets didn't go through the body, else I would have been drenched in blood. As it is, there is blood only on my hands, my wrists and on the sleeves of my light summer jersey. I take off the jersey carefully. Fortunately I'm wearing a short-sleeved T-shirt, otherwise that would have been blood-spattered as well. I wash my hands thoroughly, with hot water, up to the elbows. I rinse the sleeves of my jersey quickly in cold water – I'll wash it properly later at home.

When I'm done, the police have turned up already. Because I'm coming from the back of the coffee shop and nobody else has remained behind in the shop (I'm the only eyewitness who hasn't run away or fainted), I do double duty as the first suspect as well. A well-rounded female sergeant asks me to sit down at one of the tables. (Her name tag says Nkosikati Ndlovu.)

I watch a little scrum struggling to lift Buks's large body onto a stretcher. My legs are lame. My hands are trembling. The magazines that had been lying in front of Buks and the newspaper he'd been reading are drenched in blood. The blood is already starting to form a puddle under his chair as well. The emergency team at last manages to load Buks's body onto the stretcher and to carry him out by the door. My hands are trembling uncontrollably. Did I know the deceased? Not personally, but I know who he is. Did I notice any suspicious-looking person? Yes, a man in glasses and a jacket. This the sergeant finds suspicious. How could I have noticed this? (Sergeant, madam, I happen to be very perceptive.) I noticed it because it's unusual for somebody to wear a jacket like that on a hot day. What colour was it? Grey-brown, I think, with a herringbone pattern. An ugly jacket, I add, 'not very fashionable; very badly cut'. The sergeant regards me with sharpened interest. The more detail I provide, the more suspicious she finds me, that's clear. If on top of everything I find space in my statement to comment on the cut of the person's jacket, I must undoubtedly have criminal tendencies. Add to this my conspicuous and unprepossessing lip defect, and I am the prime suspect hands down. How else – the physical scar as mark of a damaged psyche. What was I doing here? I was having coffee before conducting an interview with somebody in town. I was sitting here minding my own business (even though I detest the place. Even though I'm already scheming another escape from the town. I just first have to get at the old father again). I was working on my laptop, I say. There it still is on the table where I was sitting. Thank God not stolen in the general chaos! The sergeant wants to check it. Exhibit number one in court: the laptop belonging to the harelip with the blood-smeared clothes. (When I look down, I notice for the first time dark blood spatterings on my T-shirt.) Sergeant, I say, believe me, I have nothing to do with this. By all means check my laptop, but then please let me go, I have an appointment in half an hour's time that I can't put off and I still have to freshen up, make myself decent. (Or should I turn up at the old father's with bloodstains on my clothes? Would that make his memory kick in?) Now may I please use the bathroom again? I may, but a member of the Service must accompany me. She must wait for me outside the door.

Once again I rinse my face and hands. Have a drink of water, I suddenly have a raging thirst. My hands are still trembling. I take off my T-shirt, do my best, but it's virtually impossible to remove the spots of blood without wetting the whole T-shirt. Fortunately it's not a white shirt.

The sergeant seems not at all persuaded of my innocence. She checks my ID document, takes down the number. Gets my address and other details. I must see to it that I don't leave town in the next forty-eight hours. I have to report to the police station tomorrow morning. If I should attempt to get away, they would be on my trail immediately.

*

Outside the light is blindingly bright all of a sudden. The entrance to the coffee shop has been cordoned off with yellow tape, but a large crowd of rubbernecks has already congregated on the pavement. A woman is crying uncontrollably. I am inspected with great interest when I emerge. I am probably regarded as a suspect. A camera flashes. Fortunately I was keeping my head averted. Tomorrow my photo will appear in the press. I'm not easily put off my stride, but in the car I realise that my teeth are chattering, as if I'm cold. Even though I washed my hands and face and tried to rinse the blood from my T-shirt as thoroughly as possible (just as well I'm wearing dark-coloured jeans today), I'm still not entirely clean. (Who could ever have guessed that I'd have the blood of Buks Verhoef on my hands?) I sniff at my hands, at my arms, at my shirt, and fancy that I can smell an undertone of blood. (Perhaps the old father will pick it up as well.)

The gates of the retirement village swing open once more. Miss De Jongh is awaiting me. I inform her briefly of what happened. She must thus please excuse a blood spot or two, should she notice any. If she's shocked, she doesn't let on, but I do imagine that I catch a flicker of sharpened interest in her eye – even something a trifle arch, perhaps? A girl who's game for adventure? She is once again wearing a low-cut top that displays her impressive bosom to advantage. Is this magnificent sight wasted on the old father, or does he take delight in it? Delight and more. Way back there was nothing wrong with his appetite. Although.

This time he's sitting on a cane chair on the stoep. It's still warm enough to sit outside. He has a light travelling rug over his knees. Once again he hardly glances at me. He is sitting so that he can gaze over the garden, in the direction of the dam, where last we stood looking at the koi. What will I drink? asks Miss De Jongh – a soft drink perhaps, sugar for the shock? (Sarcastic?) Make that something stronger, please, I say. She nods. An understanding. (It would be advantageous to have her on my side.) Whisky? A double, please. A conspiratorial glint in her eye, unless I'm imagining things. (I need the strong liquor. I now have the shakes, lightly. The screams of the customers still echo in my ears. Of Buks's last, beseeching glance I can't rid myself.)

The double tot calms me, but dulls my focus. The woman seems in fact not disinclined to pour me another shot on the spot. I suddenly get the impression that she fancies a drink or two herself, and she is probably the keeper of the key of the well-stocked liquor cabinet. Old father was no teetotaller, if my memory serves. Will Miss De Jongh and I become friends? Confidantes? Will she tell me how stingy he is, how badly he pays her, how she hates working for him, how she sometimes considers putting something in his drink? She's not my type. Her expression is too businesslike, too stony. A chilly glance, and not ironic – not unlike that of her employer.

Nowadays whole days pass without my seeing anybody, talking to anybody. The town I find alienating. The town centre I avoid, buy my milk and vegetables at the smaller shops, the KwikSpar, the Engen on the Somerset West road. After the excesses and indulgences of my youth I hardly drink anything any more, the whisky goes to my head in an instant. It does, though, dull the sharpest edge of the screams and the ringing in my ears. It lifts my inhibitions. I draw my chair closer to that of the professor.

'As you know by now,' I say, 'I'm writing a monograph on your sons. I would like more information from you regarding their childhood and youth.'

For the first time he faces me directly. If fleetingly. If he recognises me, he doesn't let on. If he didn't recognise me, it would not be odd. I couldn't very well hold it against him. But has he sensed something, has his interest been piqued by the trace of the smell of blood on my person, my clothes?

'What do you want to know?' he asks.

(*Now* we're talking.)

'I understand that you were the single parent to the boys for the greater part of their childhood and youth. When did their mother leave, and under what circumstances? Isn't it customary for the court to grant custody to the mother rather than to the father?'

The whisky has emboldened me too much. Wrong question. I see, or imagine I see, a momentary contraction of his pupils at the mention of his former wife. I shouldn't have put it like that. I shouldn't have given him a gap.

'The court grants custody to the father when it is found that the mother has neglected her duty or been negligent, or in the case of adultery or malicious desertion,' he says. 'When my former wife deserted us maliciously, she left the children in my care without scruple, second thought or any subsequent regrets. She ran off with her lover. Her lover at the time.' (For the time being I ignore the insinuation that there had been a multitude of lovers afterwards.)

'May I ask how old the boys were when this happened?' I ask.

'The boys were six years old,' he says.

'And did they retain contact with their mother afterwards?' I ask.

'From her side she never again made any attempt to take up contact with them,' he says.

'So from their seventh year the boys never again had contact with their mother?'

'That is correct,' he says.

'Is she still alive?' I ask.

'That I would not know,' he says.

'And as boys did they not miss her? Or even try later to get in touch with her?'

Wrong questions. Too soon to delve for vital information. I've botched the interview. Lost my focus. I still feel the dead weight of Buks in my arms. The smell of blood lingers on in my nostrils. The whisky has clouded my judgement. Olivier – quite rightly – ignores my question, turns to Miss De Jongh, who, with legs crossed, is sitting diagonally across from him on a garden bench, smoking, and gestures with the broad yellow-pale hand. (I have remembered the shape of his hand very precisely.) A sign that the interview has been terminated. She steps on the cigarette with her heel, gets up, and shortly afterwards accompanies me to the front door. It's cool when I walk to my car. I sniff at my arm, at my T-shirt. Unmistakable still the warm, meaty iron smell.

Janetta and I had gone to have a drink at the hotel on the outskirts of the town. Like wolves we ran together everywhere, in cahoots. She was pretty, with a broad forehead and cool, grey-blue eyes. Two men sat across from us in the pub. There was a cosy fire in the fireplace. I recognised one of them straightaway, he was a professor of history at the university, high profile. After a while they asked if they could join us, buy us a drink. Certainly, why not? After quite a few drinks the friend made a proposition to Janetta. I went with Olivier to his room. (Why the two were booked into the hotel for the night I don't know.) Why did I go with him? I would have done anything at the time for the sake of the adventure, just for the hell of it. Even so, I wasn't prepared for what followed. We'd hardly got to his room, when without preliminary he sat me down roughly on the edge of the bed, came to stand in front of me, opened his fly, grabbed my head firmly and pushed it down, tried to force his penis into my mouth. I bit him. He slapped me, on the side of my head, hard, so that my ears rang. I kicked at him. He grabbed me by the arm, jerked me upright, pressed me against one wall, banged my head against the wall, slapped me in the face, so that my nose started bleeding. (I wondered whether it was strictly necessary for him to be quite so murderous.) I brought my knee up hard between his legs. In the few moments that he was off balance, I grabbed my handbag on the bed and cleared out. With bleeding nose and without shoes I ran back to town. It was raining. Did I report him to the university council, or whatever? No, what for. At the time I believed that if you got into trouble you had to get out of it as well as you could. The next day Janetta and I laughed about my narrow escape. Even though I was far gone at the time and mainly on a suicide mission, I was damned if I was going to let myself be raped by such a cold fish, such a stupid cunt. I never saw him again. Shortly afterwards, in any case, I left town. I left when Janetta left. Without her the place was even less to my taste.

*

I go home. I rinse out the jersey. The water turns a pale red. I scrub myself vigorously under a hot shower. I'm fed-up with myself for having botched the interview. Perhaps the old father won't even want to talk to me again. So now I'll patiently have to regain his confidence. Think up some alternative strategy. First talk to him about his own work. I'll flatter him. He's probably the kind of man who thrives on soft soap.

The next day I buy a newspaper. There is a blurred photo of me, head averted, taken as I was coming out of the coffee shop. At this stage no clear motive for the murder has been established, maintain the police, but they're doing their best. Yes, for sure. The town is shocked, to a man. *A beloved inhabitant dies*, says the newspaper headline. Everywhere on trees the posters: *Shock death of well-known artist*.

In a weird way I want to return to the coffee shop where Buks Verhoef was shot. (For the time being that's not possible – clearing-up operations will probably take a while.) I feel the need to anchor the – still unreal – event. I replay it again and again in my memory. It happened so suddenly that it's as if it never happened. And poor Verhoef's last gaze, at first despairing and then resigned – like an animal before it's executed.

I meet you in town for coffee. I tell you what happened, how Buks Verhoef died in my arms. How I still find it difficult to believe what happened. You are shocked. You can imagine that it's difficult to believe – such a violent event – so unexpectedly and without any warning. (We must both be thinking of the death of Jacobus.)

I'm well, you say, when I ask you how you are. I don't believe you. Your lovely eyes still seem sorrowful. I believe, like you, that you'll never be entirely well again. His death tore a hole out of your heart, you said once. Irreparable, something like that. From now on you'll be limping along, you said. Crippled. Of everyone and everything you loved him best.

*

Marthinus phoned in the early morning.

'Have you seen the newspaper?' he asked.

Nick had been dreaming of a bed of black lava ash in which his father said they should plant peas. He was still groggy with sleep.

'What?'

'Buks Verhoef was shot and killed in a coffee shop in Stellenbosch.'

Nick was shocked. His first (guilty) thought was that he now no longer had a buyer for his house.

'What happened?'

'The police don't know yet. But a suspect has been apprehended.'

Now Nick was sorry that he hadn't sold his house on the spot to Buks Verhoef. Although that probably would not have been of much use. He'd have gotten the money only once the estate had been settled. But now that the sale had fallen through, he was less than ever inclined to stay in the house. Perhaps he should let it immediately and go and live in his studio.

Marthinus said: 'I told you, didn't I, that you shouldn't sell your house to Buks Verhoef. He's mixed up with all kinds of crooks and swindlers.'

'He wasn't necessarily shot by a crook or swindler,' said Nick. 'Was the coffee shop robbed?'

'Nobody else was injured,' said Marthinus. 'Nothing or nobody was robbed. Apparently the man came into the shop, shot Verhoef and then ran out.'

'That doesn't sound good,' said Nick.

'No,' said Marthinus. 'Verhoef's death is in all probability connected with his shady dealings – illegal art trade and all that, it wouldn't surprise me one bit. And those are exactly the kind of shenanigans Victor would be involved in. That's exactly the kind of criminal activity that would appeal to him.'

Nick groaned. 'Oh, come on, Marthinus,' he said. 'Now you're going too far. Victor can't have a finger in every pie!'

'Why not? Oh Lord. I have a very strong intuition that that man is back in the country with a definite agenda and is cooking up some scheme somewhere behind the scenes. Guerrilla tactics – the robber gangs and protagonists and all sorts of bit players striking all the time in unexpected places. Just as they do in his novels.'

'But, Marthinus,' said Nick, 'surely you can't jump to that kind of conclusion just because things happen like that in his novels!'

'I can't?!' said Marthinus. 'Why not?'

'It doesn't work like that,' said Nick.

'So how does it work?'

'Marthinus, I don't know. I don't know how it works, but it doesn't sound right to me.'

'Think about it again,' said Marthinus. 'Remember – Victor Schoeman isn't your man in the street. With him anything is possible. He's not a guy who can distinguish between reality and fiction. I have a sense that all these things are related to one another.'

'But, Marthinus,' said Nick, 'at first you thought that Victor was involved in the Moorreesburg affair – the inmates who escaped from the high-security facility; then you thought that the mental case who sat here in my kitchen was one of the inmates. A calling card from Victor. In both cases you were wrong. Now you want to allege that Victor had something to do with the murder of Buks Verhoef. All on the basis of events in *The Shallows*.'

'Look,' said Marthinus, 'I know it doesn't sound very convincing, but I have a strong intuition that all these events are linked, and I can usually trust my intuition.'

'Marthinus . . .' said Nick.

'Look,' said Marthinus, 'just because you can't see it immediately, that doesn't mean there's no link. That man is back in the country with a purpose. What the purpose is, I don't know, but that it's connected with all sorts of things we've heard about in the recent past, that I don't doubt. I sense it in my bones. Oh Lord. He likes games. He likes planting clues. For him everything is play – the more reckless, the better – life and death as well, unfortunately. A strong psychopathic streak, we can agree on that. Even a full-blown psychopathy. Nowadays apparently the term is sociopath. But with this incredible imagination. Just look at the novels, just look at *The Shallows*. Underrated. Too demanding. No reviewer wanted to risk an opinion on it. Brilliant in parts. The internal monologues! The sustained and irreverent imagination! I almost want to call it a masterpiece. Something between Flaubert and that hideously astonishing Chilean, Bolaño. The same gruesome and senseless violence, the same piling-up technique – hundreds and hundreds of pages – the same cryptic dead ends and loose ends and brutal, poetic leaps—'

'I'm going away,' Nick interrupted him. 'I'm going to rent a room somewhere. I don't want to receive Victor in my house. I don't even want to *know* about his plans and his psychopathic activities. Sorry. In any case, I don't like my house any more.'

'Oh come,' said Marthinus. 'Don't let yourself be scared off unnecessarily. Are you coming to watch *The Man Who Wasn't There* with us tonight?'

*

Later that morning Nick bought a newspaper. On page three there was an indistinct photo of the suspect who had shot Buks Verhoef. He examined it more closely – the man looked suspiciously like the Chris Kestell double that he'd met earlier that year in the coffee shop! And the coffee shop was the exact same one where he'd been accosted by the same man. Although at close quarters the man had looked less like Chris Kestell (the meandering eye). But in any case he liked all of this not at all. He didn't want to tell Marthinus about this. It would only confirm his suspicions and encourage him to further far-fetched deductions. He didn't want to abet Marthinus in his flights of fancy. He didn't know him well enough to know how reliable his intuitions were. He wasn't going to say anything. He was going to leave it to Marthinus to notice the resemblance, or not to notice it. Perhaps, in fact, the resemblance was coincidental. The photo was not very clear. Perhaps he had Chris Kestell on his mind, at the instigation of Marthinus.

Sixteen

Marthinus invited him for a beer and they sat outside on the stoep, even though the autumn air already had a nip to it. This evening Alfons was there as well, and Selwyn Levitan. Alfons had lively blue eyes and an upright, dignified, patriarchal air.

It was a near-moonless night. Lights were twinkling in the bay. Marthinus had previously pointed out the location of the urban farm to him, and behind it the informal settlement where Tarquin and company sometimes hung out. Nick fancied that he could see faint lights in that vicinity, like tiny fires, but he couldn't be sure. The people probably kept a low profile, especially at night. If not, they'd be detected, targeted and driven out – back to where they came from.

They talked about the murder of Buks Verhoef.

Selwyn asked what had happened.

Nick said the man was shot and killed point blank in a coffee shop. For the time being he didn't mention that he thought the suspect looked like the Chris Kestell double that he'd come across by chance in the same coffee shop a few weeks earlier. If Marthinus were to hear that, he'd make another meal of it.

Marthinus said that he'd read that a memorial service would be held in the town hall. Verhoef had had so many hangers-on and admirers and friends that that was the only hall that would be big enough to accommodate them all. But he would be buried from the Shofar Church.

Satanism light, said Alfons.

'Satanism,' said Selwyn, 'mustn't be taken lightly. A very real force to be reckoned with. Call it Satan, call it whatever you wish.'

Nick thought of Karlien, so blonde, so expressionless, so drawn to satanism. He wondered where the fascination lay for her.

He'd seen him once, said Selwyn about Buks Verhoef. 'A very lost soul. Very permeable barriers. Very open to malediction. Very little psychic protection.'

'Oh Lord,' said Marthinus. This pronouncement of Selwyn interested him. 'Permeable barriers, you say,' he said. 'Fascinating. Does that mean that perhaps he wouldn't have been shot if he'd had more psychic protection, less permeable psychic barriers?'

'Who knows,' said Selwyn.

'I just thought he was a lard-arse and a crap artist,' said Alfons.

After Alfons had gone to bed and Selwyn had disappeared into the night (in a taxi, ordered and paid for by Marthinus), Marthinus told Nick that Selwyn's Jewish name was Menasse. 'He's your hyper-intuitive character,' said Marthinus. 'Very finely attuned to the world. Profoundly schooled in the Kabbalah. You'd never say it – by day he's an estate agent. Good intuition for the emanations of a place. Buyers trust him. Very spiritual. He's interested in the chariot.'

'What chariot?' asked Nick.

'Ezekiel's chariot, his chariot of fire,' said Marthinus. 'The Ma'aseh Merkavah. Ask him about it! He likes sharing his knowledge!'

Nick considered it, though Ezekiel and his chariot were not for the time being a burning issue in his mind.

*

Charelle did not react to his calls or text messages. Nick wanted to talk to her. He wanted to propose a meeting in a neutral space. He wanted to know that she was okay. If he could understand why she'd left, he might perhaps reconcile himself to it.

On Monday he went to the art academy to enquire about her in person. At first they wouldn't give him any information. Then the secretary said that the student Charelle Koopman was no longer registered with them. She'd dropped out of her course.

When?! asked Nick.

The date the woman mentioned was about the time when he'd last seen her, when she'd come to cancel her lease.

Did she give any reasons? he asked. But the secretary stuck to her guns. She could give no further information.

That afternoon Nick phoned Marthinus and said that he thought they should perhaps pay Tarquin and company another visit. Maybe *they* could cast some kind of light on the affair.

For the second time they ascended the slope to the settlement on the hill. Early autumn, still warm. Past the kitchen and recreation area, the prefab buildings to the left. Two elderly men and a woman were working in the vegetable garden. In the orchard a few children were playing under the trees. Everybody greeted them exuberantly as they walked past. At the top of the hill they turned right again, the bunker-like buildings in front of them.

'When Jurgen Wesseker took over here after the founding father left,' said Marthinus, 'he started getting rid of the almighty pile of junk in the bunkers. Actually lorry-loads of the stuff. It was a sight to behold. Workers and residents spent days carrying out things. When everything had been carried out, the city's poor were invited. Taxi-loads of people with shopping bags turned up from Khayelitsha and surrounding areas. They descended like blowflies on a carcass. Clapped-out bakkies carted off loads of booty. People erected makeshift stalls and bartered some of the things that they'd plundered. There was something of everything: building material, crates and boxes of all sizes filled with every conceivable and inconceivable thing; there were old magazines, books, newspapers, kitchen equipment, crockery, garden tools, broken garden and indoor furniture, empty bottles, string, wire, half-full tins of paint, masses of nails, screws, locks, hinges, thick ropes and thin ropes, bottles full of elastic bands, stuffed animals and birds, old curtains, mouldy and tattered sheets and blankets, cushions, paintings, corrugated iron sheets, pieces of Masonite. Broken toys.

Old clothes, shoes, hangers. Man, too many things to name. At last, when everything had been carted off, the place stripped, Jurgen moved in with a team of cleaners. Cleaned, painted, converted the bunkers into dormitories for the widows and orphans. Got funding from the Department of Welfare. They were probably overjoyed that the place had now passed into other hands and was under responsible management. Jurgen makes a good impression and he had a fully worked-out twelve-point plan. As I said, a chap with vision. With a sense of vocation. An orderly mind – you need something like that to run such a show. More than just a refuge for widows and orphans. A model community, or that at least is what he has in mind. Whether that's how it's going to turn out, we'll have to wait and see. There are some violent forces knocking about here – chaotic forces that are not going to allow themselves to be thwarted by any visionary or crusader. I've mentioned it before. You should hear Menasse on the subject. He has a supersensitive apprehension of revolutionary powers – it's his Jewish, Eastern European genes. Quite apart from his mystical bent.'

By now they'd passed the bunkers on the left, and were trudging up the footpath. Nick became aware of sweating in anticipation. Marthinus was wearing a kind of bush hat, khaki shorts and boots. Shapely, sturdy calves. Tanned. Today he looked like a tour guide or forest ranger. Nick also had sturdy calves, but he wasn't as fit as Marthinus. He was battling up the hill.

'Menasse is one of the most intriguing characters I know,' said Marthinus. 'The original wandering Jew. Highly intuitive. Enigmatic. Mad about sport – cricket, tennis – self-assured, but very spiritual. A mystic, in the spirit of Ezekiel. If you look carefully, you'll see – a brow as adamantine as that of the ancient prophets. Acquainted with both the awakening and the extinction of the soul. Knowledge of the sphere of the demons, the dark side of the creation. Once when I was manic, he laid the healing hands on me.'

They had now reached the hole in the fence. Was Nick imagining things, or was this fence sagging even more than the previous time?

This time it was not Tarquin sitting outside, but a different man. One of the Main Men, Marthinus whispered behind his hand. Nick didn't know what he meant. Main in the gangster world, Main in the settlement? Up here or down there in the city? The Main Man had high cheekbones, Oriental eyes, prominent nostrils, a swarthy complexion, but with a dark-red flush, and straight hair. The high cheekbones made him look like Genghis Khan. Tarquin had to be called first. He emerged, taciturn. How often would he hang out here? Nick wondered. The hut was makeshift, not very big, certainly not adjusted to the likes of Tarquin, with his gold neck chain and expensive shoes and taste for all sorts of luxuries.

The drill was the same as before. They all sat outside, Nick and Marthinus on plastic garden chairs. But this time Marthinus presented a bottle of whisky that he produced from his rucksack. It was accepted in silence (for services to be rendered), and poured by the girl. This time round Nick had prepared himself in advance, but he still found it difficult to down the liquor as quickly and with the same nonchalance as the others. He wished that, like Marthinus, he'd had a hat. The girl went off again to fetch the man with the albino dreadlocks.

Nick was sweating. He dreaded what he might hear.

Once again the litany of rapes and murders. Everything was received in silence by Tarquin and the Main Man. Neither of them reacted to the list of horrors. Business as usual. Three children were raped in the last week in Grassy Park, two boys were killed in a shooting incident in Hanover Park. A girl's body was found on the Flats; she'd been strangled and raped. Ten children were raped in Delft. The youngest was a three-month-old baby. A child was raped by other children at a school in Delft East. A farm labourer from Lynedoch was murdered by fellow prisoners in a cell in Pollsmoor. They kicked him, beat him up and strangled him with an electric cable. Two gang members were shot and killed in Mitchells Plain.

'A girl,' said the albino, 'was abducted and raped down in the city there by the art school.' Nick thought his heart would stop.

'How long ago?' asked Marthinus.

The man considered. 'About ten, fourteen days ago.'

'Is she dead?' asked Marthinus.

'No,' said the man. 'She got away. Another laitie helped her.'

Nick and Marthinus glanced at each other.

'Could you perhaps get more information on this incident?' Marthinus asked Tarquin. He nodded. 'Who was responsible for the attack. Any information.'

Tarquin nodded. They took their leave. Going downhill, Nick's legs almost gave way under him.

'In the vicinity of the art school,' he said. 'That was almost exactly when she disappeared. What are the chances that it was her?'

'It doesn't sound good,' said Marthinus, 'but you can't really tell for sure whether it was her. This kind of thing happens all the time. At least somebody helped her to escape.'

But Nick felt sick with dismay. 'Something bad must have happened to her, she was serious about her course, she wouldn't have dropped out for nothing. She was different, she wasn't herself when she came to cancel her lease. She didn't even want to look at me. Never mind talk to me.'

All the way down Marthinus tried to reassure him. Nick shouldn't blame himself for this, he said. These things happened. If it was her, if it had happened to her, remember, it didn't happen because she was renting a room from him.

How did he know that, asked Nick. How could he say that with any certainty?

No, said Marthinus, he probably couldn't say that with a hundred per cent certainty, but the violence in this city was too often unmotivated

– a question of the wrong person in the wrong place. Too often just a question of bad, bad luck.

But this was of no consolation to Nick. He would have to get in touch with the woman with the turban.

Seventeen

Marcus Olivier informs me via Miss De Jongh that he will not grant me any further interviews. No reasons are given. (He would, though, have sniffed something suspicious in the air – no doubt he would recognise the smell of blood.) I messed up the interview. Asked the wrong questions too soon. Mucked in with questions about the mother of the boys – a matter that should have been touched upon later and with greater circumspection. My judgement impaired by the double whisky, and rattled by Verhoef's death, my timing was completely out. I should have softened up the old father first in the course of a few interviews; I should have patiently reeled him in like a fish.

When I arrive home the next day, after having tea with a woman friend (one of the few) in town (the coffee shop not yet open to the public – the floor tiles have to be scrubbed clean first and one long table sanded down and special offers devised to tempt customers back to the place of death and disaster), I find, sitting on the pavement, a lithe black animal, a greyhound. She must have run away or got lost, because she is not bewildered, just very thin, and exhausted. I take her inside. Give her water, give her a bit of raw mince with a raw egg. She eats and drinks eagerly. Then she curls up on the sofa and goes to sleep. She must indeed have been very exhausted.

Later she comes to sit by me, where I'm working in the bedroom. The bones of her pelvis and her ribs are clearly visible, but she's no stray, the black coat is shiny, well tended.

I hold her narrow head in my hands, the high-born creature. I look into her eyes – almost transparent, the colour of amber. She looks back. A gaze full of trust, a compassionate gaze. A gaze of ancient knowingness.

I stroke her smooth head, her lean flanks. She has something of the smooth, satiny coat and head of an otter. Her ears are cool. Now and again she turns her noble head in my direction, and regards me with her compassionate gaze. Then again she looks ahead fixedly.

I make her a soft bed of folded blankets next to mine, but she must feel the cold, because in the course of the night she jumps into bed with me, crawls in under the blankets. All night long the noble animal sleeps up close to me. I turn around carefully so as not to disturb her sleep.

The next morning I contact Animal Welfare. A dog conforming to her description has indeed been reported missing: a young black greyhound bitch, missing for three days. A young yuppie couple come to fetch her from my house. The woman is overcome with joy to have her back. She carries the motionless animal to their car in her arms.

*

The death of Buks Verhoef remains with me. Not because I shy away from violence, but because the unstaunchably spurting stream of blood from his wounds has called up a profound melancholy in me. And because we shared the moment of his soul's departure from his body. In the whole coffee shop (and universe) there was nobody else who heard the soft hiccup, or sob, with which his soul took flight. I was the only one, with his mouth close to my ear, my cheek next to his.

Five years ago I was employed by a prominent man in town. He was already ill at that stage. For three years, the last three years of his life, I was something between a caregiver and a female companion to him. I had responded to an advertisement in the local rag. (He and his only daughter, visiting from Canada, had conducted the interview. I found her unsympathetic. I suspect I wasn't her first choice for the appointment, but I was his.) I was initially appointed for three afternoons, later full-time, so that I no longer needed to earn my keep with freelance work. (The emolument was excellent.) At the beginning, while he was still mobile, I took him to do his most essential shopping, walked with him in the park, accompanied him to his special exercise sessions at the local gym. I needed the money. My life had been going nowhere for many years. That is, in fact, still the case. The man was an exceptionally well-to-do businessman, refined. Towards the end I sat by his bedside for hours reading to him. I wiped his brow with a damp cloth. I made him take little sips of fluid through a drinking straw. I fed him the meagre mouthfuls of food that he could take in. I held the bowl for him when he vomited. I trimmed his nails carefully. I listened to the regrets that he expressed about his life – the people he had wronged, his children with whom he had no strong ties. He said that his faith had never been particularly strong, but that now, in the face of death, it wavered more than ever. He was scared, he said, of the great darkness. I said that was understandable, and held his hand. For two, almost three months I sat by him like that. Towards the end, the last weeks of his life, virtually day and night. I watched with sorrow as he deteriorated. The private nursing staff – the day and night sisters – cared for him professionally, but from me he expected something different. A very close bond was forged between us. It must have been in the light of this that he had changes made to his will. (This I only found out after his death.)

While he was still strong enough to listen, before he slipped into a kind of shadowy half-world in the last weeks, I read to him from, among others, the following books: *The Secret Agent* and *Typhoon* by Joseph Conrad. He liked tales of the sea, he said. *Moby Dick* by Herman Melville. Hours and days on end we spent with Ishmael and Captain Ahab on board that ship. The tale of the white whale engrossed us completely. There was no space for reservations or despair for either of us while the reading was taking place. If it was something like a voyage that we'd undertaken together, I'll remember it as the most meaningful, the most intimate voyage I have ever in my life undertaken with another person. I was with him when he died.

Now I have a house in Stellenbosch and money in a trust fund in the bank. My benefactor had, in spite of his illness, summed me up accurately. This was not a woman you left with a pile of money in a bank account. He had once gently touched his finger to the scar of my lip and asked whether I wanted his name, it would entail several benefits – considerable financial benefits – but in the nature of things also problems. (His children had never trusted the harelip with their father.) I gently declined his offer. But I was profoundly touched by his proposal.

At the beginning, once one afternoon when he was reminiscing – he'd been an influential man, who had among other things served on the university council – he said that in the business world he'd come across plenty of crooked and devious behaviour, but he had seldom met a greater conniver than Dr Marcus Olivier, professor of history.

*

After the departure of the meek animal, there is for the time being nothing to keep me in town. I pack a weekend bag. I get into my car. I have been plunged into a sense of loss over the animal, the noble bitch. I take the road to the West Coast. Oesterklip seems like a good destination. Although still a cop-out and a compromise. I want to get out of town. The autumnal beauty of it gives me the creeps. Everything becomes too prettified and pleasing to the eye. I prefer a more stripped environment. If indeed I am fated to be confronted with the nothingness in myself, then let it be in a place without any pretence of abundance and salubrity. I decide on Oesterklip – probably by now already too touristy – because I was there once before on my own. In extremis. At the time there was no appreciable tourist activity. It was winter, the beach was deserted, it stank of kelp. I stayed in the hotel. I was soul-sick with longing for something undefined. The care of a mother? The acceptance of a father? I was soul-sick with the intimation of something unyielding in my psyche. When I walked next to the sea, I did not know what to think. I must have eaten in the dining room, but I don't remember anything of it. I remember only the hours that I spent lying on my bed in my room. A man approached me in the dining room. Apathetically, I complied. What did it matter to me? We sported in my room. On neither of our parts was there a grain of emotion. Beforehand he showed me some pornographic magazine. Presumably to whet my appetite. I was not particularly interested. I seem to remember that he had colourless eyebrows. I had a strong desire to walk into the ocean, entangled in the stinking kelp, sinking all the way to the bottom, there to find peace as a sea slug. Then after a few days got into my car again and drove back to Stellenbosch.

At Oesterklip I check into the hotel. Long since zooted up, bearing hardly any resemblance to the place I visited years ago. In the bar a song by Bobby van Jaarsveld is playing. The barman is exuberantly corpulent. At little tables two young couples are sitting tweeting, with quite a few shooter glasses in front of them. The sea is as flat as a hand. My room has floral spreads and curtains. The small space is dominated by a wooden wardrobe, dark, like the rest of the furniture. Overbearing. I look out of the window. From the direction of the parking lot a large, clumsy man comes walking with a box under his arm.

Eighteen

That morning Nick had once again to discuss the satanism project with the Karlien girl. Perhaps he should once and for all dissuade her from carrying on with it. She wasn't making any progress. She'd clearly bitten off more than she could chew. She got no further than the idea of a blanket with a tiger or a leopard on it. She clung doggedly to the photo in *You* or wherever she'd come across it.

The previous week he'd unmistakably, for a moment, when she sat down in front of him, got the warm smell of blood. Menstrual blood. Warm and salty, like raw meat, slightly off. He couldn't believe it. He hadn't thought it possible that normal feminine hormonal processes could be consummated in that virtually unsexualised body.

Did she have anything to show him? (He was not unaware of the ambiguity of his question.) No, she had as in like nothing. And why not? A profound perturbation flitted fleetingly as a shadow across her perfect, vacuous countenance. He explained once again that she needed to consider the project very carefully. There had to be visual coherence and there had to be a concept, an idea, behind it, binding together these visual elements. He had no idea whether his words had made any impression on her.

It was getting to be quite fresh in the mornings, but Karlien was wearing a short top that exposed her midriff (tanned), and high boots. The little skirt was only barely of a respectable length. She was odourless today; he picked up no scent from her. If he hadn't smelt her the previous time himself, he'd still have thought of her body as scentless like that of a child. Scentless, hairless, without a trace of sweat or sex. Her countenance as empty and uninscribed as if no ripple of the tides and trials of the world had yet passed over it.

She'd thought, yes . . . What had she thought? he asked (with an effort to be patient). She'd thought that like perhaps if she . . . Karlien, he interrupted her, you can't carry on in this vein. Chuck away the *You* or wherever you saw the photo of that blanket. You're going to look at Goya's Black Paintings – *there* you'll discover something about the representation of all sorts of rituals, satanic worship etcetera – you're going to look at medieval depictions of hell. You're going to have another look at the installations of the artists to whom I referred you – even if you look only at Louise Bourgeois' *Red Room* and *Cell* installations. It's a good start, reflecting on installations – both in terms of form and content. You're going to reflect on satanism. You're going to ask yourself what it is about it that interests you, which of its aspects you want to work with. Then you're going to start assembling the visual elements. You're going to place the concept of satanism in relation to these visual elements. You've been sitting on the satanism idea for weeks now, and you've produced hardly anything tangible. Go home, reflect carefully, and come back next week with something concrete. Bring me a worked-out plan on paper. A considered concept, with a clear plan to execute it visually.

The girl stared at him. Her face was expressionless. Although once again for a few moments a cloud of perturbation flitted across her face. He had absolutely no idea whether anything he'd said had resonated in any way with this kid.

*

In this zooted-up hotel I'm not going to stick it out. Not with the floral spreads and the overbearing wooden wardrobe and the over-crowded bar with Bobby van Jaarsveld and the tweeting couples. One day and one night is all I can stand. Onwards tomorrow, in search of the last remaining wilderness. Google the coastline: Frederiksbaai, Gonnemanskraal, Velddrif. I have lunch in the tarted-up dining room with a group of Oriental tourists, the tweeting couples, the big man with the box that he'd carried under his arm from the parking lot now placed next to him on the table. (Mysterious. What kind of treasure could he be guarding in it?) It sounds as if he has trouble speaking, I heard as he addressed the waiter. After lunch I lie down on the bed in my room. In the late afternoon I walk on the beach. No more stinking kelp here. On the horizon two ships. Before dinner I have a drink in the bar. A depressing space, and not the music of my choice: Captain hoist the sails/ Over many miles/ Captain she is mine/In the rising sun/ On the hori-zon . . . There is some kind of sporting event on the giant television set in the corner. The man with the box is staring at it transfixed; his hand protectively on the box next to him. (What kind of treasure requires that kind of safekeeping?)

In another corner sits a man in a hat, it's the first time I've noticed him. A lean, bony face and fervid eyes, staring fixedly at me. I can read the signs. He's going to approach me sooner rather than later. One of those for whom the trace of a harelip – perhaps of any conspicuous scar, in fact – is an erotic stimulus. And who can hardly contain himself at the very thought of the possibility of a cleft palate.

*

And indeed it's not long before he comes up to my table and asks whether I mind if he joins me. I don't fancy this at all, but he doesn't leave me much of an opening. Could he get me a drink? No thanks, I say, I don't drink. Religious objections? he asks. Yes, I say. Seventh Day Adventist.

And what is the name of the Adventist? he asks.

Magdalena Cloete, I say. He is no more going to give me his real name than I'm going to give him mine. I don't have the slightest desire to exchange personal details and assorted chit-chat. I know without the shadow of a doubt that I have to get up *now* and clear out. The man is not to my taste.

He leans across the table with extended hand: Vincenzo Anastagi, he says, but you can call me Vince for short.

I shake his hand briefly. It's warm and dry. Something about him reminds me of Joseph Beuys. The same hollow cheeks, high cheekbones, bony nose, fucked-up gaze. He's removed his hat and his hair is close-cropped, convict-like.

'And what brings you to these parts, Magdalena?' he asks.

'Nothing in particular,' I reply.

My lack of enthusiasm does not deter him in the least. He has only just returned from abroad, he says. He's on his way to visit his birth farm in the interior, in the Eastern Transvaal, apparently now Mpumalanga. The farm is called Darkwaters. It will be a nostalgic return to a meaningful place from his past. The almost twenty years that he's been abroad feel like a lifetime. You never escape the hankering, he says. There's always the desire to return to the beloved country.

(Something about the man's way of talking and about his gaze puts me on my guard. I still don't know why exactly. I don't believe a single word he says. I feel intuitively that I must reveal as little as possible about myself. I must give this man not so much as the tip of my little finger. And I note how his gaze every so often lingers caressingly on my lip.)

He's returned to the country on business, he says. Unfinished business. But first he has to visit the farm, and on the way there go and look up an unfortunate family member who has ended up in an institution. A high-security psychiatric institution on the other side of Moorreesburg. A cousin of his. As children they used to play together. Then one day the cousin lost his marbles with a vengeance. It seems as if there's a streak running through his family, he says, a lamentable tendency to psychical disturbance.

I've still not said anything. I find this conversation highly suspect. Why dish up all these things to a stranger? The man has an agenda. It's not for nothing that he's sitting here talking to me. It almost sounds as if he's rehearsing some part or other.

'Would you be interested,' he says abruptly, 'in exploring the country with me for a few days?'

This I had not seen coming. It wrong-foots me totally.

'No,' I say, 'thank you. I'm expected back in Stellenbosch soon.'

The moment I've said this I realise it was a mistake.

'Oh, really,' he says, 'Stellenbosch. That lovely little village. Home of the recently deceased artist Buks Verhoef. What a tragedy, don't you think?'

Willy-nilly, I feel the blood flushing up in my neck and face. (It must be the unexpected recollection, in this improbable context, of the dying Buks in my arms.) Of course the man notices it immediately.

'Oh,' he says, 'you knew him? A personal friend of yours?'

I just shake my head in denial. Now I've had enough. 'Please excuse me,' I say, getting up.

'We could have an exceptionally pleasant journey together,' he says as I turn around to leave. I can't make out whether he's saying it in dead earnest or in jest. The whole situation has flustered me so much that I can't get away quickly enough. I can feel him watching my retreat.

I hurry to my room. I sit down on my bed. My image is reflected in the wardrobe mirror. I look bedraggled, with the bewildered expression and the burning cheeks. When I am upset, like now, the scar turns red, and becomes more conspicuous. Just as I thought – most probably somebody with an interest in the deviant. It was clear from the manic stare, from the nature of the conversation. Exactly the kind who would hit on me. And a fucking swindler to boot, somebody I wouldn't trust as far as you can trust your hand in the dark. I know, I felt it very clearly. And he's not had enough by a long shot. I can't deal with that. I'm upset that I'm so upset. I'm leaving tomorrow morning before sunrise. Destination as yet unknown. As long as I can get away from here as fast and as inconspicuously as possible.

That evening I nevertheless – in order to calm myself– continue writing my monograph on the Olivier brothers. I write:

'The Olivier brothers, Joseph and Benjamin, identical twins, are regarded as modern masters of the stop-action film. For this they use puppets, which they make themselves – mainly carved from wood – and sometimes also real figures. It is especially the unusual spaces in which these puppets are filmed that are characteristic of the brothers' style. They were initially influenced by the surrealists but over time they developed their own characteristic voice and style. The short films, seldom longer than twenty minutes, are based on, among others, the tales of Franz Kafka, Bruno Schulz, Robert Walser, Jorge Luis Borges and the contemporary Chilean writer Roberto Bolaño. Because the films, with a few exceptions, feature no dialogue, music is an important component. Among the music they use are works by Stockhausen, Terry Riley, Alban Berg and Laurie Anderson, as well as Jewish and Greek folk music (rebetika), and a considerable amount of contemporary electronic music, such as that by the Georgian Natalie "TBA" Beridze.

'They were trained at an art school in Cape Town, South Africa, as painters and graphic artists, not as film-makers. After leaving the country, they gradually started incorporating, apart from the graphic, also filmic (cinematographic) and theatrical (scenographic) elements into their work.

'Little is known about their personal lives. After their studies they went to London, where they have been resident since the mid-nineties. The brothers have collaborated over the years, seldom appear in public, and very rarely grant interviews.

'The work of the Olivier brothers is preponderantly dark, with an ominous tonality and a strong underlying obsession with violence, with the erotic and with the obscene.'

Thus I start to establish the most important themes and motives of the monograph on the brothers.

*

In the late evening I do after all risk having a last drink in the bar. I didn't have supper in the dining room – I was scared the hollow-cheeked fellow would be lying in wait for me. So now I'm hungry as well as thirsty. I am very cautious, I first spy out the lie of the land. If I were to spot the man, I would promptly turn on my heel. He upset me. I'm still not quite sure why. It's not as if I'm not used to being accosted. It's also not as if I'm not used to fighting my corner. But there was something in his gaze – something manic and obsessive that did not appeal to me. And I saw how his gaze slid caressingly over my lip, and lingered there. And it's not as if he made any effort to disguise it.

I sit down at one of the little tables outside. The moon is shining on the water. I sit so that I can keep an eye on the door. There aren't all that many people left in the bar at this time of night. A few hardened drinkers at the counter. In the far corner, the man with the box. And it's not too long before he comes up to my table outside with the box in his hands. May he sit down? He talks with difficulty – some speech defect? The vestige perhaps, as in my case, of a cleft palate. A big head, high, square forehead, large face, of which the individual components look as if they've been joined together arbitrarily – a more acceptable version of a Frankenstein face. Friendly, but also somewhat concerned of expression. I wait for him to speak, but he places the box in front of us on the table and looks at the sea.

Since I don't have any desire to make small talk either, we sit in silence. Unlike the other man, the hollow-cheeked swindler, I don't find this man's presence disquieting. In fact, I find his taciturn presence reassuring. I'm drinking whisky, he's drinking something in a tall glass that looks like tonic. After we've sat like that for a long time, he suddenly produces from the large box a smaller box which he places next to the larger one. This second box, I note, has holes in it. So then there must be an insect or several insects inside. I lean forward slightly to sniff for a clue as to the contents. I close my eyes. The smell of mulberry leaves.

With my ear against the box I hear it – the almost inaudible sound of munching worms.

'Silkworms?' I ask.

He nods.

For a long time we sit like that, in companionable silence, the soft sound of the silkworms drowned out by the rushing of the sea, before I get up, wish him a good night, and go to my room.

*

In the course of the night I imagine I can hear a soft shuffling at my door, but I sleep on, at the mercy of the indecipherable logic of a dream. When I get up the next morning at the crack of dawn, intent on getting away before the man with the bad-luck eyes can accost me again, I find on the floor in front of my door the box of silkworms. I immediately go across to the window overlooking the parking lot. The vehicle in which the large man with the Frankenstein face arrived the day before has gone.

Yesterday I could more or less deal with things with equanimity, but this morning – after the conversation with the hollow-cheeked Joseph Beuys lookalike the previous afternoon, and the box of silkworms at my door this morning – my courage deserts me. A great despondency descends upon me. I can never escape my situation. Freedom of movement is not granted me. Thoughts in that vein.

Give me a break, I think. What am *I* supposed to do with the fucking worms?

I take the box inside and open it. Seven worms, five white ones and two zebras. (Five loaves and two little fish and a miracle waiting to happen.) How sought-after the zebra silkworms were at school. How comely the fully rounded buttock of the zebra. How elegant the flanks of the extinct quagga. How pretty the zebra-like markings on the back of the nautilus. The leaves are yesterday's, almost gnawn bare, only the veins remaining. The worms have clearly munched their way energetically through it all, and equally energetically shat it all out at the other end, because there's more excreta than leaves in the box. The seven worms lift their heads in hungry unison. I have urgently to find fresh leaves for them somewhere. Where I could have walked unhindered into the sea on some remote beach, had I wanted to, I now have to go in search of mulberry leaves.

What do worms do? They lay eggs. They hatch. The worms eat and grow. They spin themselves into a cocoon and change into pupae. The moth crawls out of the pupa and lays eggs. A cycle repeated into all eternity.

*

The moon waxed once more. Nick, Selwyn Levitan (alias Menasse, with the prophet-like adamantine brow), Anselmo Balla, Alfons and Marthinus were sitting on Marthinus' wide front stoep. Nick thought of the Astor Court, which he visited at the Met, where the master of the house would gather with friends to enjoy the full moon, to read poetry, play a musical instrument and test and savour a new tea. No poetry was read here tonight, no tea drunk. But the moon waxed and their little group sat there with the master of the house, in companionable silence, drinking wine. Apart from the waxing moon there were fleecy clouds in the open sky tonight, and the moonlit outline of the great mountain loomed behind them to the right. This was good enough, thought Nick, he could certainly live with this.

Anselmo did not sit still for a moment. He wriggled and fidgeted, he tapped his foot rhythmically, he sputtered, he snorted, he talked non-stop. Menasse with his gentle voice occasionally steered the conversation in a different direction. Marthinus, normally an unquenchably enthusiastic talker, was quiet tonight. He sat, he drank his beer peaceably, he rolled and smoked his cigarettes. It was not as if he was distracted; he was still attending to the conversation, he just did not take part.

At one stage Nick got up, let his eyes wander to the left, towards Signal Hill, first to the farm area, and then, further up the mountainside, to the refugee camp, at night only a dark splotch. There where Tarquin Molteno and the Main Man sometimes hung out (crazy about dogfights and boxing, but a church and family man, according to Marthinus). Once again he imagined that he could see the flickering of lights in that area, the light of small fires. Every time he thought of the albino saying a girl had been raped in the vicinity of the art academy, his heart contracted with fear. It couldn't possibly have been her, he told himself. Troubled, he sat down again.

Anselmo Balla said: We are brought forth from nothing and we return to nothingness.

Menasse said: The human being is equipped to comprehend both good and evil, and on his choice depends the balance of the world.

Anselmo Balla said: We are the nothingness that scrutinises itself. (He moved his head from side to side when he spoke, he groaned and snorted and looked straight ahead of him when somebody else spoke.)

Menasse said: Man initially came into being as a metaphysical potential in the mind of God.

The moon was moving swiftly, occasionally veiled in light cloud. The night was cool. Marthinus was still sitting taciturn in the corner. Below them lay the city, the harbour. What was he going to do about the sale of his house? Nick wondered.

Anselmo Balla said: St Augustine said that time is the locus of uncertainty. It is a locus of uncertain and perilous transition because anything can happen there – both good and evil. But as soon as time comes to an end, history comes to an end – then evil has run its course, then no rectification is possible any more. Then time vanishes. It is replaced by eternity.

Marthinus stubbed out his cigarette and sighed.

133

Nick sat on a long time after Balla with the egg-shaped head and Menasse with the adamantine brow had departed (in the taxi that Marthinus had ordered and paid for) and Alfons had gone to bed. He did not want to go home. He was scared of his empty house. He was scared of the feelings that could overwhelm him there. Buks Verhoef, who had made him such an attractive offer on the house, also, God knows, dead.

Marthinus said: 'Balla thinks he's a lapsed Catholic, but in fact he can't get Catholicism out of his system. Menasse, again, speaks from his immersion in Jewish mysticism. Friends, but the two of them will never convince each other till the end of time. Old Testament, New Testament, I can't decide myself. Buddha – the lord Siddhartha, or Jiddu Krishnamurti – the anointed of the Theosophists? (Even though he sent them packing quite early on.) Oh Lord, I keep harping on two, three thoughts for ever. The Koran. Each has its own appeal for me. I don't even want to think of the possibility of Orthodox, because ever since childhood I've been attracted to graven images. To drink from the Holy Communion cup, to kiss the altar or the hem of the Virgin's robe, the glory of the richly painted interiors, the chanting of the Byzantine choirs, oh Lord. If I'd been an Israelite, I'd have danced up a storm with the best of them around the golden calf. But then there's the burning bush as well. Any manifestation, I have such a weakness for manifestation. The burning bush! I'd have given my front teeth to experience it. To know for certain what it is a manifestation of!

'At the end of his life Jiddu Krishnamurti said that an immense energy, an immense intelligence had occupied his body for seventy years. He did not think, he said, that people realised the extent of this intelligence. But now the body could support it no longer. Nobody could comprehend what his body had endured. Nobody. And let nobody pretend to be able to do so. And now, said Krishnamurti – ninety years old at the end of his life – after seventy years it had come to an end. Not the energy and intelligence – those were still there, every day, and especially at night. But after seventy years the body could endure it no longer. You don't come across it again, he said, not for hundreds of years. When this body went, that also went. No consciousness would remain of *that* consciousness, of that energy and intelligence. People would pretend or imagine that they could access it. But nobody had ever been able to do it, nobody. That was what he said ten days before his death.

'Old Jiddu,' said Marthinus. 'Now *there* was a man who could anticipate and intercept every feint and stratagem of consciousness. I read him and my mind boggles.'

He sighed again, and lit a cigarette.

For a long time yet Nick and Marthinus sat on the stoep, while the moon rose higher and higher in the sky, later to usurp the heavens as the only and the brightest light – proud ruler – and bathe everything below in a milky sheen.

Then Nick got up, took his leave of Marthinus (the master of the pavilion), and returned reluctantly to his own dark house.

Nineteen

Now I have to get away from this place as quickly as possible, before the hollow-cheeked man waylays me again, or another Frankenstein figure accosts me with a bizarre request. The worms are hungry, but I don't have time to tarry any longer in this town. And away I go, but I've miscalculated. It's some distance to the next town, and it's hot this time of year. The worms will have to put up as best they can with the conditions. The box is on the back seat, I've draped a scarf over it to keep them cool. In the garden I picked a few leaves that to my mind seemed most like mulberry leaves. If I poison them with the leaves, then that's a great pity, but at least I didn't abandon them on some doorstep.

I drive up the coast, skirting the stinking and turbulent sea. Arrive at last at a hamlet, not much more than a main street with a garage, a few little shops, and something that looks like a general merchant. Some or other pristine holiday destination, with quaint little cottages further along, on the sea. How pretty the surroundings are, everything parched white by the sun. In a cloud of dust I pull up, spattering gravel and pebbles in my wake. I get out, see to it that the box is properly shut, I really don't want to hunt for fugitive worms as well. Lock the car. Go into the cool store. It is nothing more than a large, virtually empty space. In one corner are a few shelves, half-empty. In the opposite corner is the counter. In the centre a wire rack with a small selection of vegetables: bunches of wilted carrots, a few onions, gem squash. A packet of apples. Behind the counter, an Oriental. If I had to guess, Chinese. He does not seem friendly.

I address him in Afrikaans, but he does not react. In English I ask him whether he has fresh leaves for silkworms. Surely the Chinese know all about silkworms. Isn't that where they come from, and didn't some dowager empress love her silkworm cocoons more than her subjects? It doesn't look as if he understands. Leaves, I say, from trees, or beetroot leaves. For silkworms to eat. I perform self-feeding motions with my hand, and chewing motions with my mouth.

He doesn't sell worms, says the man. (He pronounces it 'wolms'.) I don't want worms, I say, I want food for worms, silkworms. Fresh leaves. No leaves, he says. No worms. Only the items on the shelf. I'll show you, I say. I fetch the box from the car. Place it on the counter in front of him. Open the box.

Is it my imagination, or are they already a mite smaller and darker? Food, I say, fresh leaves. For the worms. The man looks, interested. How much? he asks. No money, I say, food, about ten large leaves. He'll give me fifteen rand for the box, he says. I don't want to sell them, I say again. I want food for them. Leaves. He should know, I say, don't silkworms come from China? He doesn't come from China, he says, he comes from Benoni, Gauteng.

Outside, after the cool interior, I am blinded by the sun for a moment. Next to the steps is a black garbage bin. For a moment I consider chucking the box into the bin there and then. Or turning back and selling the worms to the Benoni Chinaman for fifteen rand. (I could perhaps negotiate a higher price.) But neither outcome would be a worthy end to the worms – beautifully fat and gleaming as Nguni cattle when they were left in my care.

Back in my car, and on my way, the enticing odour of the cold, salt sea in my nostrils. To feel the cool of the water enfolding me. Box under the arm into the sea. Deliver me from impious intentions.

*

I decide not to continue further up the coast. I'm not going to find a single mulberry or beetroot leaf on this barren and deserted West Coast. I turn back and take the R399 to Veldenburg, where I find fresh beetroot leaves for the starving worms, and from there to Frederiks-baai, where I check into the small hotel by the sea. Here I can settle, the worms gorging themselves. May God grant that they speedily transmogrify and take flight into the dark night. Now I carry on writing the monograph on the Olivier brothers.

I write: 'The brothers have been pioneers of the stop-action film technique for twenty years. Because they work in such an individual and innovative way with the fusion of different genres: collage, stop-motion, live action and special effects, their influence on other artists is limited, and their whole oeuvre escapes the confines of a specific genre classification. Since leaving South Africa and settling in London, the brothers have made more than forty moving-image works. One of the main characteristics of their short films is the blending of the erotic, the metaphysical and the mystical. "The enchanting metaphysics of obscenity" – as their work has been referred to.'

*

It was bitterly cold, the coldest time of year. It rained incessantly. I sat in the house not knowing what to do, where to direct my attention. Everything was as cold as ash. It was like a fire that had been doused. The most vital memory was of him in his coffin. However unreal his death had been, as he lay there, *that* was real. At first Willem Wepener and I had stood at a respectful distance, then approached timorously. It was he, and it was not he. You had not wanted to go, because you did not want to remember him like that. Nor did you ask me about it afterwards. You did not want to know. At this time you mostly kept your head averted. I had never seen you so motionless. You were at times untouchable as a statue. I felt misery in the pit of my stomach, heavy as a stone. My kidneys were cold, my womb was cold, my sex was cold, my stomach and my liver were cold, my lungs were cold. My entrance and my exit were cold. My heart was as cold as a lump of lead.

My limbs, too, were cold, my hands and my feet. My eyeballs were cold. My nose was cold and my ears. The roof of my mouth was so cold that I fancied I could feel the scar of the rectified cleft, every cicatrised stitch of it. I touched my upper lip, felt the tumid, cold ridge running to my nose, and still the tears would not come.

Twenty

Marthinus phoned Nick a few mornings later to tell him that he'd just read in the paper that a stash of stolen paintings had been discovered in Buks Verhoef's workshop, including a Pierneef and a Tretchikoff, as well as a whole pile of other valuable stuff. Somebody found it who'd come to value Verhoef's works. Nick said to Marthinus he mustn't even think of saying it. Marthinus said he wasn't saying anything. Nick said he knew what Marthinus was thinking. Marthinus said he couldn't deny that he was intuiting something. Don't even mention it, said Nick. Why not, asked Marthinus. Because he did not want to hear again that Victor was behind this as well, said Nick. Marthinus said right on, he wasn't saying it. Nick said, well then, let it go. Marthinus said right on, he was letting it go. Nick said, don't even *think* it. Marthinus said right on, he wasn't thinking it. Nick said, of course he was thinking it, he couldn't very well stop him. But he thought that Marthinus was over-interpreting – he saw Victor's hand where in all probability it was not. Nick said he knew Victor was a schemer and a plotter, but he reckoned that Marthinus was now going too far in ascribing events to him. Marthinus said yes, Nick was probably right, he was inclined to get carried away with things.

Poor Buks. Nick still found it difficult to see the poor overweight, clumsy, apologetic, asthmatic Buks as a villain. He'd been intending to buy the house and to convert it into a private gallery. What he'd meant by that, heaven only knew. Perhaps he'd wanted somewhere to store his stolen goods – his Tretchikoffs and Pierneefs – or a place where he could peddle them. A smokescreen for his unholy transactions.

After the conversation Nick wandered from room to room in his house. In the front room, opposite his bedroom, some of the boxes were still unopened. Since Charelle had left, the house felt even emptier, less inhabited than before. A stopover. He ate here and slept here, but most of his time was spent in his studio in Woodstock, when he was not at the art school (where he actually also wanted to be as seldom as possible). Only the kitchen, that was the only room that had ever had a shred of conviviality for him, and even that only when he and Charelle had had supper there together.

*

In the same week, early one morning, Albrecht Bester, the principal of the art school, woke Nick with a phone call. A terrible disgrace had befallen the school, he said, he was afraid it could adversely affect their future numbers. One of their students had almost bled to death the previous evening in the course of some ritual. And three of their other students had also been involved, and that with some satanic ritual, he didn't know what he was going to tell the governing body. And the girl, he was sorry to say, was one of Nick's students, one Karlien Meyer. Nick instantly sat up. What happened?! he asked. Ever so terrible, said Albrecht, terrible that something like that should be associated with the school. And on top of it all some of those implicated were among their most promising students. (Here Nick thought he could detect a sob in Albrecht's voice.)

Nick asked what indicated that the ritual had some connection with satanism. Well, said Albrecht, on the scene – in the living room of the flat, no less – all kinds of objects were found. Razor blades, black candles – things that he had no idea where one would get hold of them. Perhaps from one of the Chinese shops in Bird Street. Apparently the ambulance covered her up just like that in the blood-soaked blanket on which she'd been lying and took her away. And just in time, too. How badly was she hurt? Nick enquired. Difficult to say at this stage, said Albrecht, but apparently so badly that, as he'd said, she'd almost bled to death, and in all probability would not be able to complete her course this year.

Nick thought, should he go on his knees in gratitude that he'd been released from the girl and her idiotic non-starter of a project? The wretched kid – she could have been dead! He should have discouraged her from the outset, nipped the whole damn half-baked satanistic idea in the bud right there and then. He should have known that behind that pale, expressionless countenance a multitude of unholy thoughts was brewing.

Look, said Albrecht, the two of them would have to go and see the parents. They'd have to visit the girl. As soon as possible. The father was an important donor. They couldn't afford to lose his financial support. Was it really necessary for them both to go? asked Nick. Oh yes, said Albrecht firmly. She'd after all been Nick's student. They had to go and demonstrate their empathy. Flowers, they'd have to take a big bouquet of flowers. She was still in hospital. As he'd said, she almost died.

*

That afternoon Nick dropped in on Marthinus to tell him about the incident. He said he didn't know whether he should laugh or cry. There the student sat in front of him week after week making no progress with her project and in the meantime she and her friends were probably passing the time every evening with all kinds of absurd satanic rituals that one fine day got out of hand so that she just about bled to death. Probably on the very blanket or cloth with the tiger or leopard on it that she'd wanted to use for the installation.

An idea popped into Nick's overheated brain. 'Marthinus,' he said, 'for god's sake just don't say again that it reminds you of something in *The Shallows*.'

'D'you know ... now that you mention it,' said Marthinus musingly, 'I'd almost forgotten. There's that beautiful – well, not beautiful, but powerful scene in *The Shallows* where the people are dancing around this effigy of the devil, a kind of folk-dancey dance, to the tune of some folk song, if memory serves. Listen, gruesome but forceful. I'd always read it with Goya's *Witches' Sabbath* as background. But carry on. Tell me about the girl.'

'Thin. Blonde. Physically perfect, like a Barbie doll. The parents came to see me once. The father's an arsehole, but the mother was worried about the project that the child was planning. Karlien, her name is Karlien. One of those people who look as if they're going through life untouched. I never knew if she was registering anything of what I was saying. She struggled with the project, made no progress. I suppose I should have probed a bit deeper. I really just wanted her out of my office as quickly as possible every time—'

'Wait, wait,' Marthinus interrupted him. 'Come over this evening. I'll get Menasse to talk to you. He knows everything about this kind of diabolical condition. He'll probably say that the girl never had a chance, she was already trapped in some or other demonic sphere. Don't judge yourself. It was out of your control. Menasse will confirm that.'

He wasn't judging himself, said Nick, and he doubted if there'd been any diabolic or demonic spheres involved, for that the students had too little imagination.

After their conversation he went to his studio anyway and finished the half-bottle of whisky that he always kept there. He slept restlessly on the sofa, and when he woke up, in the late afternoon, and everything flooded back over him, he thought he was going to slit his fucking wrists, there and then, that was how utterly shit he was feeling.

*

He forced himself to get up rather than to just carry on sleeping. He dropped in on Marthinus. Going home was out of the question. The very next day he would put his house up for rental. And if somebody wanted to buy it at a good price, all the better. Marthinus said nothing, but fried some eggs for Nick and made him coffee. Nick ate wordlessly, grateful for Marthinus' solicitude. Later that evening Menasse with the adamantine brow arrived. (Marthinus must have commandeered him specially, though Nick had not thought it necessary.)

They sat on the stoep. The conversation veered from this to that. A bit later Marthinus referred to what had happened to Nick's student. Menasse did not seem in the least surprised or perturbed. Probably used to all kinds of bizarre goings-on, if he really was acquainted with the demonic spheres, as Marthinus maintained. Menasse questioned Nick cautiously. Nick told him about the girl's interest in satanism. About the project that she'd planned and could never get going. How she'd got stuck on the photo with the blanket with the tiger on it. Menasse listened attentively. It sounded to him, he said, as if the girl had ended up in two intersecting circles, that of good and that of evil, which were almost inextricably intertwined in the Asiyah, the lowest world. She'd clearly, reckoned Menasse, already been enticed, blinded, drawn into or coerced into a domain of ignorance and darkness. A domain in which her soul was in peril of being destroyed.

Nick said that as far as the domain of ignorance was concerned he'd grant Menasse's case, but he wasn't all that sure of the possible peril to the girl's soul. That was to say, he said, if she – and for that matter he too – had such a thing as an immortal soul. Menasse smiled unperturbed. It would nevertheless benefit Nick, he said, no matter what his convictions, to regard the girl in her plight with a positive energy.

The moon was half a disc tonight, alternately visible and veiled by fleecy clouds as eerie as a painting by Friedrich. To the right behind them the colossal, ominous mountain lay veiled in darkness. Charelle had been scared of the mountain when she arrived in the city, the day she had menstrual pain. He'd been shocked that she could tell him something so intimate. The temporary settlement behind them was lost in darkness, a patch of darkness in the night. There where Tarquin Molteno hung out with his fancy sneakers and his gold chain. A man of no fixed abode.

Meanwhile Nick was determined to sell the house; even letting was no longer an option. More than ever tonight he dreaded the idea of going back there. He was scared he'd hallucinate or something. He was scared that something would be revealed to him there – something about Charelle's plight.

*

'Do you believe what Menasse says?' he asked Marthinus later in the week. 'Everything he says about the lowest world and the domain of ignorance and darkness, and so on?'

'Look,' said Marthinus, 'I have the greatest appreciation for Menasse. I see him as somebody with exceptional gifts. That I admire and respect, even though I may not believe everything he says. The superior man commands respect – Confucius. I have on occasion seen him intercede between two warring factions. Impressive mediation. He's assertive without pushing himself to the fore. In short, a lovely person. I stand in awe of the Kabbalah, even though I've never immersed myself in it. As you know, my attractions and interests lie elsewhere. But I don't think there's any harm in taking cognisance of his slant on things.'

No, said Nick, there probably wasn't any harm in it.

*

Soon after the girl's discharge from hospital, Nick and Albrecht (at the insistence of the latter) went to visit her at her parents' home. They were armed with chocolate and an enormous bunch of flowers. (Bigger even, Nick noted, than the one Liesa Appelgryn had received.) The residence was on a wine farm with a view. The mother received them.

She introduced herself as Mignon. An attractive woman, with those lush eyelashes; small, perhaps slightly too thin. The father was not at home at the moment. (Nick rejoiced greatly at this small mercy.) The sitting room was spacious, with an impressive blend of antique Cape Dutch pieces and contemporary furniture; the right paintings (among others Irma Sterns, Pierneefs, an Alexis Preller, a Christo Coetzee and a number of Maggie Laubsers); exotic vases, expensive carpets, kelims. The bunch of flowers was summarily delegated to the servant.

The mother proposed that they should quickly look in on Karlien, before having tea. But no questions please, she stipulated, Karlien was still in a state of shock after the unfortunate incident. The girl was lying in a wide bed, waxen, her eyes shut. One arm, bandaged to the elbow, was resting on the bedspread. Around her neck, too, there was a bandage. (Nick felt a slight shudder at the thought.) Next to her on the bed, a collection of soft toys. The colour scheme of the bedroom – off-white and shell-pink. (In this space the prospect of a dried frog or a black candle or a cat skull was not even to be contemplated.) The girl opened her eyes languidly, but without really reacting to their greeting.

The woman ushered them out again with equal adroitness. Tea, canapés and a variety of pastries were served. But when she proposed wine, Nick was only too ready to oblige. He got the impression that the woman was frail but feisty. She didn't say much, told them briefly what had happened. Karlien's flatmate had phoned them at three o'clock in the morning, in hysterics, to say that there was big trouble. The ambulance had got her to hospital just in time. After that Albrecht Bester, his moustache atremble, fortunately did most of the talking. He expressed his absolute shock and dismay at the incident, his sorrow that something like this should befall this talented child, and assured the mother that the culprits would speedily be brought to justice. Nick admired Albrecht for the skill with which he got all this said, while at the same time delicately shovelling in several petits fours and canapés and delivering appreciative commentary on the paintings, the colour scheme of the room, and the choice of furniture. The mother received all this in well-bred silence.

When they said goodbye and Nick shook her hand, the woman looked up at him, and for a few moments they exchanged a glance that – in retrospect – in its flagrantly sexual invitation, was totally inappropriate to the occasion.

In his car, on the way back to Cape Town, Nick groaned – no, he thought, no, not that as well.

Twenty-one

In the early morning I take a walk on the beach. The dunes in front of the hotel are cool. I want to crawl around in them on all fours, so lovely is the colour of the sand, the delicate little red dune plants, the small white shells.

When I get back to my room, the box with silkworms has gone. I placed it on the table in front of the window, so that the cool breeze could waft over them after their hot journey yesterday in the back of my car. Honestly, I can't get that worked-up about their disappearance either. I cared for them when they were left in my care. Now the next person, the one who took it upon himself to remove them from here (to steal them), is welcome to go looking for fresh leaves for them. In actual fact I'm relieved.

I like the hotel, it's unadorned, unlike the revamped hotel at Oester-klip. The double doors in the dining room open onto a cement stoep with a low whitewashed wall. The sea is so close that I can feel the dampness of the spray on my cheeks. Here I have breakfast this morning. I almost feel myself cheering up, and taking heart. Here, perhaps, I'll be able to work undisturbed for a few days.

While waiting for my breakfast I look at the newspaper. On the front page is a report that the suspect in the murder of Buks Verhoef has been sent for psychological observation. There is a photo of a laughing Verhoef, and an indistinct photo of the man with glasses and oily hair who shot him that day.

I become aware of a crawling of the skin on my neck, seconds before the man pulls out a chair and sits down at my table. It's the fucking hollow-cheeked disturber of the peace. The man I had at all costs tried to avoid at Oesterklip.

'I have something for you,' he says, and places the box of silkworms on the table in front of me.

'What makes you think I want it?' I ask.

'In that case,' he said, 'I'll get rid of them here and now.' And he makes as if opening the box and throwing the worms over the low wall.

My immediate impulse is to stop him, but I control myself.

'Did you follow me here?' I ask.

'What gives you that impression?' he asks.

'Because it can't be pure chance that you should turn up here this morning, or that you stole the worms from my room.'

He laughs. 'Pure chance,' he says, 'do you feel like defining pure chance for me?'

'No,' I say, 'I don't feel like doing anything for you. But I say again that it can't be pure chance that has brought you here this morning to disturb my peace.'

(I realise that in fact I should not engage in conversation with him at all.)

'No,' he says, 'you're right, it's not pure chance. I followed you from Oesterklip.'

'Why?'

'You interest me. And I wanted to see what you'd do with the worms. I – by pure chance – saw you yesterday leaving with the box.'

'I don't want to do anything with the worms,' I say. 'You're welcome to have them.'

'Worms give me the creeps,' he says. 'I had an unpleasant experience with silkworms as a child.'

'I don't want to hear,' I say. 'Keep your story to yourself.'

'As far as I'm concerned,' he says, 'all worms belong in the Garden of Eden. I can see no need or niche for them in the modern world. Isn't silk nowadays manufactured synthetically anyway?'

'That I couldn't say,' I reply, 'but unfortunately these seven worms still need fresh leaves every day.'

His eye falls on my newspaper. He picks it up quickly and scans the item.

'Buks Verhoef,' he says, 'the poor murdered Buks Verhoef. Did you know him? I've asked you that before.'

(For a single moment I'm scared that he will recognise me from the – fortunately – indistinct newspaper photograph, taken on that afternoon as I was emerging from the coffee shop after Verhoef was shot.)

'No,' I say. 'I only knew who he was.' (I'm not going to tell this man that I held the dying Buks Verhoef in my arms. That my face was the last thing that the poor Buks beheld in this life.)

'Who would want to shoot Buks Verhoef? Who'd want to harm the poor fellow?'

'Did you know him?' I ask, reluctant to pursue this conversation.

'Didn't know him. Did though meet him once or twice before I left the country years ago. I've got nothing against him as a human being, but he was a howlingly mediocre artist. Perhaps he deserved to die just for that. What do you think? He was exceptionally successful, apparently. Built up a kind of art empire, you might say. Though rumours are circulating that he no longer made his own stuff, but employed a little team. An art factory. Something akin to Jeff Koons's modus operandi. It makes sense, because I have grave doubts whether the poor Buks could as much as draw a donkey – let alone fashion a hyena or a warthog – to judge by his early work. But he saw a gap in the market – give the devil his due. Struck a rich touristy vein. And now it would seem as if on top of that he had stolen paintings in his possession. Tretchikoffs, Pierneefs, Sterns – which he would have got from where? And what does one do with stolen stuff except traffic in it? A shrewd operator, our Buks, though this time he was too clever by half; he overplayed his hand, it would seem. What do you think? Did he deserve to live, in so far as any one of us deserves to live?'

He does not wait for a reply. Looks at the report again. Puts down the paper.

'And the suspect is sent for psychological observation. What do you make of *that*? Mentally disturbed, apparently. Mentally disturbed people – that's to say, severely disturbed people, like my poor cousin in the high-security psychiatric institution – often act at the instigation of higher powers. That is to say powers from the unconscious. A domain to be reckoned with. Those voices are not to be disregarded lightly.'

He picks up the paper, holds it out for me to look at.

'What do you think,' he says, 'does the man seem disturbed to you? Do you think he acted at the instigation of voices from his unconscious? Or is he someone absolutely ordinary – like you or me – who one day had just had enough of the tyranny of mediocrity, and decided he was going to get rid of Buks Verhoef for the sake of society's aesthetic survival?'

I don't like the way the man looks at me. I've not liked it from the outset. I'm starting to wonder whether perhaps he saw me that day in the coffee shop. I don't like him. I have a hunch – an intuition – that he's better informed on the whole Verhoef affair than he's letting on. Hollow cheeks, bony nose, the suggestion of a freckly tendency on his skin, a slightly weathered, ruddy complexion (of whom or what does it remind me?), his eyes are of an indeterminate colour, but with a manic glint.

Unexpectedly he leans across the table and strokes my upper lip, before I can slap away his hand. 'Your lip,' he says, 'suggests something of a criminal tendency. Has anybody ever falsely accused you of untrustworthiness?'

I don't reply. That is the best defence. That way there's least danger of compromising myself in one way or another.

He leans back in his chair. Takes up the newspaper again. Looks at it. Puts it down again. Looks down, at the table in front of him. Looks up, peers in the direction of the sea. (Grey and flat this morning – like his eyes, it suddenly occurs to me.)

'Blinky Booysen,' he says, musingly, 'ever heard of him? Now *there* was a talent. Without a doubt. One fine day simply disappeared off the face of the earth. Or at least disappeared from the city, from Cape Town. I'd swop any Tretchikoff, Pierneef or Stern for one of his paintings any day.'

I know of Blinky Booysen. The Olivier brothers refer to him in an interview. They came across his work at art school, where he'd been a year or two, three before them. They mention him as one of the formative influences on their work. But the man does not have to know that either.

'Come with me,' he says. 'We'll make an unforgettable journey of it.'

I don't reply. Enough of this. I get up, take the box of worms, greet him.

'Magdalena Cloete isn't your real name, is it,' he says.

'No,' I say, 'and Vincenzo Anastagi is really a ridiculous choice for a false name.'

'That is true,' he says. He laughs, but with little real joy.

And that is where we leave it.

*

That afternoon I sit in my hotel room indecisively. I have to get away from this place. Worms and all. Away from the hollow-cheeked disturber of the peace. He's not going to let me get away, that much I know. He's going to carry on asking me to go away with him. I find it disturbing that he remains so relentlessly on my track. I begin to suspect that he's more than just a fetishist who's turned on by my lip. I could go back to Stellenbosch, try once again to induce the old father to grant me another interview. Or I could carry on further up the coast. I could find a suitable spot, a deserted beach, and walk into the sea, box and all. Two birds with one stone. While the hollow-cheeked terrorist spies on me with binoculars from a dune, lights a cigarette when he is satisfied that I have disappeared under the waves for the last time, washes his hands of me, gets into his car again, and goes to visit his cousin in the high-security psychiatric institution. I don't believe a word of all his stories – neither the cousin nor the family farm. The man has a different agenda. Where and how I fit into it, is not clear to me.

I must make up my mind, I can't sit here shilly-shallying for ever. In the late afternoon I am vouchsafed a sign. The silkworms start spinning themselves into cocoons. I'm relieved. This means that they're no longer eating; I no longer have to provide them with fresh leaves every day. This gives me greater freedom of movement, if I should want to carry on up the coast. But actually this simply confronts me with an even greater dilemma: at what stage do I get rid of them? The seven worms spin themselves into cocoons, after a set number of days (I have yet to check this out on the internet) seven moths emerge. The seven moths lay their seven eggs. (Why does it all sound so biblical?) How many eggs do seven moths lay, because it certainly can't be only seven. In fact, it can't be a trifling number. I can hardly start farming silkworms.

What am I to do? At what stage do I abandon the worms to their destiny? I can't release the seven moths into nature. The moths, I read on the internet earlier, can't fly. Silkworms are domesticated, as dogs are domesticated – they can't fend for themselves in an unprotected environment.

I reach a decision. I'll go back to Stellenbosch. I'll take the pupae to a pet shop, or to a school. I'll let myself be guided by the circumstances.

Thus I allow my movements to be dictated by seven domesticated worms. I pack my weekend bag. Pay my bill. Try to get away quickly. Hope the pervert doesn't spy me from somewhere and descend on me. Or even worse – follow me again. At a hundred and forty kilometres an hour I race back to Stellenbosch – that place of limited potential – with the seven spinning worms on the back seat of my car. I listen to Jack White singing: 'I want love to walk right up and bite me/ grab a hold of me and fight me, leave me dying on the ground/ . . . Yeah I won't let love disrupt, corrupt or interrupt me any more.'

That is what I want, I think, while the landscape flies past me at high speed, for love to grab me and fight me, leave me dying on the ground. Yes, (all the same) I won't let love disrupt, corrupt or interrupt me.

Twenty-two

Back in town, back in my house. So much for my little trip to Oester-klip and Frederiksbaai – rudely disrupted by unforeseen events. I don't have much time, it takes the worms about three days to spin them-selves into cocoons. The cocoon, I read, provides a vital protective layer during the defenceless, near-immobile pupa phase. (The mystery of that motionless transformation process interests me.) I have to get rid of the cocoons before the moths emerge, couple and lay eggs. More than 350 eggs at a time, I see on the internet. I could take the box with the seven half-spun cocoons to the nearest primary school. I could try to make a case for the educational value of the silkworm cycle. But I can just imagine the reaction of the teachers – the distrust with which they will regard me. Therefore, on the second afternoon after my return to town, I stalk the nearest primary school like any paedophile. At the gate, on a pillar, half-hidden under the leaves of a creeper, I leave the box like Moses' wicker basket in the bulrushes. I can only hope that some child will discover it and like Pharaoh's daughter insist on taking the box home and caring for the cocoons. More than that I cannot do. Even though I feel dastardly at abandoning the worms – by now in an advanced pupal stage, entrusted to my care by a man bearing a strong resemblance to Frankenstein, and very possibly mentally disturbed – in this way to their fate. Fare you well, transforming cocoons, I whisper to them, may you be vouchsafed an eternal and uninterrupted cycle.

*

For the time being I focus on the Olivier brothers again. This is what I'm doing, and I engross myself in it. When I'm watching their films

– which I do again and again – it is as if I see in every one of them, always and all the time, the presence of a character: most often a hand-carved Punch and Judy puppet, but sometimes also a real human being, who in the way in which he features in the specific film, in the music announcing and accompanying his appearance, in the themes associated with his character, in his movements, in the way in which he is lit, in the actions he performs – operating levers leading to trapdoors, climbing stairs, pursuing characters, bringing about their undoing, peering through a magnifying glass – brings to mind the person of the father, Marcus Olivier.

*

In one of the interviews with the Olivier brothers there is a photo of their mother at twenty-one, in tennis clothes, with a racquet. She was pregnant with them at the time. An exceptionally beautiful woman, as far as I can judge from the little photo – tall, blonde like the boys, and apparently equally sporting. In the interview they claim that she played tennis at national level. So that is the woman by whom Marcus Olivier, academic, had his sons. On the face of it a sporting star was an improbable choice of wife for him. He must also have been quite a bit older than she. After they separated, Olivier did not marry again. In none of their interviews do the brothers make mention of their father, and there is no further mention of their mother either. At some stage she must have disappeared off the scene, but I can't discover anywhere in my research exactly what happened. This is one of the things that I want to try to find out from Marcus Olivier, and *that* is exactly where I botched my previous interview, by introducing the matter too soon and with too little circumspection – still under the impression of and stupefied by the shock of the dying Buks Verhoef in my arms, the smell of his blood still on my hands and in my clothes.

In the place of the stricken Karlien, Nick acquired another student to supervise. He had recently noticed the chap, a new student – tall, with abundant shoulder-length hair, a moustache and eye make-up. Jan Botha was his name. Clearly a very different proposition from the dilatory Karlien. He knew exactly what he wanted to do. On the desk in Nick's office Jan spread out his preliminary sketches, he showed his multitude of notes, and even produced a small model of the installation he was planning. A dark installation, it would appear. It made the wretched Karlien's plan for her satanism installation seem even more pathetic. Nick wondered how this guy had ended up *here* – he was so obviously in a different league from most of the other students. He was not inclined to indulge in personal chit-chat, he was focused and to the point. Let not the thick mascara and conspicuous eyeliner suggest otherwise, or the shiny – and probably fragrant – hair. (Nick had the urge to press his nose in it and take a deep sniff.)

Jan Botha brought new drawings to show Nick every day. The man evidently drew reams of stuff, if that was his daily output. He was clearly a fount of creativity. There was apparently nothing that deterred or intimidated him. Had he known the student who was involved in the satanism incident? Nick enquired cautiously one morning. Not personally, said Jan Botha. In any case not his type, too passive, too little spunk. Nick could go along with that, the girl certainly had remarkably little drive. For a moment he was tempted to tell Jan Botha that he'd smelt her one day, much to his surprise, because he'd assumed that she was odourless – well, odourless in terms of female reproductive processes. He thought better of it.

What did he think of the whole affair, of the fact that it was apparently connected with satanism? Nick asked him. He thought it was a ludicrous business, said Jan Botha. The students messed around with things they knew nothing about. They were too squeamish or too inexperienced. They could learn a thing or two from the gangsters and criminals of the Flats and Khayelitsha and places like that. The students here thought they were cool, but they knew zilch of the real world. They should pop into the Salt River mortuary for a look-around sometime. That would show them the real world. He did volunteer work there over weekends. He knew what bodies looked like when people really meant business. Even when they were ready to be identified, patched up after a fashion, they still didn't look their best.

After a fashion, asked Nick, meaning what? Cleaned up a bit after the postmortem – the worst of the blood mopped up, the more obvious gaping wounds discreetly closed up. The viewing was through a window in any case, which softened the impact for the viewers, said Jan Botha.

And how did he find this volunteer work? asked Nick. He wondered in passing whether Jan Botha wore his eye make-up there, at the mortuary, and whether he tied up his abundant hair there (he probably had to). It did not ever seem to bother him while he was drawing, or discussing his work. (His fragrant hair, in which Nick wanted to bury his nose because it filled him with longing.) Interesting, said Jan Botha. And what was the nature of his work? asked Nick. Very menial, said Jan, cleaning up, wheeling bodies on gurneys to where they had to be – to autopsy rooms, viewing rooms, back to the fridges. Sometimes going out to collect bodies, taking photos of the crime scene, that kind of thing. Things didn't look too great there, he said. The times were very violent. The daily intake of dead people was huge. There were hellish backlogs on everything. People couldn't keep up.

*

Since Charelle's departure Nick spent much more time at Marthinus' house than when she'd still been at home with him, and he'd regularly cooked for them. Also because his own house seemed more inhospitable by the day. Winter was approaching. They wouldn't be able to sit on

Marthinus' stoep for very much longer. (Nick still associated this stoep with the pavilion in the Astor Court.) This evening Anselmo was present again, with his clever, egg-shaped head, and Menasse with the adamantine brow. The moon, which had been new quite recently, was starting to wax again.

Anselmo said: To be subject to time, means to be subject to constant transformation. Time destroys everything it touches. Newton thought that the earth was six thousand years old. His friend the Reverend Thomas Burnet, an Anglican priest and fierce anti-papist, did not question the Biblical chronology, any more than Newton did, but he was searching for a law of nature. He tried to understand why so many events could have taken place in such a short while. He had a bizarre theory of the Flood: All the water on earth had gathered under the first crust of the earth and had exploded one day, hence all the water. Everything transforms, said Anselmo, except particles. They don't evolve. But as soon as the particles form themselves into atoms, and the atoms into molecules, at that moment time takes its toll. Time applies only to forms, to systems, not to elementary materials. Everything coming into being in the universe is subject to the irreversibility of time. And ultimately to death and destruction, to dissolution, and to a rearrangement of the original elements from which it was formed.

Menasse said: Time existed before the beginning of the universe. God's time is not measurable.

The moon rose, and waxed, and the night sky changed, and the breeze got progressively cooler. The bay lay stretched out and scintillating below them, and the mountain to the right of them. Nick felt his own thoughts coming and going, coming in and going out, like waves, sometimes closer, sometimes further, sometimes calmer, sometimes more turbulent. As if he were moving in and out of Anselmo's monologue. But the basic undertone of his mind remained restless and troubled.

What Menasse was making of Anselmo's monological verbal deluge was not clear. He sat calmly gazing out before him, always with the cap on, the little smile, secure in the knowledge of the Kabbalistic truth, of God and the angels and the spheres and the shedim. Nick wasn't sure of the exact reach of Menasse's faith, what mystical knowledge he had at his disposal – apart from his sensitivity to the emanations of a place, which according to Marthinus made him such a reliable estate agent.

Anselmo Balla, the lapsed Catholic, was unstoppable this evening, though the more he talked the less coherent he became. As the moon rose in the sky and the rest of the company fell silent, he conducted his monologue ever more assertively. He looked at nobody directly, he never sat still. He quoted St Augustine (Marthinus had claimed that he could never escape Catholicism), he spoke about an enormous molar to which the saint referred in *The City of God*. Nick pictured a gigantic molar washed up on the beach, as big as a whale. History was unpredictable, said Anselmo, not because it was illogical or depended on chance, but because it was not controlled by natural laws. Then again he was on about apocalyptic movements, which according to him were always revolutionary by nature.

Menasse remarked that the apocalypse was rooted in a very vigorous Jewish tradition – just look at the writings of the prophet Isaiah in the Bible. Anselmo did not respond to Menasse's comment – or to anybody else's – but spoke once again about the end of time (to which he returned constantly). When you talk about civilisation, said Anselmo, you talk about loss, because only an infinitesimal part of what has ever existed on earth – whether natural objects, whether man-made, cultural artefacts – has survived. We are in any case ignorant of the greatest part of the whole of creation, he said.

Nick thought of his brother, dead for so many years now. His brother who no longer existed. His father and sister had had to go and identify the body in Namibia after the accident. His mother had not been up to it. When they came back, Nick had wanted to ask how it had been, but he didn't know how. His father was dumbfounded and his sister was her usual undistractably focused self. He wanted to know whether his brother had been disfigured beyond recognition, but he didn't know how one asked such a thing, he was fifteen years old, and he lay awake night after night wondering what his brother's dead body had looked like. If he'd lived, his brother would have been almost sixty by now, a middle-aged man. Nick sometimes felt as if his brother had aged along with him. As if he had an awareness of his brother, still older than he, right behind his left shoulder, an unpredictable, reckless, devil-may-care presence. A presence from which he still in a weird way took his bearings.

Twenty-three

In the third week of May, more or less three weeks after the incident in which Karlien had been involved, Albrecht Bester turned up in Nick's office one morning. He was breathless with dismay. His cheeks were flushed, his perfect coiffure in disarray, his eyes bloodshot. For a moment Nick thought the man was going to confess to a night of reckless passion or an unrequited love.

The police had just been here, he said. The three students who'd been involved in the incident had now also been charged with drug dealing. Can you believe it, groaned Albrecht, and that three of our most promising third-year students! (This was news to Nick, that apart from Jan Botha there were other promising students in the place.) What was our governing body going to say about this? How was it going to affect our numbers in future?

Nick said it wasn't Albrecht's responsibility what students did in their free time. But Albrecht moaned that the charges against the students still reflected abysmally on the school.

*

Jan Botha intrigued him. Nick was grateful that at long last there was a student whose work interested him. Jan Botha was older than the other students, he took his work seriously. He was unusual of appearance, with the abundant hair and the eyeliner. Work-shy he was not (unlike most students). Sturdy of build, not the effete, over-refined designer look that so many of the male students cultivated. His work reminded Nick of that of Ed Kienholz, or Joseph Beuys, but with a stronger contemporary feel, and more confrontational. Much of his imagery clearly originated in the mortuary – figures on stretchers, on gurneys, in fridges. Some of his drawings were crude, almost pornographic. He confronted every taboo head-on: race, sex, death. One of his drawings, a dead figure on a steel slab, reminded Nick of Holbein's panel painting of the dead Christ. Isabel had told him that when Dostoevsky saw it, it made such an impression on him, he was so gripped by it, that his wife had to drag him away to prevent it from inducing an epileptic fit in him.

*

Albrecht now regularly came to bewail his lot with Nick. Fortunately he did not expect any response. Nick simply carried on doing whatever he was busy with. Today he was looking at a book on Japanese battle art, while Albrecht was telling him hand-wringingly that the girl's flatmate had also been taken in for questioning, that in all his years nothing like this had ever befallen him, that he'd been under the impression that what they offered there was more than a mere art education, that they were shaping their students into well-adjusted adults who could fill their proper places honourably in society, and now it had transpired that they were dedicating themselves to satanism, the lowest, the most perverse activity conceivable. Not to mention drug trafficking. Nick was looking at the reproduction of the *Night Attack on the Sanjo Palace* from the Heiji era. It depicted the bloody war between two clans during the last half of the twelfth century. A host of fighting soldiers in heavy battle garb were engaged in a fierce battle in the foreground, while the whole scene was dominated by the massive flames of the burning palace. Stylised flames, billowing and curlicuing like waves or clouds. He felt his personal honour impugned, said Albrecht, he did not know where it would all end, but it did not bode well, because it could have far-reaching implications for the continued existence of the art school, and for everything he had dedicated his life to. The soldiers were engaged in brutal man-to-man combat, as was usual in these civil wars. Blood spurted from a decapitated neck, a soldier was held to the ground while another was cutting his throat – quite a few were headless. Decapitation was apparently de rigueur. Couldn't have been difficult, Nick thought, he'd seen some of those Japanese swords. You impaled your opponent on it, right through the heavy battledress, like a caterpillar threaded onto a thorn. He didn't know what he was to do, said Albrecht hand-wringingly, he didn't know what they had to prepare themselves for, because perhaps everything was lost, everything that all these years he'd been able to pride himself on, everything that had made this school a leading, sought-after institution. (Nick had been under the impression that it was considered a very mediocre school.) He'd taken a photo of Isabel in the Metropolitan Museum standing next to a display case containing five of these sets of Japanese suits of armour. He didn't know how he'd persuaded her to pose for the photo, because she'd not wanted photos of her taken anywhere. Her expression on the photo was reproachful. She was still prepared for love on one condition, she'd said, and that was that he did not look at her face-on. Don't look into my eyes, she'd said, the intimacy hurts me, I can't handle it. It had wounded him, it had made him feel unworthy, because he'd still desired her. He looked at the representation of a Japanese suit of armour from the Edo era. Lacquered iron and silk brocade. Used for equestrian battles between the tenth and fifteenth centuries. The woven, harness-like outfits were reminiscent of the ornate markings on some insects. A special metal flap over the heart. The soldiers wore similar harnesses in the night attack on the Sanjo Palace with the billowing flames like clouds. But in spite of the elaborate precautions for the safety of the wearer of the outfit, it was apparently possible to decapitate the enemy effortlessly. The razor-sharp blades sliced through the necks like butter. Still agonising, Albrecht left the room again.

The single student, apart from Jan Botha, who had shown some promise and whose work had still interested Nick – the images of headless seagulls, hotels with broken windows and wax figurines of a child with eyes sealed with pins – had dropped out on account of depression, despite his happy childhood. (Apparently he'd not been able to process the loss of the bygone idyll.) Jan Botha was for the time being his only student. Jan did not need Nick, because Jan knew exactly what he wanted to do. Nick didn't know what he himself was still doing there. The woman for whom he was substituting would be returning in the fourth term. As soon as Albrecht had recovered from the shock and regained his equilibrium he would assign Nick new students. Nick didn't know whether he felt up to this. He pictured an endless sequence of Karlien clones – the one as indecisive as the other, but each with a head filled with dark, brooding intentions.

*

He told Marthinus, when they were having a beer again on his stoep that evening, that the business with Charelle had really thrown him. He wouldn't rest until they'd had a proper conversation, but she hadn't responded to any of his calls or text messages. It was clear that she did not want any contact with him, and he couldn't understand why not. He still feared that she'd been assaulted by the guy who'd stalked her earlier, who might have thought that she and Nick were having a relationship or something. He no longer wanted to stay in his house or be involved with the art school. Especially now after the ludicrous episode with his student. Perhaps he should do something drastic, he said, like going to study Japanese gardens. He was strongly attracted to Oriental art. He thought it could be good for him to rake gravel. If he'd had a predilection for it, he'd have gone off somewhere in isolation to meditate. Rake and meditate. But actually he was talking total crap and nonsense, he said, because raking and meditating were so totally not his scene. *Totally* not – it was actually a bit ridiculous to have mentioned it at all, because he completely lacked the propensity for it. It didn't accord with his temperament. He thought he had a strong tendency to hedonism – although his equally strong tendency to melancholy probably tempered it somewhat.

Marthinus laughed softly. Who knows, he said, Nick might just possess abilities he hadn't exploited. He doubted it, said Nick. If he sat for long enough under a pine tree, he might turn as green as Milarepa, said Marthinus. Nick thought for a moment that Marthinus was mocking him, but Marthinus was still gazing ahead solemnly. Oh Lord, he said, Milarepa is a fascinating figure. One of the most important teachers in Tibetan Buddhism. Trained as a sorcerer. In later life he said that he had committed black deeds in his youth, but practised innocence in his maturity. Imagine that, said Marthinus, to practise innocence. At long last, said Milarepa, he'd been released from both good and evil, and saw no further reason for action. I am an old man, he said, leave me in peace.

Nick said that that was what he desired as well – to be left in peace. He was god knows not up to supervising another student like Karlien. Once was more than enough. (He recalled the charged, sexually inviting glance the mother had given him when they parted. It had – to his surprise – totally wrong-footed him, *and* properly hit home, that glance.)

They drank their beer in silence. Nick's eyes wandered to the settlement against the mountain. On whose side were Tarquin and company *actually* in the end, he asked. Did they collaborate with the police or with the gangs or what? They were mainly on their own side, said Marthinus. They collaborated with whoever suited them at any particular moment. But one thing was certain, they had their finger on the pulse through their extensive network of informants. Did Nick think they should at some point go up there again to see if Tarquin and company had after all discovered something? he asked.

No, said Nick, no, he didn't think it would be any use. The best thing that could happen would be for Charelle to get in touch with him herself.

*

Nick covered the large, horizontal sheets of Fabriano paper, 150 x 110 cm, on which he worked, with a few layers of gesso to give them a rougher surface. He drew on this with koki pens – mainly sepia-coloured, with accents in dark brown and red. Numerous figures – exclusively men – committed acts of grievous bodily harm on one another: suffocation, strangulation, decapitation, torture. Sometimes he added shallow graves, car wrecks, chopped-down trees and smouldering tree stumps. All under a sky of billowing white summer clouds.

Twenty-four

It's the third week of May. When the early morning is not overcast, the sunrises are magnificent. One morning, as I'm getting up, an immense, opaque cloud mass is hovering just above the horizon. The outline of the mountains is still solid. The rising sun, not yet visible, illuminates this cloud mass from below, so that it starts glowing blood-blue from underneath, a darker blue above. Except for this cloud column the sky is virtually empty, marked with a few smears of cloud. I can't take my eyes off the sight. It reminds me of a painting by Andrea del Castagno: the *Holy Trinity with St Jerome*. God is supporting his Son on the cross, they are depicted from above. Christ's body terminates midway, in two reddish-pink winged cherubim. The effect of this is that his body appears to be bloody, the organs visible, the ribs and the kidneys. The colour of the clouds in this painting is the exact shade of the undersides of the cloud mass above the mountain.

I once again contact the secretary of Marcus Olivier. Is there any possibility that I could speak to the professor again? She will find out from him and come back to me. This time I mustn't botch it. I must be tactful, I have to reel him in gradually like a fish.

I am not at my ease. I'm scared the hollow-cheeked fetishist is following me. He's quite capable of doing it. Something tells me the man has an agenda. It's not for nothing he's in the vicinity. The story of the cousin in the psychiatric institution and the so-called intended visit to the family farm are fabrications. I read him as someone who enjoys playing games. I can feel it in my bones. For the time being I avoid the coffee shop where Buks Verhoef died in my arms. I have a strange premonition that if I encounter the man somewhere it will be there. He has some or other connection with Buks, and also with the suspect.

Of that I'm sure, though I have no proof to back up my hunch. He knows that I didn't give him my real name, and that my Seventh Day Adventism was a joke (stupid of me) – but that's exactly what he enjoys, that's why he followed me. That man's native territory is fabrication, counterfeiting and intrigue. I find it offensive. But if it's true that it may just fascinate me as well, I must be careful.

In the newspaper I read a small report that three students at a private art school just outside town have been charged with assault and drug dealing. It seems as if the charge of assault is connected with a satanic ritual that went wrong and in which a fellow student almost bled to death. In the small newspaper photo the injured girl looks like every second girl in town: pretty, with a long blonde ponytail.

*

I meet up with you again in the café where we met earlier this year, soon after your return to the town. The day when it rained so hard. We haven't seen each other for a long while, because you've been busy and I've seen nobody. There are lines next to your mouth that I haven't noticed before. But you once again smile with your eyes, although in unguarded moments they still seem wounded, as if sorrow has been indelibly imprinted on them. How are you? I ask. Better, you say. The ground feels more solid under your feet. You're not quite so cast down any more. You can laugh again. Sometimes for short spells you do again experience something like joy. And you? you ask. I tell you that I'm making headway with the monograph on the Olivier brothers. I've spoken to the old father twice, and the second time fluffed the interview, I say.

We sit in silence for a while. Drink our coffee. What happened? you ask. It was the day that Buks Verhoef was shot, I had the last interview with Marcus Olivier immediately afterwards. There were still spatterings of blood on my shirt. I fancied that I could still smell the blood on my clothes and even on my hands, even though I had rinsed them thoroughly. The yelling of customers was still echoing in my ears. I saw Buks's face before me. He couldn't believe what was happening to him. I told you about it. I was totally put off my stroke. No wonder you fluffed the interview, you say. Do they know yet who did it, and why? No, I say. But the suspect has been sent for psychological observation. Who would want to murder poor Buks Verhoef? you ask wonderingly. Perhaps Verhoef was not as innocent as he appeared, I say. He always looked as if he couldn't harm a fly, you say. He, perhaps not, I say, but his enemies, or his friends, might. Yes, you say, and look down. A while ago I found a black dog on the pavement in front of my house, I say. A beautiful animal. Narrow, noble head. She slept next to me on the bed that night. The next morning her owners came to fetch her. She must have got lost. They were glad to have her back. Are you more reconciled to your life here? you ask. You know how ambivalent I am about the place, I say. I hate it, it makes me claustrophobic, I feel I can't breathe freely, and yet I return to it every time. It's autumn in particular that I'm ambivalent about. So much self-evident beauty makes me restless.

I can still not forget the expression in Buks Verhoef's eyes, I say. And what's more, it was a moment of intense intimacy between us. It's almost as if I hanker after it. It's as if at that moment a special bond was established between me and Buks. You understand, you say, it makes sense to you. Who could ever have thought that I would feel like that about Buks Verhoef? We shared the moment of his death, we were at that moment as intimately connected as it's possible to be to another human being. I've noticed, I say, that I think of him often. He's somebody for whom previously, before his death, I felt nothing but the greatest contempt. And now I harbour this strange, inexplicable tenderness towards him. It's almost as if I long for him, strange as that may sound.

It makes sense to you, you say. Quite unexpectedly, sudden tears start up in my eyes. My eyes burn, my throat aches with holding back the tears, because I'm embarrassed; I'm ashamed of my tears. It's almost,

I say, as if our souls got entwined at that moment. And you know how I feel about the soul, I add wryly.

I say nothing about my visit to Oesterklip. I say nothing about the silkworms. I say nothing about the man who followed me. I say nothing about my suspicions. You are the person closest to me. You've always been my only confidant. I'm scared you'll ask me a question to which I don't have an answer.

*

Marcus Olivier's secretary reports that it's in order, I may have an appointment. But it cannot be a long interview, the professor's health was dealt a severe blow by his recent flu, and no personal questions, please. I assure her that I'll keep it light. Just a few little general questions. For some or other strange (perverse?) reason I'm tempted to go and sit in the same coffee shop as on the day when Buks Verhoef was shot. Call it obsessive behaviour – compulsion, call it a tempting of fate. My appointment is at four o'clock. At three o'clock I sit down in the coffee shop, at the same table as on the fateful day. The sky this morning was uniformly bright, no cloud mass, no dramatic spectacle where the sun was rising, but further to the west there was a long, low, indigo-coloured cloud. Further along, only faint daubs in the sky and a tender rosiness in the east just before sunrise.

As I pass through the back section of the shop to the toilet, somebody unexpectedly grabs hold of my arm from behind. It is, sure enough, the man (was I not *looking* for trouble, didn't I foresee it?), his two fanatical eyes close to my face. Even so, I'm almost paralysed with shock. We are standing between the shelves, with bottles of preserves and muesli on the one side and a table with tins of fudge, cheese straws in packets and round panfortes on the other side.

'What do you know?' he asks.

'What do you want me to know?' I ask.

'What do you know about Buks Verhoef?'

'I didn't know him.'

'He died in your arms.'

'It was pure chance.'

'Now *you're* talking of chance.'

I don't reply to this.

'Come with me for a few days,' he says.

I try to tug free of his grasp, but he only tightens his grip.

'Had you noticed the suspect before around town?' he asks.

'No,' I say.

'The man is totally cuckoo,' he says. 'But that you probably know.'

I say nothing.

'Come with me,' he says, 'we'll make a pleasant little trip of it. I promise.'

His face is close to mine. On his breath I smell coffee, cigarette smoke, something meaty.

'I've looked you over very well,' he said, 'you don't scare easily. You like a challenge. A girl very much to my taste. And the lip . . .'

I turn my head aside before he can stroke it again.

'You intrigue me,' he says close to my ear. I keep my head averted.

I turn to him, look deep and intimately into the fucked-up eyes and say: 'Let me go or I'll scream.'

He laughs merrily. 'There speaks a forked tongue,' he says. 'On the one hand it says fuck off, and on the other it says, yes, why not?'

The next moment I take him by surprise by screaming very loudly and at the same time pulling loose of his grip. A bone-piercing scream that makes customers as well as waiters freeze in their tracks. A shocked silence ensues. Everybody is staring in our direction. For a moment I see in the man's face an expression of confused surprise – he hadn't expected that, I did indeed catch him unawares – before he turns on his heel and quits the shop swiftly.

A few members of staff rush to my aid. The man who was harassing me has left, I say, he's just left the shop. One of the waitresses says she saw him come in. He's dangerous, I say, watch him if he should come here again. I sit down with a beating heart. My hands tremble when I drink my coffee. I must calm down now, I admonish myself, otherwise I'll be off balance again when I talk to the old father.

*

I am still slightly off-kilter when Miss De Jongh (still with décolletage) opens the door for me. Can she offer me anything to drink? I ask for a glass of water. (She may have hoped that I'd have another double whisky and shoot myself in the foot.) Once again the old father receives me on the stoep, the same travel rug on his knees, but this time he's wearing a thick, check dressing gown and a scarf. Still no sign of recognition on his part. He acknowledges my presence with the merest nod of his head.

Did the great success and international recognition of his sons come as a surprise to him? Not in the least, they had distinguished them-selves from an early age. From an early age in an artistic direction? I ask. No, he says, on the sports field and academically. He never needed to discipline them, as far as their work was concerned. (I wonder in what he *did* discipline them.) (I'm tempted to ask whether, like their mother, they were good tennis players, but have resolved not to mention the mother this time round.) Does he find it difficult that his only children have settled in a foreign country? No, why should he? They visited South Africa often, and he travelled frequently when he was younger. (I note that he uses the past tense. At some stage, then, the contact must have become less frequent.) I take it that he is thoroughly acquainted with their work? Yes, they regularly send him videos and catalogues of all their exhibitions. In this way he remains informed about everything they're doing. Does he find their work resonates with him? Yes, why wouldn't it? (Do I detect something defensive in his tone?)

The video titled *Kafka in Long Street*, I say, is exceptionally dark, with all kinds of suggestions of sexual indecency, was that his view too? He shrugs, everybody is free to interpret the work as he wishes, he says. (I get the impression that he's not familiar with this video.) It is said that their work exhibits more than just an underlying obsession with violence, with erotica – even with pornography and obscenity – would he agree? It's not for him to pass a value judgement on their work, he says. It's not a value judgement, I say, merely a description of its nature – could he go along with that? I can see him hesitate. What are you driving at, Miss? he asks. (More than just defensiveness, I now hear aggression in his tone as well. Touched on a sensitive spot here?) And on that he signals to the woman that the interview is concluded. Have I gone too far once again, got his back up?

I thank him copiously for his willingness to talk to me. I say that he has no idea how valuable I find the conversations with him. I don't wish to place him in a position of having to answer awkward questions. I do value immensely his willingness to talk to me at all. I have so much admiration for the work of his sons, and I don't know anybody locally with whom I could have anything approaching an equally valuable background conversation.

He still does not look at me. He acknowledges my thanks with a single nod of the head, but his jaw remains inexorably clenched. I suddenly recall with indecent clarity the violence with which he slammed my head against the wall in the hotel room. If I hadn't re-sisted, would he have inflicted even greater bodily harm on me? He hadn't stopped even when my nose started bleeding. What precisely do I want to know from him – or just *want* from him? Do I want him to look me in the face and tell me, thirty years ago I took you to a hotel room, tried to ram my penis into your mouth, slapped you so that your nose bled, and knocked your head against the wall with all my might? Perhaps, I don't know.

I go home. The sun sets in full glory. Pink and gold and all that is gaudy and over-the-top. The beauty depresses and intimidates me. The hollow-cheeked man is in town, as I feared. He is here either because he has something to do with the whole Buks Verhoef affair or because he's following me, presumably because he thinks I know more about Verhoef's murder than I'm letting on. Just what I need – to be followed by a fucked-up hollow-cheeked stalker and Joseph Beuys lookalike.

Twenty-five

I can feel the year relentlessly bearing down upon the winter solstice. Helter-skelter. The stolen paintings were confiscated, and then they disappeared from police storage. It's mysterious, and I brood on it. What part is played by the disturber of the peace, and does he in fact have anything to do with it? He knew just a little too much about Buks Verhoef. He wanted to know what I know. He's following me; somewhere he's going to lie in wait for me. I wonder how the cocoons are faring. Three weeks, I read, for the stealthy process of transformation to run its course. Then the moth crawls out, lays her eggs and dies.

The morning sky is wide and wet. It's grandiose. It's sublime. It's all of these things for the receptive of spirit. The last few nights I've been dreaming of the corrupter of my youth. According to report, he's dying in another province. I was too young to do justice to the subtlety of his offensive.

The man, the hollow-cheeked stalker, won't believe me that I know nothing. Perhaps it really isn't chance that Buks Verhoef died in my arms. Perhaps I know something that I don't know I know. I consider leaving town again, anything to flummox the man. But where to? Thanks to him and the Frankenstein double who left me the worms, my trip to the West Coast was prematurely cut short. For the time being I'm done with the old father. Reached a dead end. What was I thinking? I decide to lie low, until a plan of action presents itself.

*

Albrecht Bester was now sitting in Nick's office every day bewailing his lot about the students who had been released on bail. He didn't know whether he should permit them to attend classes again until their case was heard, because it could take months, he said, and he could under no circumstances tolerate the presence of undesirable elements at the school, but on the other hand they probably had the right to continue their studies. Oh sweet jesus he didn't know how to deal with the situation. Thus, hand-wringingly, he sat with Nick.

One afternoon at the beginning of June, when Nick arrived home, Charelle was sitting on the stoep. She must have let herself in, she knew the code to the gate. It was bitterly cold, the first cold front of winter had arrived. The first thing Nick noticed was that her hair had been cut short. She was thin. She was tense. His heart started beating wildly. He invited her in; at first she seemed uncertain, then consented to come in. She wouldn't stay long, she said.

In the kitchen she sat down at the table. He filled the kettle to make tea. She wasn't going to stay long, she said again. She owed him an explanation, she said.

'I treated you badly,' she said. 'You were always kind to me. I want to explain.'

His hands trembled as he placed the tray on the table and sat down. All of a sudden he knew what was coming. He feared the worst. He did not want to hear it.

He poured their tea. She told her story in a neutral voice. When she was coming back from the art school latish that Friday afternoon, a minibus stopped next to her, somebody jumped out, gagged her and pushed her into the minibus. They took her to a remote site and there the three guys took turns raping her. They'd first tied her hands behind her back with a rope. They hit her with their fists, they kicked her, they dragged her around.

She was having her period, she said, there was blood everywhere. They jeered at her because she was bleeding. They penetrated her from behind because she was bleeding. One of them must have felt sorry for her or something, because he said to the others that was enough, they had to leave before somebody found them there. Then they left in a hurry.

At first she'd just lain there. Then she'd worked her hands loose. Then she'd got up. That at least she could still do. Then she made her way to the main road. Somebody picked her up and took her to the hospital.

He wanted to say something but couldn't. A hollow sensation in his belly.

In the beginning it was bad, she said. She couldn't sleep, she couldn't eat. She'd gone to stay with Desirée. She was still staying there. She hadn't wanted to go home to her parents, because once she'd left Cape Town, she knew, she'd never come back. She dropped out of her course at the art school. She couldn't work. She didn't have the will to do anything. She was in therapy now. She thought it would be a long time before she was okay again. Emotionally recovered.

He asked whether she knew who it had been. No, she said, they had cloths tied over their faces. It wasn't perhaps . . . But she shook her head before he could complete his sentence. Had she gone to the police, he asked. Yes, she said, for what it was worth. He called her by her name: Charelle . . . he said. These things happen, she said, some girls get off quite a bit worse than her. Quite a bit. That didn't make it less terrible, he murmured. She didn't know about that, she said. She was different, he saw. She was stricter. Less forbearing. Would she go back to art school, he asked, she did such fantastic work. He felt a fool saying it; a feeble and inappropriate remark. She shook her head. She'd not been able to take photos again yet, she said. She was going to enrol for a nursing diploma. But wasn't that a waste of her talent! he exclaimed. Is it a waste of talent to help other people? she asked sharply. He felt reprimanded. Sick to the pit of his stomach. A weight like a rock resting on his chest.

But she was so furious, she said, so terribly furious. That they could *do* that to her. That she still regularly felt so terrified, so *pathetic*. Their aim had been to do her bodily harm and to humiliate her. They'd succeeded.

She'd been so totally powerless. That was what she was so furious about. That *they* should have had such power over her.

He just nodded. Dumbfounded. When she'd finished her tea, she got up. She had to go. She'd just wanted to come and say. She was sorry she said nothing that day when she came to fetch her stuff. She'd not yet been able to talk then. That's okay, he said, she shouldn't feel bad about it. He understood. Could he give her a lift to Desirée's? No, she was good, thanks. She could at least now use public transport again, she said, with a faint laugh. He walked her to the gate.

Just before she went out, she turned round to him for a moment, and for a few seconds they exchanged an intense, mutually beseeching look. Something welled up instantaneously and violently at the back of his throat. Tears perhaps. He wanted to hold her with this look and bind her to him. But it lasted for only a few moments, then she turned round and went out through the gate.

*

When she'd gone, he sat at the table in the kitchen for a long time. The table that he'd bought way back at an auction in Johannesburg. Isabel had liked it. It was dark by the time he got up, got into his car and drove to his studio in Woodstock.

As he went up the stairs in the feeble light to his studio on the first floor, a man was standing on the landing. In the faint light his face wasn't clearly visible; he was wearing a cap. As Nick reached his door, the man, in one lightning-fast movement, was standing next to him, shoving him against the wall, and pressing a knife to his throat.

'Give,' he hissed, 'or I cut.' Nick smelt him, the liquor on his breath.

With a low cry he violently shoved the man away from him – he had the advantage of sobriety and greater heft – so that the man lost his balance, fell, rolled down the stairs, came to his feet nimbly when he hit the bottom, and cleared out.

Nick unlocked his studio door with trembling hands. He immediately poured himself a whisky. He sat down on a chair and looked at his current work, the large drawings on the wall. He saw that it was rubbish, what he was doing. Worthless rubbish. Isabel had been right. It was indecent, what he was doing. Indecent rubbish, all of it. She was tired of the male obsession with the pornography of violence, it gave her the shits, she'd said. Men wanting to level everything with the ground, wanting to drill and ram and fuck it into the ground. Her eyes as pale as her skin and her hair as white as flax. She's ill, he'd thought, see what she looks like, see how pale she is, see how manically her eyes glow, how thin she is; she needs help more urgently than ever.

He drank more whisky. When he was properly inebriated, he lay down on the sofa. He woke up with the first pallid morning light shining in at the window. His first thought was of Charelle. His thoughts felt like harpies descending upon him and pecking at his eyelids. He had to go in to the art school, but he didn't feel he could face the day.

Twenty-six

He went to work. He had a massive hangover and a throbbing head-ache. He was grateful that he would not have to talk to Albrecht that day. In the evening he went to have a beer with Marthinus. He couldn't sit at home on his own, he was still too upset.

It was cold. Marthinus had made a fire. They sat in the sitting room. Nick was grateful for the warmth. Only now did he tell Marthinus about Charelle's visit. Oh no! he said, oh Lord! It could be the girl the dreadlocks guy spoke about last time at Tarquin and company's, he said. That was possible, said Nick. They could go and find out from Tarquin who the people were who did it, by this time they should know, or they could find out, said Marthinus.

'Of what use would that be?!' Nick exclaimed passionately. 'It's too late *now*! The deed's been done! She'll never be the same again. She doesn't want to take photos any more. She wants to do a nursing diploma. Of all bloody things she wants to do nursing. She's an extraordinary photographer, she's got all the makings of a good artist, she's got more talent and she's more committed than just about any student at the art school. And I can tell you she's made more sacrifices to be able to do her course than any of them.'

'Oh Lord,' said Marthinus. 'Heartbreaking. Perhaps she'll take up photography again later on.'

Nick said nothing, he thought of the way in which Charelle looked different, stressed and thin, as if she were running on her rims, as if she'd been robbed of all her softness; and of the determination with which she wanted to take up nursing, as if she were trying to throw off her old life with violence. When he thought of her, of what had happened to her, he still felt it in his body, in the region of his stomach, his heart. His heart felt as if it were being compressed between two heavy objects. He didn't want to dwell on what had happened to her, but he couldn't help returning to it again and again.

*

Jan Botha invited him for a beer in town. He was grateful for the invitation, because he felt the need to get away from the claustrophobic atmosphere of the art school (and from Albrecht Bester's hand-wringing agonising).

They had a drink in the bar where the Chris Kestell lookalike had followed him that day, the man who was now the suspect in the Buks Verhoef murder. Nick was still interested in Jan Botha's job at the Salt River mortuary. Did he sometimes attend the forensic autopsies? Sometimes, said Jan Botha, when he didn't have too many other jobs. As he'd said, things were pretty hectic there at the moment. The people couldn't keep up. South Africa was a violent society, he needn't tell Nick that – gunshots, stabbings, rapes, road accidents. Every year more than three thousand bodies were examined at Forensic Pathology. If you worked there, said Jan, you were very close to the pulse of the city's violent heart.

How did he stand it? asked Nick. Oh well, said Jan Botha, it's a job. He was used to it. He found it interesting. It was real. The kids at the art school didn't know what real was, that was why they flirted with life-and-death games, then things went awry. Too much time and too little talent. Too much time, too much money, and bored. Most of those students were bored out of their tiny minds, said Jan Botha, so then they went looking for all kinds of cheap thrills and instant gratifications.

And did the work feed his art? asked Nick. Yes, said Jan Botha, it certainly did that. It was real. What he saw sometimes elicited a very visceral response in him – he found that important for making art, he said.

They drank their beer. Nick watched the man covertly. The warm, curly, shoulder-length hair, the eyeliner and mascara. An inscrutable guy. He wondered what Marthinus would make of him. He had no idea of Jan Botha's sexual orientation. The man sent mixed messages – the sexy, fragrant, feminine hair, and the robust, no-nonsense macho vibe. A matter-of-fact bloke, focused, with no affectations. If he retained his focus he could turn out to be a good artist. He had the passion, the singularity of vision, the technical skill.

What was the general procedure followed after a murder? Nick asked. When they got a murder call, Jan Botha explained, the forensic police went out to collect the body. He sometimes went along. It depended whether there was anybody else to help. Forms were filled in on the spot, the Forensic Pathology Service was contacted by radio as soon as they got to the location, and again when they left. Photos were taken; he sometimes helped with that as well. The body was put into a white plastic bag on a gurney and strapped down. The gurney was wheeled back into the van. At the mortuary the body was weighed and measured as soon as it arrived, that too he often did. Then it was taken to the refrigeration room. There it stayed till the autopsy was done. The forensic pathologist then had to determine the cause of death. In most cases the violence had been committed under the influence of alcohol. The details were documented, the toxicology samples were sent away and added to the file when they returned. Only after the autopsy could the family come to identify the body. A death certificate was issued. The court case was more often than not delayed. The family could be thankful if the forensic report was ever opened. Generally the backlog was too great. Except when people had money, said Jan Botha; if they could pay, they could speed up the whole system.

On the way back to his car Nick walked past the coffee shop where Buks Verhoef was shot. He saw a man sitting in the window, reading a newspaper. His heart almost seized up with shock – the man was Victor Schoeman. He could fucking-well swear the man was none other than Victor Schoeman. He did not want to linger, in case the man looked up, but he did want to double-check. He walked past, went and stood on the stoep of the shop next door, and went back in the direction of the bar from where he'd come. Then he walked back, his head averted, but in such a way that he could catch a second glimpse of the man. It was Victor Schoeman, it was him for sure. Older, thinner, but him without a doubt. The same bony face, now even more like the older Willem Dafoe in the role of villain. Even bonier than before, his hair close-shaven on his head like that of a bloody convict.

That evening Nick went to see Marthinus to tell him. Menasse was there. They sat in the sitting room. Marthinus had once again made a fire. Marthinus and Menasse were rapt in conversation when Nick entered. Menasse was turned towards the fire, his hands on the arm-rests of the chair. While talking, he stared intently into the fire, as if beholding eternal verities in the glowing flames. Marthinus was sitting on a bench, his face tilted towards Menasse. Menasse was talking.

They stopped when Nick entered. Don't interrupt your conver-sation, he said. He went to the kitchen, got himself a beer, and joined them in front of the fire. He didn't want to interrupt them, but he was itching to tell Marthinus about Victor Schoeman.

Here, in Marthinus' sitting room, in front of the fire, he and Menasse in conversation, Nick felt safe. He thought if he hadn't had this refuge, he'd have gone under. Menasse was wearing what he always wore – running shoes, an old pair of jeans and a windbreaker (he was dirt poor, Marthinus had said once). Marthinus was wearing sheepskin slippers, wide, high-quality tracksuit pants and a white woollen jersey that looked as if the wool had been spun by hand in Peru or on one of the Greek islands and the jersey hand-knitted somewhere. Exclusive.

Menasse said: God counts the stars, and names every one.

Lovely, said Marthinus. Lovely.

The human soul is clothed in a physical body – almost like a pupa in a cocoon – that enables the soul to function in the physical world, said Menasse. Our deeds, our speech and our thoughts could be seen as the vestments through which the soul expressed itself in this terrestrial sphere. The Shlemut referred to the non-duality of God. God consisted in Ayin – the imperceptible nothingness and complete unity, and Yesh – perceptible being, manifested in the diversity of creation. This non-duality was sometimes manifested as metziut – created being, and sometimes as non-metziut – the nothingness preceding creation. (Nick suddenly recalled the silkworms he'd kept as a child.)

Menasse had maintained the other evening that time existed before the beginning of the universe, said Marthinus, and he found that an interesting idea. He liked the idea that the beginning of the universe had not been the first beginning, but that the idea of a beginning was more complex, with endless consequences.

Menasse nodded dreamily. His gaze was still fixed on the flames, in which he no doubt saw the secrets of creation and of God's nothing-ness as well as of his perfect unity with everything. Nick envied him this extensive system of truth and coherence. His own life felt as if it was fast scattering asunder.

The drink, the heat of the fire, the restful conversation between Menasse and Marthinus about the eternal things, about God's unity with everything and about the complexity of the idea of a beginning, all these acted soothingly on Nick's turbulent state of mind, so that he gradually started to relax and unwind, and the idea of Victor Schoeman no longer felt quite so unpleasant. So what, he thought, if he'd seen the fucker.

After Menasse had left, Nick told Marthinus about Victor. Nick half expected Marthinus to reply that he'd known intuitively that Victor was in the vicinity, he'd *known* (intuited) that Victor was going to turn up sometime soon. But Marthinus said nothing of the kind.

All that he asked was whether Nick was one hundred per cent cer-tain that it had indeed been Victor.

He was ninety-five per cent certain, said Nick.

That was good enough, said Marthinus. But what was it, he asked, that Nick had against Victor Schoeman? Look, said Marthinus, Victor was an offensive fellow, and he'd often enough indicated to Nick that he suspected that Victor was the instigator of a whole lot of things that had recently happened – criminal activities and so on – but did Nick have any reason to feel that Victor could harm him personally?

No, said Nick. (He didn't want to tell Marthinus that it had in fact been *he*, with all his talk about Victor, who had made him even more wary of the man.) Victor owed him a lot of money, which Nick had in any case written off long ago, but that wasn't the worst. Victor had admittedly fucked him over properly with the *Shallows* thing, but in the end that was nothing. The money was nothing. Much worse was that in a way – perhaps unjustly – he held Victor responsible for what had happened to Blinky. Perhaps he was making a mistake. Nobody would ever know what exactly happened there. And that on top of it Victor had taken Marlena with him when he'd left for overseas. More than that? No. But he'd never liked Victor. The man had pissed him off from the outset. And his dislike of him had over the years only grown stronger. The very thought of having to look into Victor's scheming mug gave him the creeps. That was more or less his position as far as Victor was concerned.

'Okay,' said Marthinus. 'I understand. Oh Lord.'

*

The following morning the agent phoned him. Was he still interested in selling, she had a buyer with a very good offer.

Twenty-seven

I avoid the town even more assiduously than before. I do only the most essential shopping early in the morning at the small Spar supermarket around the corner. During the day and even at night I avoid public places. I watch the Olivier brothers' videos. I watch series on my laptop. Anything, I'm no longer particularly choosy – series about vampires (God hates fangs), about detectives, about drugs. I become a recluse. No, I become a prisoner in my own home, because I'm scared of coming across the stalker somewhere. If I can keep myself out of sight long enough and well enough, he may lose interest in me and clear out. Did he not have on his agenda a visit to his cousin in the high-security psychiatric institution near Moorreesburg, and a visit to his birth farm in Mpumalanga? All of it lies and fabrications of course, but nevertheless. He must have other matters on his agenda, it can't be for nothing that he's come back to South Africa, unless that was also a pack of lies.

When I do venture out onto the streets, I am hypervigilant. I look around me constantly, and behind me, to see if I can't perhaps spot him out of the corner of my eye. I wonder if he's instructed people to spy on me. How else could he have followed me into town and accosted me in the coffee shop, and that by chance in the place where Buks Verhoef was shot? He wants to know something from me about Verhoef's death, something that he thinks I know, and I'm afraid he's not going to leave me in peace until he's had an answer.

But I'm on the lookout not only for the hollow-cheeked man, but also for friends and acquaintances. In these days I lack the patience or the appetite for making small talk. With the exception of you (who are in any case not in town at the moment) and one or two others, there are very few people that I wish to have contact with nowadays.

I slip out one evening to see a documentary about a South African artist. The film is showing at a small private theatre in the student centre of the university. I've never been here before. I have no particular interest in this specific artist, but I do have a very strong need to get out of my house. It's a bitterly cold evening. This morning there was snow on the highest peaks of two mountains. Winter solstice is in ten days' time. It's evidently going to be a cold winter. The artist is a showman. He has well-developed calves and a lot of money. Some Chinese person arranged a retrospective for him in China. Angels and flying figures are an important motif in his work. Take away the cross, he argues, and it looks as if Jesus is dancing. (I'm not so sure of this.) He executes an exuberant Jesus dance to exuberant music, dressed in a loincloth and wig, his body painted brown. As far as I'm concerned, the whole documentary could have consisted of this dance, because it's very amusing. Very imaginative, very joyful. He does it on one of the verandas of his home (an extensive mansion), with two statues, one on either side of him. But the scene doesn't last long enough to make out whether they are two effigies of Christ, or if the statues are supposed to represent the two thieves on the cross. His paintings don't say much to me, and his artistic process and his ideas even less, but towards the end he dances again for a gathering of guests, presumably once again at his home (pine trees and mountain in the background), dressed in pointed-toe green leather shoes, and an enormous blow-up suit with two stylised women's breasts drawn on it, and with a kind of Malay skullcap or Christmas hat on his head. This dance I also enjoy greatly. The director is present tonight, and at the end there is a question-and-answer session with him, which seems to me to last for ever, because people ask all sorts of irrelevant questions. All of a sudden I become very restless, because I can just picture the stalker in the meantime sneaking into the theatre, and lying in wait for me next to the curtains, or, even worse, grabbing hold of my arm in the foyer.

The man, my benefactor, the man whom I had cared for full-time in his last months, died at this time of year, at the beginning of winter. While I was reading him *Moby Dick*, we both of us identified so closely with that novel that it was as if we were on that ship, with Captain Ahab and Ishmael. I started reading to him in the afternoon, just after his afternoon nap, and sometimes carried on until dusk fell, and I had to switch on his bedside lamps for more light. It must have rained at times, but I don't recall that. It always grew dark very gradually, almost imperceptibly. Towards the end of the novel I carried on reading until the night nurse reported for duty. Then he and I – each in our own manner – had to detach ourselves from the world of the novel, and refocus on our immediate surroundings: the room in which he was lying, the sick chamber, the room to which he had been confined for weeks by his illness. He must certainly have refocused on his bodily discomfort, on his pain, presumably; I on trifles, probably. The atmosphere of the novel remained with me for a long time every day, and I think the same was true for him, even though he was progressively slipping away into a twilight world on account of the heavy sedation for pain.

*

It is now about a year ago that Mr Mandela fell ill and was admitted to hospital. Although everybody was awaiting it, he took a long time to die. Even when they had already started digging his grave at Qunu, he still did not die. One afternoon, I remember, I had a vision. I was standing at one of the windows of my sitting room at about a quarter to seven. I was looking at the wide western skies. On the horizon there was a glimmering and a few dark, drifting clouds. Bare branches were etched against the darkling sky. There were still dark leaf clusters here and there on those trees that had not yet lost their leaves. Then I saw the heavens open and our tata ascending unto them. Straight up he floated, smiling, wearing one of his pretty shirts. He was waving. Slowly he ascended, as in all of history only the Virgin Mary had managed before him. (Think: Titian's *Assunta*.) Below him the sea at False Bay was opening slowly, as in my Children's Bible the Dead Sea had opened at the behest of Moses for the Israelites to pass through. A multitude of things, I saw in the vision, was revealed on that exposed sea bottom. Weapons, cartridges of bullets, banned writings. Documents, reels of film, tapes with interviews – all the incriminating exhibits the apartheid regime wanted to get rid of – everything full of slick and slime and seaweed and some of the objects covered in barnacles. Some things had already almost turned into coral. Recent bones – the bones of black and white people (indistinguishable, naturally), but also a multitude of fossils from the Cambrian era, from the Permian and Cretaceous eras, and many larger bones from the time of the dinosaurs – even these were exposed. Also the skeletons of fish – large and small. In a room I saw Graça, Mandela's wife, seated very still on a chair. Her hands were folded in her lap. She was wearing a black veil and she was inconsolably sad. Winnie climbed into a black Mercedes and stepped on the accelerator. I could not read the expression on her face, but she was also clad in black, totally; the ornate gold embellishment on the temples of her dark glasses reflected the light momentarily. Then all of a sudden the old tata was no longer visible. The heavens had swallowed him. Then I blinked my eyes, and the vision was gone. I remember thinking we – my people and I – had done him an injustice but he had prevailed. A few months later they showed on television how his grave was being dug at Qunu among the aloes and the koppies.

You are out of town for a while and sometimes, in this time of isolation, I yearn for the black dog, the noble animal that I had the privilege of housing for a day and a night. It is almost as if it never happened, as if she never slept tight up against my back for a night and regarded me with her compassionate gaze.

In the meantime I keep a close watch on the newspaper for any mention of the man, any revelation of his true identity.

*

The house left to me by my benefactor is not big, but it is in an old, established area, with a view of Stellenbosch Mountain from the sitting room, the stoep and the main bedroom. (There is nothing more lovely than the full moon rising behind that mountain.) I could never have imagined myself as a homeowner. Drinking my early-morning tea, I have a view of the mountain from my bed, and in these days specifically the sunrises are often achingly beautiful. It gets light late, first light becomes visible only at half past six. There are still a few days to go before the shortest day. At times the sky is completely clear (like the past few days) – after days of cold, wet weather. At times there are clouds just above the horizon, just above the outline of the mountain, and half an hour before sunrise the radiance gradually turns to gold. At times the sky is as clear as on the first day of creation. The mountains in silhouette etched in velvet against this lambent light. At times there are great cloud masses, mainly in shades of muted blue, with their upper edges in warmer pinks, on account of the glow of the rising but as yet invisible sun. Some mornings, when the weather is worse, there is a mighty spectacle of dark clouds, with only fragments of clear sky in between. High clouds, often, gravid with rain. As it gets lighter, the clouds assume a less threatening aspect. But every day the spectacle is thrilling, the beauty of it seizing me by the throat and forming a – frequently sublime – transition from night to day, from the oppressive intensity of night-time dreams to the anxiety of daytime reality.

For a considerable time now I have found the company of people wearying. Actually ever since the death of Jacobus. Even as a child I was uncommonly reserved and for all of my adult life never particularly sociable (this was undoubtedly largely due to my blemished mouth), but my tendency to withdraw from the world has probably in the last few months assumed unnatural proportions. It may be why, I now think, I regard my last, intense community with people, in the time around

Jacobus' death, as a thing apart – as sacred! (And so help me God, sacred is not a word commonly occurring in my vocabulary. It is, truth to tell, a word I find deeply suspect. So much the more meaningful that I can so easily invoke it in the context of the death of Jacobus.)

My tendency to self-withdrawal must surely also be one of the reasons why I handled the interviews with Marcus Olivier so poorly – irregular interaction with other people has rendered me less nimble in precise timing in a social context. And also why, indubitably, I experienced the few minutes with the dying Buks Verhoef in my arms – I have no idea how long it lasted – as searingly intimate.

For the last few months, since returning to the town, I have sought refuge in writing the monograph on the Olivier brothers. I believe, tell myself, that I don't need anything other than that. In this state of mind it's easy to feel threatened, to feel somebody is following me, intent upon invading my privacy. But that the man, my stalker, is an unsavoury character, and probably a thug as well, embroiled in all sorts of criminal activities, of that I become ever more convinced.

It must surely signify something that the man is following me so relentlessly – from Oesterklip to Frederiksbaai and from there to Stellenbosch. It would not surprise me if he found my cleft palate condition exciting (sexually stimulating) – I've encountered that often enough. And then because he thinks I know something about the murder of Buks Verhoef – probably because he himself had something to do with it.

*

Because my benefactor died at this time of year, at the beginning of winter the year before last, I frequently need to think of him again.

When – at the beginning, when he was still mobile – I took him for his special exercise sessions at the local gym, I used to sit on a bench next to the swimming pool while he was doing his exercises.

He waded at the shallow end, he moved slowly in the water, which reached only up to his waist. I never encouraged him, that was the job of his special personal trainer (a young man with freckles). He was still robust of build, his chest broad; covered in grey hair (the way I like it). He must have been a heartbreaker, because he was still handsome, with the broad face, dark eyes and solid masculine torso. His penetrating gaze was fixed on me throughout, and when our eyes then met, there was something like a shudder, a sexual shudder palpable between us. I remember it, the heavy smell of chlorine, the vapour against the windowpanes, the patient, freckled young man, his trainer, with him in the water, and my benefactor slowly wading towards me in the water, holding me captive in his fierce gaze. As if he wanted to compensate with the penetration of his gaze for his physical debilitation. By then he was already weakened by his disease, there was a big age difference between us. Because he was attractive, and influential, I believe there must always have been more than one woman in his life. Later, when he was completely bedridden, disarmed by his illness, and he had few physical secrets from me – by this time I was familiar with every phase of the disintegration of his body – I still loved him, and he me, like a man and a woman. It was, I like to believe, the chastest, most selfless love either of us had ever experienced.

*

Last year, in late winter, after the death of Jacobus, when I was staying in the outside room with my friends in the Eastern Cape, when I got so interested in the work of Nancy Spero, in the time when my bones felt as if they were constituted of ice crystals, and I thought I would never again be warm, I was sitting on my own one afternoon in my friends' large living room. I can't recall why I sat there all afternoon. In the fireplace were the ashes of the previous night's fire. Above the fireplace there was a rose in a slender vase. Through the window, if I turned my head slightly to the left, one could see the bluegums in front of the house, and, across the valley, the long, flat hill with the quarry. On top of the hill there was a deserted house. I associated it with the house of the hanged man, as in the painting by Cézanne. I was surprised at how robustly my heart was still beating in my chest, robustly and rhythmically, reliably. There was a chill in the room, although it was not particularly cold that day, and the room was cosy. Outside the air was thin, but clear. Inside the light was cold, the walls had an unusual blue tinge. It was dead quiet. Three o'clock, half past three, four o'clock, half past four, five o'clock. I thought I was never going to get away from this place, time was passing too torpidly. Time is the obstacle. It's time that handicaps me; time has taken hold of me. Time is going to restrain me first, then extinguish me. Outside there was a slight stirring in the bluegum leaves. Later the late-afternoon sun shone warmly on these leaves and the hill opposite was bathed in sunlight. A long, low, warm hill. Then suddenly the sun was gone, the sky on the horizon turned a pale pink and the earth cooled down as if at the sudden cracking of a whip. In the room was a dustiness, as if the most rarefied layer of dust was covering all objects. Just at half past five I got up and went to my room.

One evening I saw three figures in the flames of the fire that my friends had made in the fireplace. It reminded me of Daniel and his friends in the Bible – in the furnace, unscathed by the flames. One of these three figures, I could fancy, was Jacobus. Jacobus who had trans-mogrified and could now manifest himself in various embodiments. Jacobus who had been liberated and was no longer shackled by time. Jacobus for whom time had ceased, and who could now move freely – no longer confined to one single medium, and who could now make himself visible in flames. That evening I stayed by the fire until all the others had gone to bed, and the fire had burnt to ashes. Then I was overwhelmed anew by Jacobus' searing absence. Then I felt anew the icy cold in my bones.

At this time I engrossed myself in a book on the work of Nancy Spero, and in medical handbooks, especially *Gray's Anatomy*. I was often furious, a helpless fury, of which I did not know the origin. Sometimes the fury seeped into my body, then I was cold as ice on the outside, my limbs like ice, but so dark and burning on the inside that I felt I was standing on the rim of a crater, into which I could plunge and by which I would be instantly swallowed up.

*

Nick told Marthinus: 'I have a buyer for my house and I don't have a good feeling about it at all. To tell the truth, I don't even want to know who the person is.'

Twenty-eight

Marthinus was always eager to come and see Nick's work; he looked long and attentively, he asked questions, he made comments, sometimes he whistled appreciatively, and then he invited Nick to come and watch a DVD with them that evening.

Nick was grateful for every invitation from Marthinus, because every invitation was a reason not to return to his cold house. So, since Charelle's departure, they had made their way through a whole pile of DVDs. The most recent was *Solaris* by Tarkovsky. Afterwards he and Marthinus sat for a while in dead silence, in one corner of the sitting room, where they always watched DVDs on the big flatscreen television. (A room in which the hand of a woman was visible.) The atmosphere of the movie grabbed Nick by the throat – something elusively desolate. He saw in that film a perfect mirror of the state of his own mind. The cryptic turbidity, the searing feeling of loss, of guilt and betrayal. He remained under the influence of the mood of the film for a long time, of its muted colour, of the evocative, sombre, inexplicable images. It grabbed him by the throat and it wrung his heart. The film was for him a reflection of his failed relationship with Isabel. It plunged him into recollections of her.

He thought of her in her blue dressing gown, in New York. One evening she was feverish, she complained that she didn't feel well. She nevertheless consented to lovemaking, but kept her face averted throughout. He held her burning, feverish body under his hands like a heathen idol. He was practising idolatry, he knew, that was what he was doing. He would empty himself into her, he knew, he could not hold back anything of himself, even if nothing remained of him or of her, even if they both spontaneously combusted. Immediately afterwards she turned her face to him, and something like a drift of tenderness washed over it. She allowed herself to be held in his arms, and sighed.

*

Five days before the solstice (Nick kept a weather eye open for this) the agent made an appointment with him to meet the prospective buyer. He had as little enthusiasm for this event as for the Second Coming.

*

On a cold, overcast day, three days before the solstice, the agent brought the two prospective buyers to Nick's house. From the very first sight they turned him off. The younger one had a sly, sneering jackal-face, with beard and leather jacket. He looked arrogant and presumptuous. The older one had a shaven head, his eyes were a perfidious pale-green, and a tattoo crept out from under his collar. Low-class scum, Nick thought.

They hardly looked at the house, and offered Nick a large sum – even more than poor Buks Verhoef. Were they going to live in the house themselves? Nick asked. Oh no, said the younger one, and the two exchanged a swift glance, the house was going to be converted into a private gallery. It was so exceptionally well situated. Were they in the art business? asked Nick. No, they were actually buying on behalf of a client. The client was in the art business, he was an overseas art dealer. The person was very interested in South African art, said the older man. (Tell me another, thought Nick. What kind of bullshit was this.) The client was very knowledgeable, and he already had a large art collection. He was hoping to use the house as a kind of showcase. He didn't perhaps have a few paintings by the artist Blinky Booysen in his collection? Nick asked. Again the two exchanged a swift glance.

No, said jackal-jaw, he really couldn't say. But the name did ring a bell. (Really, thought Nick, I think you're a fool and a swindler and a charlatan.) And were the two of them also interested in art? he asked. Oh yes, said the tattooed guy, but they weren't as knowledgeable as their client, they were really only facilitators. Middlemen, said jackal-jaw. So the name Buks Verhoef, the Stellenbosch artist, also meant nothing to them? Nick said. Again the quick, sidelong glance between the two. No, said jackal-jaw, heard of him, but didn't really know anything else about him. Also not that he was shot – fatally? asked Nick. Jackal-jowls laughed, heard something of the kind, yes, but as they were saying, the art world wasn't *really* their speciality.

Now Nick just wanted them out of the house. He didn't want to have to listen to their fabrications any longer. Give him a few days to consider the offer, he said. Goodbye. He couldn't buzz them out of the gate fast enough, also so that he could phone Marthinus.

'You won't believe it,' he said to Marthinus, 'I don't know if I've gone totally paranoid now, but this time *I* think Victor Schoeman is behind the whole house-buying saga. Or at least has a share in it.'

Marthinus laughed. 'Oh Lord,' he said.

'I don't know if you've infected me with your talk,' said Nick, 'but I see Victor's hand in this. Must be since I saw him in the flesh the other day.'

'Oh Lord,' said Marthinus.

'I just know something's not kosher with these damned buyers and I'm afraid Victor is behind it.'

'Perhaps he's just a front man,' said Marthinus (with somewhat less conviction than usual), 'for somebody else.'

'So why are *you* soft-pedalling now, Marthinus?' Nick said. 'After all, *you* thought he was behind the killing of Verhoef. You were in fact fully convinced of it.'

Marthinus laughed softly again. 'It was all just speculation,' he said.

'You can't say that *now*! It's too late to backtrack now! What are the portents from *The Shallows*?'

'Oh Lord,' said Marthinus. '*The Shallows*. That compendium of horrors. No, listen, the emphasis there is on other things, bigger debaucheries.'

'But you said at the beginning,' said Nick, 'with the murder of the businessman in Moorreesburg, Malmesbury – where the hell ever – you said you were sure that Victor was behind it all!'

'That's true,' said Marthinus. 'But then everything was much more clear cut. The escaped prisoners from the psychiatric institution. The marauding bands. It was all straight out of *The Shallows*. The man here in your kitchen as well. What he said conformed so exactly to that one scene in *The Shallows*. Oh Lord. I could have put my head on the block. Even at first with Buks Verhoef. But now I'm starting to think the murder of Verhoef is too obvious. It doesn't fit Victor's modus operandi. Do you want to sell or not, how do you feel?'

'I don't know,' said Nick, 'on the one hand I've not been able to stomach this house for a long time. On the other hand I don't want it to become some smuggler's den or nest of crime either. The idea doesn't appeal to me.'

'Oh Lord, yes,' said Marthinus. 'I can imagine that. We'll get Menasse to come and have a look. He'll be able to gauge the atmosphere. He's very good with that kind of thing. Clients trust him. He has an exceptionally reliable sensitivity to many things.'

Nick agreed to this. It was fine, he now needed an outsider to help him. An impartial third party. Menasse, so engrossed in the secrets of the creation and of God's nothingness and His complete unity with everything, now had to come and say what he made of the situation. (While he was about it, he could also pronounce an impartial verdict on Nick's whole life, not just the house.) With his exceptional sensitivity to atmosphere and emanations he could perhaps pass judgement on the house and even on the auras of the two scoundrels, traces of them surely still lingered in the air.

Nick wondered why he'd ever bought this damned house. What a pity that he hadn't befriended Marthinus beforehand. Then Menasse could have advised him on the purchase – gauged the atmosphere of the place in advance. But then he'd probably never have met Charelle. Perhaps, he thought, that would have been better for him and especially for her.

*

A day or two later Menasse came to inspect the house. He came one morning with Marthinus. His brief was to analyse the atmosphere of the house. Nick's hopes were fixed on him. He was going to be led by Menasse's findings. For himself, he no longer knew whether he should sell to the scoundrels, accept the substantial offer, or refuse to sell to them because he suspected them of criminal activities.

Menasse took his time. (Always clad in the same running shoes, worn jeans and windbreaker, and the cap, of course, which concealed his adamantine brow like that of an Old Testament prophet, although Nick felt the need today to see the proof of his prophetic powers.) Menasse walked slowly, from room to room, through the house. He took his time. He lingered for a long time in each room. Marthinus and Nick sat waiting for him at the table in the kitchen.

When Menasse had finished, he came to sit with them. Nick made tea for them.

The house basically had a good energy, said Menasse. But this good energy had been disturbed in a few places. Notably in the front bedroom. But also in the passage and in the sitting room. (This did not surprise Nick at all, considering the negative thoughts and bad dreams that he'd had in his bedroom. And the unopened boxes in the sitting room must certainly have impeded the flow of good energy.) But the situation was not irreversible. With application and with good energy it could be repaired.

What did he mean by application? asked Nick.

With a dedicated meditation on the Good in these rooms. But it could take time. Nick should not be in a hurry. It couldn't be fixed overnight. But if Nick were to do it regularly, with the requisite focus, he could succeed in gradually dispelling the negative energy in the rooms. Especially in the front room the harmony was completely out of equilibrium. There was an almost palpable – Menasse demonstrated with his hands – cloud of regret, melancholy, negative energy. 'Very oppressive,' said Menasse. He'd advise Nick provisionally not to use that room. The 'powerful emanations' could adversely affect his spirit. (Nick glanced at Marthinus covertly, but his facial expression betrayed nothing of what he made of Menasse's words.)

Menasse was extremely complimentary about the tea. Nick made another pot. Menasse approved of the emanations in the kitchen. A very salubrious room, 'beneficial for the soul'. Just as well that it was the only place where he and Charelle had ever met, Nick thought.

Nick said that he was not acquainted with any meditation techniques. No problem, said Menasse. It could be acquired. All that it required was an open mind and 'a commitment to the Good'.

(Once again Marthinus' face was inscrutable.)

What is the Good? Nick asked, hesitantly.

The Good is a concentration on that which is Divine, said Menasse. That was the short answer. The long answer was everything that the Kabbalah taught us about the nature of the Good. Very complex. Perhaps some other time.

He'd like to ask Menasse another question, said Marthinus, one that didn't altogether relate to this one, but one that he often puzzled about. (Menasse nodded. No problem. A small man, fine, shapely hands, well-kept nails, cap pushed back on the head, the prophetic brow now exposed.) How did Menasse interpret Ezekiel's vision?

Merkavah is the word for chariot, said Menasse. It was derived from the Hebrew word rakhav, which meant to ride. The chariot was a metaphor for God who 'travelled' from His unknowable state to a 'place' where He could be known, that was to say, visualised.

Marthinus was clearly taken with this reply. He was now immediately going to reread Ezekiel with enhanced understanding, he said.

Shortly afterwards Menasse left. Nick thanked him for his time and trouble. No trouble, Menasse assured him, and thanked him profusely for the tea. Menasse didn't have a car, said Marthinus when Menasse had left, he walked everywhere where he had to be, or took a taxi. Or sometimes he ordered Menasse and Anselmo a taxi, on those evenings they visited him. Menasse lived on a shoestring. But he was very particular about good tea. With that one could always please him greatly.

Nick and Marthinus remained sitting at the kitchen table. He told Marthinus that what Menasse had said made sense to him, but he didn't have the dedication or focus, and especially not the ability, to sit in each of the rooms every day and meditate until the negative energy had been dispersed. It was too extreme. It was too remote from his own take on things. And the Good wasn't really a concept that meant anything to him. He'd rather practise art. That was the area he was best acquainted with. Perhaps he should take the easy way out and sell the house. If the buyers wanted to convert it into an art brothel, if the two guys were part of an underground art mafia, then so be it. And whether or not Victor had a share in it, that had ceased to matter all that much to him.

He understood, said Marthinus. Oh Lord. Perhaps Nick should consider going away for a while before reaching a final decision. In the meantime he should come and watch a DVD with them. He quite felt like something by Sokurov. Perhaps *Father and Son*.

He'd seen it, said Nick, at some film festival, and it had depressed the hell out of him.

Marthinus was interested. In what way? he enquired. He didn't know, said Nick, he couldn't remember any more. The relationship between the father and son was just too intimate. Uncomfortably intimate. Too complex. And the absence of the woman was just too palpable.

Then they'd watch something else, said Marthinus, no problem!

Twenty-nine

My very good friend, Willem Wepener, is back in town. He's been away on a six-month-long artist's residency in Paris. I missed him sorely in this time. He is a painter, and Jacobus was his best friend. It was with him that I went to view Jacobus' body at the undertakers that day, in that wretched little back room with the Mr Price curtain. Willem and his long-time partner live in an old house, in the centre of town. This is where Willem has his studio. His partner is an architect (as outgoing as Willem is reserved, a cordial man; a life artist, Willem calls him). Willem Wepener (Louw Wepener, the Boer commandant, was an ancestor), is, if at all possible, even more unsociable than I. Tall, thin, intense, with a broad, thuggish face (which offers no clue to his extremely sensitive nature) that at times reminds me of Michel Foucault's. Or when he wears a woollen cap in winter, of a villain in a French detective film. Jacobus' death hit him very hard. It took him a long time to get over it. For months afterwards he still dreamt of Jacobus. (How I envied him this, because Jacobus never appeared to me in dreams, whereas I yearned for it to happen to me.)

Willem invites me, two evenings before the solstice, to have a drink with him in town. (He never receives anybody at home.) Like me, he avoids the public gaze as much as possible. He is a dedicated artist, almost obsessive about his work. He makes small paintings, in oils, non-figurative, although not conforming to the conventional rules of abstraction – indeed, he strives wherever possible to break these rules. He works with complex forms, layered and interwoven, with added highlights, and shadows to suggest depth. Every canvas is meticulously constructed with layer upon layer of paint. He is uncertain of himself, full of diffidence about his work, in spite of his considerable success.

He is the one who gave me the idea of the monograph on the work of the Olivier brothers, after he'd seen a retrospective of their work a year or two ago at MoMA in New York. He brought back a book on them and a catalogue, which immediately intrigued me, with, of course, the additional knowledge that they were the sons of Marcus Olivier, the old father.

I tell him about the man who is stalking me, and about the death of Buks Verhoef. I tell him that now that he's back in town I feel less threatened, as if I have an ally. Even if it's just the thought that he's there.

Willem tells me about Avigdor Arikha, an artist whose work has recently impressed him tremendously. He is also intrigued by the way in which Arikha writes about art, and the painter's remarkable knowledge of a wide variety of artists. Arikha writes among others about Poussin – he even made a reconstruction of the kind of brushes the painter must have used. Willem also tells me that Arikha believed that a painting should be completed in a single sitting. That sometimes he did not paint for weeks on end, until a theme – the chance correspondence of a few objects – so grabbed hold of him that he then *had* to paint it. Thus he once cut short a foreign trip to go back to paint a theme that had engrossed him at home. And none other than Samuel Beckett, Willem tells me, was Arikha's best friend. He made several portraits of him. It took quite a number of years before they addressed each other as 'tu'. They listened to music together. Arikha was fascinated by polyphonic music, in particular the music of Heinrich Schütz. Beckett preferred Beethoven's chamber music and works for piano, as well as Schubert, Haydn and Mozart. They also listened together, Willem recounts, to Schoenberg, Alban Berg and Webern. Beckett was particularly drawn to Webern's fragmented melodies. Together they also read poetry aloud: Dante, Hölderlin, late Goethe and the work of the strange eighteenth-century German poet Matthias Claudius. In his last days, when Beckett was slipping away into the haze of his drawn-out coma, he still murmured the names of Arikha and his wife, and the words of the poets they had once read together. After Beckett's death Arikha visited his grave every day. So great was his despair at his friend's death that his own health was affected. For a while he couldn't even paint. *Sam's Spoon*, one of Arikha's most beautiful paintings, says Willem, is of Beckett's silver baptism spoon that he'd given Arikha's eldest daughter on her baptism. The painting, not large, depicts the little spoon on a cloth of white linen. The only colour in the work is the slight copperish tints in the spoon. Beautiful, says Willem, poignant.

For a while we both sit in silence, thinking of the remarkable friendship between the painter Avigdor Arikha and Samuel Beckett.

Now Willem feels, he says, that abstraction has reached a dead end for him. He's considered for some time returning to figurative work; even painting from life. Especially now that he's so strongly under the impression of Arikha's work. But he's vacillating. It would be a radical break with his way of painting. And he doesn't even know if he *could* paint from life at all, he's never really done it. He also doesn't know how it would be received.

Willem and I are having a drink in one of the town's more luxurious guest houses. (I don't anticipate meeting my stalker there.) It's conveniently situated in the centre of town, and the lounge is convivial, and more private than most other places where one can have a drink in town in the evening. After we've drunk a considerable amount of whisky, and Willem has left, late in the evening, I remain sitting in the lounge for a while. Diagonally opposite me a woman has been sitting on her own all evening, of whom I was only vaguely aware, because the conversation with Willem totally absorbed my attention. Now that he's left, she comes into sharper focus, also because I become aware of the fact that she's watching me.

She is older, I would put her deep in the fifties, with a finely chiselled face and a supercilious expression. Short grey hair, stylishly dressed, slender build.

After a while she gets up, and just before she ascends the staircase to the bedrooms (so she's a guest here), she stops, and turns to face me for a few moments. I pay for my drink, get up and follow her.

Her bedroom door is ajar. She invites me in, makes me sit down in one of the deep armchairs, and introduces herself. She's British, involved here in the country with a project on poverty. She pours us each a whisky. She tells me about her project. Her glance is sardonic, reserved. She's not over-friendly, actually quite offhand. Unusual eyes. Attractive.

After a while she gets up and puts out her hand to me. Wordlessly I follow her to the bed. Wordlessly I let myself be undressed by her. We crawl into the heated sheets. Lightly intoxicated by the whisky and the intense earlier conversation with Willem, I submit to her expert manipulation of my body. She handles my body with the ease and confidence with which I imagine her to drive a car. When at last a trembling passes through my body – an almost ecstatic thrill – it is Buks Verhoef's dying face that I see before me momentarily.

*

We must have slept for an hour or two. When I wake up, I get up, get dressed. I take my leave of her softly and thank her; she murmurs something in her sleep. Then I slip out by the door. Outside the streets are quiet. A fine drizzle is falling after some heavy rain earlier in the evening. Still pleasantly befuddled, my body relaxed into well-being after the sexual surrender and the sleep, I am less alert, less inclined to fear that the man may be lying in wait for me at home.

*

I can't bring myself to visit the grave of my benefactor. I don't want to think that he's lying there, the once potent male body reduced to bones.

207

At times I still feel as if he's extending a sexual invitation to me – from beyond the Styx, from the domain of the dead – to which my body spontaneously never fails to respond.

*

All the time I have an urge to go back to the coffee shop where Buks Verhoef was shot. While I know without a shred of doubt that that is the one place I must avoid, because that is the place most likely for my stalker to hang out. There is undoubtedly something about the place that exerts an irresistible attraction upon both of us. For me because Buks Verhoef died there in my arms, for him because he could have had something to do with the murder (a criminal returning to the scene of the crime?).

I also have a desire to visit once again the little room behind the undertaker's. I don't know under what pretence. I don't know how I would announce myself and how I would describe the purpose of my visit. Perhaps that I wanted just once more to be in the space where for the very last time I could lay eyes on my beloved dead friend. Perhaps the room is now being used for another purpose, presumably it's becoming ever less common to view bodies before the funeral.

I also consider returning to the guest house, to see whether I can recover the woman who surprised me so, and provided me with such bodily pleasure. But I suspect that in broad daylight I will be less reckless. And the intensity of that encounter is probably irrecoverable. So I decide against it.

*

With the passing of the days, I start hoping that the stalker may have beaten a retreat. Perhaps he is already on his way to the family farm in Mpumalanga, via a visit to the disturbed cousin in the high-security psychiatric institution in Moorreesburg. Who knows, perhaps the cousin is the guy who shot Buks Verhoef, the suspect who was sent for psychiatric observation. His severely disturbed cousin, according to the man. Perhaps that's why the stalker so chronically wants to know about Buks Verhoef from me. Anything's possible, that much I've learnt.

Thirty

At the time of the solstice it rains in the early part of the night, but it ceases during the latter part, and by a quarter past seven in the morning it starts clearing. An enormous, solid bank of cloud hovers over Simonsberg. From one end of the horizon it extends, as far as I can move my head. Gradually this cloud bank becomes lighter and smaller, as if dissolving, starting to fray downwards into wisps of cloud. I drink my tea in bed and behold it all. Gradually it starts to grow light, the outline of the mountain becomes more visible, the solid bank of cloud becomes less solid, and another, lighter cloud slowly starts shifting in behind the mountain. By degrees the cloud bank grows ever lighter, the mountain more solid, but still hazy, until by half past seven the massive cloud bank is long, extended and elliptical, smokily soft. Very gradually the light becomes radiant, the cloud shrinks ever smaller, the mountain assumes more presence. In the distance I hear the scolding of geese, and hadedahs, very far away, almost out of earshot, and the sound of small garden birds intensifies. Further to the right the next mountain range is much more emphatic of shape (not easily visible from my bed) and the greens in it are already distinguishable. And then, all of a sudden, at a quarter to eight, a cloud appears behind the mountain, rosily illuminated by the rising sun – still invisible. How glorious it is, the single, rosily glowing cloud behind the mountain.

I feel the breath of time blowing down my neck. I feel time hunting me down. My friend Willem Wepener commented that only at times does he succeed in standing still and looking at things, without being constantly driven, conscious of the susurration of passing time in his ears.

*

He had three options, argued Nick. (Four, if he took seriously the notion of taking up the study of Japanese gardens, which he naturally had no intention of doing.) The most radical, most extreme option – by far the least probable – was to adopt Menasse's suggestion: telling the agent he no longer wanted to sell; acquiring the art of meditation; sitting for hours (days, weeks) in the polluted rooms, and focusing on the Good and the Godly. A second option was to sell straightaway, regardless of whose criminal clutches would take possession of the house and to what purpose it would be put, looking for another habitation, carrying on with his life and never looking back. A third option was to adopt Marthinus' suggestion: telling the agent he needed a few days to make up his mind; going away for a while; seeing if distance would bring clarity.

He decided on the last option. The art school was closed for the winter break. He had time. He would lock up his house, ask Marthinus to keep an eye from time to time. Or get Jan Botha to stay in the house. He thought Jan would be proof against the powerful emanations Menasse had picked up there. If he could last that long in the Salt River mortuary, where the emanations would most certainly be less than positive (much more powerful than regret and melancholy), he would probably also be resistant to whatever negative energy he was likely to encounter in Nick's house. And it was important, thought Nick, that somebody should live in his house in his absence, because he had the hideous fantasy that when he returned, Victor Schoeman and associates would have occupied the place. And then he would have burnt his arse good and proper.

He fixed on Oesterklip. The sea air would do him good. Perhaps he could even get fit again, jog on the beach. He had no idea what the place would look like now. He'd been there years ago. Then everything had been pristine. He'd rented a fisherman's cottage and spent a fortnight there painting. In the evenings he'd gone drinking at the hotel bar. He remembered the flatness of the sea. The beach as well. Narrow and flat, an undramatic beach. Pebbly, with washed-up kelp. Stinking. He'd experienced Oesterklip at that time as a strange, unemphatic half-disconsolate place. For him it had been a place of grey – a place in shades of grey. From lighter, warmer grey to darker, cool greys. Grey, Marlena had said, the only anonymous, the least personal colour. Grey did not stimulate, it was perceptually static. The same perceptual stasis was what Nick had recovered on the beach at Oesterklip.

*

Nick informed the agent that he needed more time to consider the offer. Jan Botha with the fragrant hair was perfectly prepared to stay in Nick's house. Even when Nick apprised him of the negative emanations. Jan Botha just laughed. Bring it on, he said. If he could cope with the emanations of the Salt River mortuary, he said, he could cope with any emanations. (As Nick had foreseen.) But scarcely had Nick asked him, than he regretted it. He didn't know if he wanted the guy in his house. He didn't know if he still wanted to go away. But it was too late now. He'd reached a decision. It was important for him to go away for a while for clarity, and it was important that his house not be left unoccupied – an open invitation to robber and scoundrel. The whole idea of so-called clarity sounded flaky to him, but a change might just help to unscramble the tangled rigging of his mind.

*

Again and again I study the work of the Olivier brothers while writing the monograph. I'm still charmed and intrigued by each of their little videos – even though I've seen some of them any number of times.

For each video they create a special set with a box-like format. Small

– sometimes no larger than 90 x 65 x 75 cm. Within this created space the puppets, hand-carved from wood, are then filmed by means of the stop-action technique. Unlike on a film set, the spaces are not reproductions of existing spaces – there is no attempt at spatial coherence or logic. The materials used are mainly wood, glass, metal and cloth. Murky street scenes (like the one in *Kafka in Long Street*), dark interiors, cabinets, cupboards, empty shelves and unexpected detail are characteristic. Often a mysterious, nineteenth-century Dickensian atmosphere prevails (as in the video *The Cabinet of Jan de Grevenbroek*). In *Kafka in Long Street*, one of my favourites among the brothers' videos, a Kafkaesque hand-carved puppet emerges from a door, and slinks down the street. He is in a night scene, of which the background is made up out of dark, apparently soot-stained panels reminiscent of industrial scrap-metal surfaces, illogically arranged in a shallow space. Small ladders, such as those used in big cylindrical storage tanks, a street light. A length of white cloth draped over one of the panels. Two flying, or suspended, objects, that look like the arms of little porcelain dolls. Ominous, inhospitable, desolate. High up, to the left, in a small opaque window, perches something that looks like a Punch and Judy puppet. The Kafka character is remarkably lifelike – the same intense facial expression, sternly staring eyes and angular face as Franz Kafka. Like all their puppets, he has an immovable face, but moving hands and limbs.

The spectator feels herself trapped within these bizarre spatial configurations. The puppets are often stalkers, voyeurs. The spaces provide spyholes into other spaces – ambivalent, fractionally exceeding the boundaries of a recognisable reality. The spectator is placed in the role of stalker herself, of voyeur.

A recurring motif is that of the cabinet – cabinets of curiosities, cabinets of memorabilia, cabinets with pseudo-scientific contents. The dominant ambience of the videos is mysterious, dream-like, ambiguous. Obscure, half-known characters and anecdotes, often relating to history, and sometimes also South African history, are embodied. (*The Cabinet of Jan de Grevenbroek*, for instance, and *The Tempestuous Dream of Doctor H*, in which Doctor H, the protagonist, in a small, almost claustropho-bic chamber on the upper level of the set, behind half-drawn curtains, is examining the genitalia of a naked, tawny woman with a magnifying glass. While he's doing this, he is spied upon through a keyhole by another character. Accompanying this are the moving string quartets of Leoš Janáček.)

In one of their interviews the brothers quote Bruno Schulz: 'Yet what is to be done with events that have no place of their own in time; events that have occurred too late, after the whole of time has been divided and allotted; events that have been left in the cold, unregistered, hanging in the air, homeless and errant? . . . Let us try to find at some point of history such a branch line, a blind track onto which to shunt these illegal events.'

I cannot but see the Punch and Judy puppet – grinning, cynical, grim, with an immovably fixed wooden eye – regarding the whole street scene from his vantage point in the little window, as a portrait of the old father, Marcus Olivier.

*

In the morning I sit in bed watching the shifting spectacle of the sunrise. One morning there is a single pink swirl of cloud, with a darker centre. A cloud as wispy as an afterthought, a blithe spilling-over from an excess of possibilities. A playful recollection of godknowswhat. And just for the hell of it, higher up in the sky, an exuberant bright-pink cloud – rosy, radiantly lit up by the rising sun. A cloud glowing in the as yet uninscribed, blanched, pellucid sky.

Thirty-one

Nick handed over the house keys to Jan Botha. He got into his car and drove to Oesterklip. The surroundings were attractive. Since his previous visit Oesterklip had grown considerably. He checked in to the hotel. The place did not look at all as he remembered it from his previous visit. If he got fed-up here, he'd move further up the coast the next day.

His room was small, dark and musty. It was dominated by a dark wooden wardrobe, dark headboard and a too-gaudy, too-floral bed-spread. He doubted whether it was going to be conducive to any clarity of mind or vision. The repetitive fish motif on the shower curtain could induce hallucinations.

One night, and tomorrow he'd move on.

In the late afternoon he took a walk on the beach. A haze hovered over the sea. Much higher up in the sky there were delicate fleece clouds. The rocks were less grey than he remembered them. They were brilliant orange in patches, interspersed with a rust-green. The beach between the sea and the plant-covered dunes was wide and almost level. Towards the edge bordering the sea it was littered with mussel shells, which crushed under his feet when he walked on them. Three times he saw a seagull flying high up into the sky, dropping a mussel onto the beach, then swooping down to gobble up the cracked-open mussel.

Some distance along he came across a dead seal. It must have been fresh, because it had no smell as yet. Close to the tail-end the skin was lacerated. The insides bulged out here like raw boerewors. There were many seagulls in the vicinity, but only two were feeding on the seal. He found this dead seal upsetting. If it was a sign, it was not a good omen. (Where was Marthinus to put him at his ease, and Menasse to interpret the premonitions for him?)

As the sun started setting, the fine fleece clouds were suddenly gone. Nick stood still to watch the setting sun. The sea was a warm yellow-green, much lighter than the sky. As the sun moved closer to the horizon, it gradually turned a darker shade of red, and changed into an irregular, flattened oval.

With a sinking heart he walked back to the hotel. Near the hotel a man carrying a plastic bag came up to him. Crayfish, Pa, he said, freshly dived out of the sea. He held open the bag for Nick to see. There was little or no movement in the bag, and an unpleasant smell. He took out one of the crayfish, flung it down at Nick's feet. There was still some feeble movement in the claws. The man had a scar running across his right cheek, from the top of his ear to under his chin. His front teeth were broken. Pa can trust me, he said, my name is Fatey. Nick said sorry, he didn't want crayfish, and hurried back to the hotel, before the man could utter another word. (Fatey – did he hear correctly?) A figure from a Bergman movie, a harbinger of death, with his bag of stinking, dead crayfish. Something medieval about him, something from one of the DVDs he and Marthinus had watched recently, *The Seventh Seal*, by Ingmar Bergman. Fatey – little destiny – with his bag of stinking crayfish.

In the parking lot next to the hotel he noticed an expensive sports car. It hadn't been there when he arrived that afternoon. He could hardly imagine that the owner of such a car would want to stay in such a crummy hotel.

That evening he ate at a pizza joint near the hotel. (The hotel dining room had not seemed promising.) Against the wall were posters from the fifties. The light was too yellow. It reflected off the jaundiced walls and the yellow-green melamine table top. A man who introduced himself as Penelope – signwriter and snake catcher – sat down next to him. (Did all the men here have women's names?! Once again, was he hearing correctly?)

Were there enough snakes here to catch? asked Nick. Oh yes, said the man, the snakes always managed somehow to slip into the visitors' cars and then he was just the guy to catch them.

Penelope had small ears and short, curly hair, cropped close to his scalp.

At nine o'clock that evening Nick went to the hotel bar. If there was any hope of clarity, and insight into his current psychic state, he'd be more likely to find it here than in his room with the dark wardrobe, the synthetic floral duvet, and the cavorting fish on the shower curtain.

His heart sank as he walked into the bar. Atmospheric it was not. The kind of space into which, if you were already tottering on the edge of a crater, you could very easily pitch headlong. Here you had to keep your eye fixed on the ball very firmly not to be overwhelmed by despair and feelings of futility.

He sat down at the bar. He'd just ordered a whisky, when a person – a woman – entered the bar. This was Mignon, the mother of his student – his ex-student – Karlien Meyer. The woman who on the occasion of his and Albrecht's visit to her injured child had given him a look of unmistakable sexual invitation. Nick groaned inwardly. For a moment he considered clearing out quickly. But unless he dived headlong through one of the windows, the only other exit from the bar was the one through which the woman had just entered.

She saw him and made straight for him.

Could she, and she nodded at the bar stool next to him.

Could he buy her a drink?

With pleasure.

She was an attractive woman. Karlien had got her slender build from her mother. Extremely lush eyelashes, emphasising her eyes. Pretty eyes, green. Her skin must have been exposed to a lot of sun (must be the horses), but she had laughter wrinkles and she smiled readily, although slightly warily. (One of those women whose ready smile constituted a defence against the world, he thought.) Darker blonde than her daughter. A more expressive face, even if only because of the light sun-wrinkles, and in spite of the slightly forced smile. For a moment Karlien's uninscribed, almost expressionless face flashed clearly before his mind's eye. He shuddered lightly. Focused on the woman in front of him. The mother.

She just *had* to get away from the town, she said. She couldn't process what *had* happened to her child. She blamed herself. She should have known. She'd not taken to Karlien's friends, especially not the girl with whom she'd shared the flat. And now they were all being charged, and with possession of drugs on top of it, and probably dealing in drugs as well. They were probably all guilty. (Not a word about Karlien's possible complicity.)

Her perfume was expensive. Her nails were manicured. There was not an inch of this woman that was not meticulously groomed. The sports car belonged to her without a doubt. She accepted the offer of another drink. She held her liquor surprisingly well. (Clearly better than her husband.) Nick took careful note of how much he was drinking.

She couldn't forgive herself. She should have known. Karlien was their only child. Her husband had been crazy about her when she was small, but communication was not his strong suit. Since her adolescence he and the child hadn't really spoken. They'd gradually drifted apart. She blamed her husband for it. He'd not been there for Karlien when she needed him. Had he been a stronger father figure, she might never have gone astray and gone overboard with the whole satanism thing. This whole terrible affair hadn't done their marriage any good either. Not that it had been that wonderful in any case (with a slightly wry smile). She didn't know why she was telling Nick all these things. He was a stranger. And yet, he was somebody who shared this tragedy (tragedy? would he call it that?) with them, because he'd been Karlien's lecturer. (She had unusual eyes, attractively framed by the lush lashes.)

She just *had* to get away from home for a while. She could no longer watch the child lying around so washed-out and listless. Physically

Karlien had recovered well enough, but emotionally she was – she could almost say – crippled. (Of course the child would rather slump around with her friends in the satanic den among the black candles than in that shell-pink bedroom among the teddy bears and other soft toys, he thought.)

There was something frail, something childishly trusting about the woman, he thought, but still, and he didn't think he was imagining things, a strong sexual vibe. He had to keep a level head. Otherwise he wasn't going to be able to stop himself.

By midnight she was leaning her tear-stained face on his shoulder. He buried his face in her fragrant neck, his thoughts whirling in tempestuous turmoil. At a quarter past twelve they went upstairs to her room. She definitely had the bridal suite. Marginally more attractive than his room. They'd held back on the cavorting fish and the floral duvet and the dark, depressing wardrobes, but went flat out with satin – satin curtains, satin scatter cushions, satin bedspread – and a variety of large, cheap Mr Price-type vases containing tinted feathers and dried plumes. At least there was a large window facing the sea, with the reassuring sound of breaking waves.

Her body was youthful. She was tanned, the line of her bathing costume still visible, although it was winter already. Her breasts were lovely – nicely firm and rounded. She surrendered herself with ardent abandon. It was the first woman he'd slept with since Isabel. His own enthusiastic response confused him.

What the fuck now, he thought, as he went back to his own room in the small hours.

*

Early morning he was awake and pondering. He hadn't reckoned on a lightning fling with the mother of his ex-student in the local hotel at Oesterklip. Instead of simplifying his life, he'd now complicated it.

What was he going to tell her? What was he going to do if her husband got to know about it and hired somebody to fuck him up? (He didn't look like the kind who could do it himself.) In his mind's eye he saw Karlien's pale, reproachful gaze bobbing buoyantly towards him.

But hardly had he eaten a hasty breakfast than Mignon came into the dining room. She was highly upset. Her car had been vandalised. She'd had to summon her husband immediately to come and see what he could do about it.

He had to be on his way in any case … said Nick.

Yes, it was better that way, she said, and gave him a perfunctory hug.

The car – the expensive sports car indeed – had had its tyres slashed and on the bonnet and doors was painted with spray-paint: *white cunt*.

(The lettering had been executed quite skilfully, with a certain stylish flair.)

*

He did not see her again before his departure. Against one of the hotel's outer walls the guy with the scar and the bag of crayfish was standing grinning in the morning sun. Fatey. Little destiny. A short distance from there, on a low wall, sat Penelope the snake catcher and signwriter. Before Nick got into his car, he checked carefully that a snake hadn't perhaps slipped into his car. When he drove off, both of them waved at him exuberantly.

*

Suddenly it's freezing cold. It's the beginning of July. There is low mist over the mountaintops. Snow is forecast. I slip out to have coffee in town. I'm starting to feel more at my ease. It's been a while since the stalker waylaid me in the coffee shop where Buks Verhoef was shot. That place I've in any case been avoiding of late. As I round the corner, on my way to a small, inconspicuous coffee bar in an alley behind Church Street, somebody grabs me by the arm. It's him, the hollow-cheeked stalker. Before I can resist, he's adroitly steered me into the coffee shop to which I'd been headed. (How did he know to find me here?)

'Sit down,' he says. 'I want to talk to you. In god's name don't scream again. I won't do anything to you. You should know that by now.'

We sit down. At this time of day there aren't many customers. A man is sitting in the corner reading his newspaper. Another man is working on his laptop in the opposite corner.

'Why don't you leave me alone?' I ask.

'Why would I?' he asks.

'Because there's nothing in it for you, following me around all the time. You persist in believing I know something I don't know.'

'And that is?'

'I don't have to spell it out. It relates to Buks Verhoef.'

He laughs brusquely. He looks tired.

'You interest me,' he says. 'I still think you should accept my offer and accompany me on a trip to the interior.'

'Don't you have a cousin to visit in the psychiatric institution, and a visit to a family farm in Mpumalanga waiting for you? Is that where you're planning to take me?'

'That can wait,' he says. 'My cousin is not going to come to his senses any time soon. In fact, I fear he may never do so. No,' he says, 'if you come with me, I don't envisage visiting my disturbed cousin.'

'You don't understand,' I say emphatically, 'I'm not going travelling with you. I happened to be there the day Buks Verhoef was shot. More than that I don't know. I did not know him. I know nothing about the motives behind his murder. I'm starting to suspect *you* have something to do with it. The way you suspect *me* of some kind of involvement.'

He laughs again. A mirthless chuckle.

'You don't understand,' he says. 'I want to come back. I'm tired of wandering about in foreign countries. I've done it for long enough. I've come to consider my options here. A kind of reconnaissance, you might say. Perhaps a couple of people I want to get even with, but that's not a priority. Old friends I want to look up. Probably not all of them are going to be equally delighted to see me. As far as your allegation is concerned: No, I have nothing to do with Buks Verhoef's murder. Murder interests me only indirectly. You could say I have a highly personal interest in it. You could say I have my own selfish uses for crime. For the rest I find it banal. Buks Verhoef's death is banal. He was a banal artist and his death was banal. As I've implied before, his death may not even have been totally undeserved. Most artists nowadays hardly deserve to live. There are only a few exceptions – Blinky Booysen was such an exception, and he's dead. Beautiful irony. What became of him, heaven only knows. Blinky and I, by the way, were never friends, even though I had the greatest respect for his work. I still have it. I can't get worked up about Buks Verhoef's death. Come with me, let's leave it all behind us. Let's take a trip together. I repeat – you won't be sorry.'

The man looks tired. He's unshaven. Dark rings under his eyes. His irises are flat, a flat milky-grey disc. His bony nose and hollow cheeks are even more prominent than before. With stubble beard and close-cropped head, he looks even more like a convict today. I remain silent. Let him have his say.

'I know enough about crime,' he says, 'to be able to guess what happened to Verhoef. He was involved in illicit art trading. But somewhere he made a mistake – the poor guy wasn't canny enough for the types that he'd got mixed up with – and then somebody was hired to get rid of him. As simple as that. Everything very predictable. Everything very banal. But what about it, what business is it of mine?'

'The suspect was admitted for psychological observation,' I say. 'Who's going to hire a mentally disturbed person to commit a murder?'

'Perfect,' says the man, 'the perfect person to use for such a thing! Somebody who can't distinguish all that well between voices from out there and voices from in here.'

'It sounds like your Moorreesburg cousin,' I say.

'For sure,' says the man, and laughs. (It's a long time since I've seen anybody laugh so joylessly. If perhaps in a moment of insanity, my judgement severely impaired, I'd considered travelling with him, this little laugh alone would have been enough to change my mind.)

'I seem to remember that you wondered whether the suspect wasn't perhaps completely normal – like you and me' (and here I shoot him a meaningful glance) – 'simply with an urge to rid the world of mediocre artists. Of the tyranny of mediocrity, I seem to remember your words.'

Again he laughs his unpleasant little chuckle. 'You have a good memory,' he says. 'But no, I don't doubt that the fellow is disturbed in some way or other. Probably severely disturbed.'

'So now you've gone and changed your story completely,' I say. 'Now all of a sudden you don't care a fig for Verhoef's death, whereas before you wanted to know all about the day and the circumstances of his death from me. One of the reasons, I think, why you don't want to leave me alone.'

'And the other reason?' he asks.

But I know what he's getting at and I'm not going to give him the satisfaction of a reply. 'Look,' I say, 'I don't even know your name. You don't know mine. Thank you very much, but there's no way I'm going to avail myself of your offer. *No* way. You're wasting my time. You're wasting your own time. Do yourself a favour and stop bothering me.'

'If you'll go with me, I'll tell you my name,' he says as I get up. 'It may well interest you.'

'I prefer that we both remain anonymous,' I say, turn around, and walk out of the coffee bar. But not without feeling the hairs bristling on my neck. Not a good feeling and the day is cold and dismal.

Before going home, I enquire at the guest house where the woman with whom I had the surprising encounter was staying. I'm told that she left the previous day, back overseas.

223

Just before driving out of Oesterklip, he received an SMS from Marthinus saying: *Buy today's paper, check the interesting item on the Verhoef suspect.*

Nick stopped at the only café in town. No newspaper. If he wanted a paper, advised the man behind the counter, he should go to Veldenburg. About fifteen kilometres from here. In the café there was not a huge choice, except naartjies, cling-wrapped bananas (overripe), tinned food and firelighters. Two gates with sensors to ambush prospective thieves. On a wire shelf, apart from the *Oesterklip Express*, three books. Two of them were Mills & Boon-type romances, the third was *Invisible Cities* by Italo Calvino. Of all things. This place was definitely not without its surprises, thought Nick.

He bought the book for Marthinus, without knowing exactly what it was about. It looked like something that might interest him. Perhaps something that Marthinus could discuss with Anselmo Balla, who was so interested in St Augustine's *City of God*.

*

Veldenburg vicinity was where Charelle came from. If he'd known her parents' address he could have seen where she grew up. She'd told him that at school already she'd taken photographs in the cemetery of all the different letters of the alphabet. She'd shown him in her portfolio the tombstones starting with the letter K that she'd photographed. In one of the town's butcheries she'd taken the photographs of herself, naked, draped in metres of boerewors. And now she wanted to do a nursing diploma. Perhaps he and Marthinus should after all visit Tarquin and company once more to find out whether they knew who was responsible for the atrocity. It was unforgivable, it was scandalous that people should go unpunished after what they'd done to her. When

Nick thought of her, he still registered it in the vicinity of his heart, it still felt as if his heart were being compressed between two heavy objects.

He bought the paper, drank something in a coffee shop. On page three there was a report that the suspect in the Buks Verhoef murder case, who'd recently been admitted for psychological observation, alleged that he'd acted on instructions from voices. Sometimes he got instructions to kill someone, he alleged, and sometimes he heard voices warning him not to go to sleep, because he'd never wake up. From the report it wasn't clear whether the man had been instructed by the voices to shoot Buks Verhoef, specifically, or whether Buks had by pure chance been the victim of his hallucinations. What did seem clear to Nick was that everything suggested that Victor Schoeman at least had not been implicated in the Verhoef murder. Which didn't mean that Nick did not still suspect him of all sorts of chicaneries.

Nick reflected that he should probably be grateful that the man hadn't been instructed by voices to shoot *him* there and then in the coffee shop or afterwards in the bar. He'd thought the guy, the Chris Kestell double, looked pretty bewildered that day, with his floating eyes. He should count his blessings, and negotiate the world with fewer misgivings.

*

From Veldenburg Nick drove to Frederiksbaai. Back to Oesterklip was not an option, and back home would feel too much like a lack of perseverance.

The hotel at Frederiksbaai seemed considerably more acceptable than the one at Oesterklip. He was sitting on the hotel stoep that afternoon watching the sea when somebody behind him said his name.

'Nick.'

He looked round. An attractive, middle-aged woman was standing behind him with a drink in her hand. It took him a few moments to recognise her: Marlena Mendelsohn.

She'd lost her lanky angularity, and her radiant blondeness, but she'd remained well preserved. Her face and figure were considerably fuller, she was groomed and made up to her eyebrows, she was smartly dressed. Absolutely not as he remembered her in her skimpy dresses and threadbare jerseys, her bare knees sometimes blue with cold.

(He could have died for the beauty of her slender feet and her bony, boyish knees.)

What was she *doing* here?

She was visiting people in South Africa. She'd lived in England for years. She'd been running a gallery there for a long time. Her husband had died recently. (Rich inheritance, he thought, that explained the gold jewellery. The manicured appearance. Had she ever worn jewellery before?)

And he?

He was living in Cape Town again. Teaching part-time at an art school.

Was he still painting?

(Was he still painting – what kind of a question was that? She was the one who'd sat with him for hours in his studio, encouraged him; evinced, for whatever reason, an intense interest in his work.)

No, he wasn't painting any more. He drew nowadays and worked mainly in three dimensions.

Her nails were polished. She wore boots and jeans. (Expensive; designer clothes.)

Was she here with Victor?

Victor? No, why would she be?

She'd left here with him.

Victor had just been a means of getting out of the country, she said. They lost touch years ago.

And Blinky? he asked, with trepidation.

She shrugged. Dead, as far as she'd heard.

Did she know where he died?

No. As far as she knew, he died in Cape Town. She wasn't quite sure when. She'd left the country by then.

'You used to be very good friends,' he said. (Accusingly?)

She looked pensively over his shoulder at the sea. 'Yes,' she said, 'we used to be. He made wonderful stuff.'

Nick had no desire to carry on discussing Blinky with her.

This was the woman who thirty years ago had charmed him out of his mind. Whatever he knew about art, he'd learnt from her (not at art school). She'd stood behind him (literally) and encouraged him. She'd sat behind him on a plastic chair in his studio talking to him while he painted. She told him about the death of Rothko, who'd been found by his assistant in a pool of blood, having slashed himself with a razor and taken an overdose of antidepressants. About Guston's father who'd committed suicide when Guston was twelve years old, about Kitaj's visits to whores in Havana, about Jasper Johns's obsession with flags. About Seurat, dead at thirty-one of diphtheria. About Goya, about Dostoevsky, about Roy Lichtenstein. She explicated the values and qualities of colours for him: black with its mystical connotations, white with its connotations of purity; grey, perceptually inert (as he'd experienced the Oesterklip beach during his first visit.) Red, yellow. Green.

She'd made him listen to Alban Berg, until he overcame his innate resistance – until something in him yielded – and he developed a taste for it, as for Schoenberg, Terry Riley, Luciano Berio. (Cathy Berberian singing Berio.) She'd made him read books. She explained the modernist project to him. She explained the minimalist backlash of Gerhard Richter to him. She made him look at Baselitz, Sigmar Polke, Anselm Kiefer. That was just before Jeff Koons appeared on the scene, photographed on a rock, naked, with Cicciolina under him in stockings and suspender belt. That was before the manifestation of Ilona's clean-shaven butthole (for Nick inexplicably uncontaminated – without any baggage, during his and Isabel's dismal visit to New York). Marlena had been one of the three most important women in his life (by contrast with the multitude of one-night stands and brief encounters); she, after her the woman he'd married, and then Isabel (her hair as white as flax).

Did she still listen to Alban Berg? he asked.

Yes, she said, sometimes. But in fact for a long time now she hadn't really listened to music.

It had been good to see him again, she said, as they said goodbye.

*

He'd slept with the mother of his ex-student. He'd encountered the woman with whom he'd been obsessed thirty years ago (he'd always thought that he'd never before or since desired anybody as much as that). Now he just had to decide whether he wanted to sell his house, then he'd have seen it all.

*

Jeff Koons was a contemporary of his, three years younger than Nick. So when he was at art school Jeff Koons was not yet known. Koons had not yet produced the photo series *Made in Heaven,* in which he and Ilona Staller were photographed in all kinds of explicit sexual positions, among others exuberantly engaging in cunnilingus on a rock. When Nick was at art school in the eighties, when Marlena had taken him in hand and introduced him to a multitude of things, Ilona's clean-shaven pudenda and anus were not yet available for general consumption.

*

That evening, when Nick was lying on his left side, his heart beat so fast that he was scared he was going to have a heart attack.

The next morning in the dining room there were a man with a pointed face, two semi-oriental women and a little boy with a dense mop of black hair. Two mail-order brides, thought Nick. One bride was a trifle more attractive than the other. Which one of the two would be the mother of the child? Nick, the man, the child and the two brides, and a large man with a coarse, Frankenstein-ish face, were the only people in the dining room, and probably in the hotel. Marlena had mercifully departed already. She'd said the previous day that she was planning to leave in the late afternoon. He still had to process the shock of their reunion.

In the course of a late-morning walk on the beach, no illuminating thought or blinding insight came to him. When he thought of the possibility of selling his house, a haze descended on his brain. Thoughts that did obtrude themselves were the aroma of the woman's neck and her enticing body, so ready to receive him. His sexual interest had been properly stimulated. He was still surprised at the total surrender of both of them. With indecent vigour they'd set sail into the night on the double bed of satin and ribbons as if on a ship. He had to smirk when he thought of that room – the bridal suite – with plumes and ribbons and baubles and bows, which they'd utilised with such unholy abandon. He could never have surmised that such a – to look at her – rich, demure trophy wife could be capable of such inventive sexual high jinks. But it wasn't an ideal situation. Were the inebriated husband to get to know about it – and they hadn't been exactly discreet, and he probably posted spies everywhere his wife went without him – he wasn't the kind of man blithely to accept that his wife was cheating on him. And that, on top of it, with the man who'd encouraged – or at least not discouraged – his daughter to do a project on satanism, which in the end had just about cost her her life. Or that was how he could reconstruct it.

Marthinus sent him an SMS: *I'm reading Ezekiel. Powerful stuff.*

Ezekiel, thought Nick. Lord knows, further than Ezekiel was at that moment from his thoughts, no prophet could ever be. But perhaps he should also read it, to guide him in these confusing times. The moon, nearly full, shone on the sea that evening. Li Po, according to legend, drowned when he grabbed at it from his boat. Li Po, the poet who sang of drunkenness. Drunk, and drunk with the image of the moon on the water.

*

The first week of July. The night before full moon, at six o'clock, the moon appears above one mountaintop. At ten past seven it is already radiant in the open heavens. It is cold. There is a light stirring in the air, but no wind. At a distance the barking of dogs, and the voices of children.

Full moon. Eleven o'clock in the evening. I go outside. All solid forms are virtually dissolved in light. Even the mountains. Especially the mountains. All is light, no shadows, no detail. The light is cool. The world is bathed in the coolness of the light of the moon. You can say what you like, but the light of the moon is cool. It's like no other light. It's like light from another time – a time before the beginning of time.

Thirty-two

A day or two later Nick had had enough of the hotel, of the beach, of the moon on the water, of the man with the two mail-order brides, of the Frankenstein figure, brooding, in a corner of the dining room. The few of them still the only guests at the hotel. Off-season. He got into his car and drove back to town.

Jan Botha had shorn his hair. Nick was gobsmacked. How could he do it? That fragrant head of hair!

'I see you've cut your hair,' he said cautiously to Jan.

'Yes,' said Jan Botha.

'Any specific reason?' Nick asked.

'Penance,' said Jan Botha. Evidently as much as he was prepared to say. Nick noted that he was no longer wearing eye make-up either.

There'd been somebody to see Nick, said Jan. His message to Nick was: Vincenzo Anastagi had been to visit him. He was on his way somewhere – Jan thought he'd said Malmesbury, or Moorreesburg – but as soon as he was back in Cape Town, he'd definitely drop by again.

'Oh, God,' said Nick.

*

Nick was glad to see Marthinus again. Victor Schoeman had visited him in his absence, he said. The person had referred to himself as Vincenzo Anastagi. It could only be Victor – typical of him. He had, after all, sent that postcard earlier in the year with the picture of Vincenzo Anastagi. He'd told Jan Botha that he would come by again on the way back from Moorreesburg. Why on earth would Victor want to see him, Nick asked, they hadn't had anything to say to each other for years. And he still wondered whether Victor hadn't after all had some hand in the house-buying business. Marthinus said he'd never been altogether sure of that. Of the other things, yes – the robber bands and the escaped prisoners and the convict lookalike in Nick's kitchen, yes, *that* he still thought Victor could have had a hand in. But common everyday criminality, he didn't think that would interest him. That was too predictable, too ordinary. Just look at *The Shallows*, Victor liked unusual angles, he liked complicating things, he liked unexpected twists, he liked ambiguity, he liked to shock and intrigue. Although it was possible, said Marthinus, that in reaching certain conclusions he'd allowed himself to be led too much by *The Shallows*. That was perhaps mistake number one that he'd made.

'But why is he in the country all of a sudden?' asked Nick.

'There could be a thousand-and-one reasons,' said Marthinus.

'Like what? What's suddenly bringing him here *now*?'

'For all you know, he's been here on a visit any number of times before. He could have business interests here. Perhaps a relative died. Perhaps he inherited money. Perhaps he's come to do research for a new book. How long ago was *The Shallows* published? As far as I know nothing's been published since. Unless he did it under a pseudonym overseas.'

'He has no relatives, as far as I know,' said Nick. 'I don't think anybody would ever consider him as an heir, he was too much of a general pain in the arse. He fell foul of everybody. If he didn't borrow money from them without paying it back, he insulted or stabbed them in the back in some way or other. Although he wasn't as bad as Chris Kestell. There wasn't a soul who wasn't rubbed up the wrong way by Chris Kestell. He was the most confrontational person I'd ever met. Confrontational and destructive. Self-destructive.'

'Maybe Chris never committed suicide,' said Marthinus. 'Maybe he just let the rumour be spread. Maybe he went off somewhere, somewhere up the coast of Africa, to smuggle elephant tusks somewhere, or to start up a cellphone empire or to smuggle counterfeit funerary art. Or to swindle and corrupt the pygmies of the Congo in some way. Oh Lord.'

'No,' said Nick. 'Chris is definitely dead. A friend of mine was present the day when they winched his body from the dam. Stone tied to the ankle. His packet of cigarettes still on the dam wall. He had a horror of water, and then he went and drowned himself. A final deed of self-spite. Chris Fungus. His equal I've never come across since.'

'That's what you get,' said Marthinus, 'if your great-grandfather was a minister of the church, and your grandfather a member of the Synod, who wrote a vindication of racial segregation. The sins of the fathers are visited upon the children unto the third and fourth generation.'

*

Initially Nick hesitated to tell Marthinus, but a day or two after arriving in Cape Town, one day when they were having a beer on Marthinus' stoep, the mountain diagonally behind them, clearly delineated in every detail, he could no longer keep it to himself and said: 'In Oesterklip I slept with the mother of my ex-student.'

'Oh Lord,' said Marthinus, 'how did that happen?'

'I don't know,' said Nick, 'it just happened.'

'What now – are you going to follow up?'

'No,' said Nick. 'Not because I don't want to, but because it would be an exceedingly bad idea. In the first place because she's married. I'm wary of the husband. He's the relentless kind. I checked him out. The kind who wouldn't hesitate to exact revenge. He wouldn't think twice about hiring somebody to shatter my kneecaps, or worse. In the second place she's the mother of a student of mine, and I still feel a bit uneasy about my share in the whole ridiculous satanism palaver. I sort of feel I should have given the kid better guidance.'

'Nick,' said Marthinus, 'what's *this* all about now?'

'Besides,' said Nick, 'somewhere, with our randy cavortings, we were trying to drive out the thought of the child, and it's not going to work. It's going to catch up with us and then sooner or later the roof's going to cave in on our heads. If the spouse hasn't already taken his revenge by then. No, however exciting our delights were, and I can assure you they were, I don't dare follow up. For my own sake and that of the woman.'

'I see what you mean,' said Marthinus. 'The wise man knows when to contain himself. And did you achieve clarity on the sale of your house?'

'No,' said Nick.

'What are you going to do?' asked Marthinus.

'For the time being nothing,' said Nick. 'Especially now that I've got the message from Victor. I first have to make sure that he's got no part in the affair.'

'And how are you going to find that out?'

'Buggered if I know. More than ever I just want to cut and run. Up the coast wasn't far enough. Run, as in to a place where there's no chance of meeting anybody from my past or my present.'

'I see what you mean,' said Marthinus. But Nick got the impression that Marthinus wasn't really saying what he thought.

That evening they watched *A Serious Man* by the Coen brothers. The film resonated powerfully with Nick. Especially the strange, cryptic opening. The curse of the dybbuk. He thought that perhaps he'd taken Menasse's stories too much to heart. But if there really were things like the emanations Menasse mentioned, then Nick wondered if it had been wise of Jan Botha to cut his hair. His strength – and his protection – could perhaps also reside in his hair, like Samson's. But perhaps, he said to Marthinus when they were discussing the film afterwards, he was confusing different things with one another: the dybbuk and the Kabbalah and the Bible, Samson and Job, and whatever else. And once he started seeing things in terms of emanations and so on, it was late in the day for him.

He couldn't see, said Marthinus, how the one contradicted the other. Weren't all these things interconnected? And he could see why Nick was concerned that his student Jan Botha had cut his hair. It made sense to him. He would have been concerned too. Marthinus was particularly intrigued when Nick told him that Jan Botha had said that he'd done it as an act of penance. And that he'd not wanted to say more than that.

'Penance, you say,' said Marthinus. 'Fancy that, eh?'

*

My dear friend Willem Wepener and I meet again one evening for a drink. We meet in the same guest house again – private and cosy, exactly as Willem prefers it.

I become aware of the fact that I'm constantly on the lookout for the woman, although I know perfectly well that she left the country a week ago. Tonight I'm distracted. Willem tells me about Paris, where he did an artist's residency. He tells me how he followed in the footsteps of Arikha. How he'd visited Beckett's grave. How poignant he finds the friendship between Arikha and Beckett. How is his own work coming along? I ask. He's struggling, but he finds it a challenge. He thinks he's making a breakthrough, although he's wary of saying such a thing. I tell him about the woman. He's intrigued. Here, in the guest house, after he left?! Yes, I say. She'd been sitting diagonally across from us all the time (I point out where), but I hadn't really been taking note, he and I were too engrossed in conversation. Only once he'd left, had I really focused on her, also because I realised that she'd been watching me all evening. Willem laughs. He finds it an engaging story. I tell him about my encounters with the hollow-cheeked disturber of the peace. Hardly encounters, I say, really more like stalkings, so much so that for some time now I've been afraid to go to town, in case he's lying in wait for me somewhere. The man wants to go travelling with you, says Willem, without your even knowing each other's names? I tell Willem about my three bungled meetings with Marcus Olivier. I recount how he'd not looked at me once, or given any sign of recognition, although we met each other long ago in very particular circumstances. (I don't elaborate on these circumstances.) It remains a mystery to me, I say, that such a mean-spirited, surly man could be the father of such magnanimous artists. Willem is at one with me on this, the Olivier brothers are exceptional.

The rest of the evening we talk about Arikha again (Willem is clearly a bit obsessed with him). We talk about Willem's work, about his relationship, about the monograph I'm writing.

*

Two days later I read in the paper that Marcus Olivier, historian, professor emeritus, has died unexpectedly of a heart attack.

I'm caught on the wrong foot. I had still hoped to talk to him once or twice. Unfinished business. What had I wanted from him? Did I want him to confess in my presence, look into my eyes and say: I know who you are? I remember every moment of that evening as if it happened yesterday. I have to laugh at the sheer improbability of this. I bungled every single one of my three recent meetings with him. Perhaps I should have had a more clearly defined agenda. Such a churlish man, so unobliging. In all probability a misogynist to boot. Perhaps it was enough to have beheld him and wondered at the fact that such a man could have fathered two such sons, such innovative, imaginative artists, whose work has provided me with so much pleasure. Perhaps it's enough to have savoured the irony of it.

He is being privately cremated, but a small memorial service will be held for him in the retirement resort where he lived. A pity that there's not going to be a proper funeral. I would have liked to stand next to his open grave with the other mourners.

Am I supposed to sympathise with Miss De Jongh? On the phone she sounds cool and businesslike. It's quite in order, I may attend the memorial service. Will his sons also be there? No, unfortunately they won't be able to make it, they're involved with some project in Alaska at the moment. What a pity, I say. Yes, she says. Did he have any other near relatives? No, only the sons. How sad, I say. Yes, she says. When did he last see them? Very long ago, she says, several years ago.

I have no desire to attend the memorial service. I can just picture it: a small gathering in the dining hall of a retirement village. Mainly ex-colleagues of Marcus Olivier. An arrangement of pink gladioli, white carnations and grey foliage in one corner. Tea, coffee and snacks – savoury and sweet. One or two of his ex-colleagues say a few words. They mention what an outstanding historian Olivier had been, how painstaking, how valuable his contribution. (Nobody refers to him as beloved. No criticism is levelled at his modus operandi, his intransigence, his obstinacy, his contracted vision, his meanness.) I picture a staid, sedate occasion. No tear is shed, nobody tears their hair in an indecorous display of public grief. Everything decently decorous. Unless Miss De Jongh were to decide she'd had enough of hypocrisy, duplicity and false decorum – she will turn this into a memorable occasion. She revs up proceedings with décolletage and a well-stocked drinks trolley. She'll see to it that her employer (slash benefactor?) is dispatched with fanfare. (One of the ex-colleagues ventures later on, behind the arrangement, to paddle a hand gently – appreciatively – over her impressive bosom.)

I'd like to ask her sometime whether Olivier had been a good employer. I can picture her shrugging. He was okay. He paid well. He sometimes came up with requests not covered by her contract – and she'd never exactly been of a charitable bent. But she had her price, as every woman in her situation would have. In general he was a cold fish, I picture her saying.

I think back to the koi in the dam at which we'd stood gazing during my first visit to him. The blue membrane over the eyes that had made the fish seem blind. Bright red, with the two protrusions on either side of its mouth. How sexually obscene I'd found the mouth, in its opening and closing palpitations. I'd wondered, that day, whether it could be a covert message from the old father, an acknowledgement of our brief tussle almost thirty years earlier, when he'd thought he could exploit my deformity to his own benefit.

*

As far as his cremation is concerned. How should I picture *that*? How ravishing it would be if I, darkly veiled, the two sons (fresh from Alaska or New York or Amsterdam), and Miss De Jongh were the only mourners in a small private crematory chapel. On the coffin, standing at the front of the chapel, the sons place a hand-carved puppet (perhaps even the Punch and Judy puppet starring in the *Kafka in Long Street* video). A puppet to accompany the old father to oblivion or damnation. Even a voluptuous female puppet, perhaps, symbol of the faithful spouse in Indian culture, who is burnt with her husband on the funeral pyre. Miss De Jongh places a copy of her employment contract on the coffin. And some or other memento that she judges appropriate to accompany Olivier's last journey. His spectacles, perhaps, or his fountain pen. I'll have to think about my own contribution.

The man from Hobkirk & Doves (overweight, in a shiny grey suit) gives a signal, presses a button, the coffin moves forward slowly; to the accompaniment of monophonic Gregorian chant it glides on metal bearings through an aperture, the curtain closes. The coffin slides into the cremating chamber, the doors are sealed. Everything is now primed for action. The oven is stoked, it's at the correct temperature already (593 °C). The coffin bursts into flame. The old father burns. His body fat burns. His muscles burn. His organs burn (the fatty heart, the sagging testicles, the limp penis). His bones burn. His bony forehead burns, his tongue, his eyeballs, his brain, everything devoured by the flames in the twinkling of an eye.

No, not in the twinkling of an eye. It takes two to three hours for the body to be consumed by the flames. Afterwards the pulverised bones are raked together with a little implement specially designed for the purpose. The urn is ready the next day for the sons to take delivery. In the meantime after the ceremony we go to have a meal in a restaurant with a breathtaking view of the sea.

Instead of scattering the ashes somewhere, the sons decide to have them made into a coral feature, that they can place in a fish tank, or use in one of their videos in an undersea scene.

Thirty-three

My monograph on the Olivier brothers is nearing completion. I still watch a few of their videos every day with enjoyment. *The Cabinet of Jan de Grevenbroek*, like *Kafka in Long Street,* enthrals me anew every time. Again and again I watch them, and each time details strike me that I haven't noticed before.

I look at the mountains. I gaze at the sunrises and sunsets as if my life depended on it. I watch series on my laptop. Good series, bad series – fantasy, horror, crime, everything on offer. Quality is no longer a prerequisite.

*

Nick told Marthinus that he wanted to pay Tarquin and company another visit. He wanted to find out whether they had any idea of who was responsible for the rape of Charelle. He felt that the perpetrators should not go unpunished.

Marthinus was perfectly amenable to this suggestion. He proposed that on their way they might as well pay a more extended visit to the farm – now that under the hand of Jurgen Wesseker it was turning into such an interesting utopian experiment. And because they hadn't got round to it on their previous visits.

But Nick said no, some other time. This time he wanted once again to keep the two visits separate. He didn't want to be distracted at first by an extended visit to the utopian experiment. He wanted to go straight to the settlement, to Tarquin and company.

Marthinus said he understood. It was fine, they'd do that. He didn't have a cellphone number for Tarquin, but he thought it would be in order for them to arrive there unannounced. If Tarquin wasn't there, somebody would in any case be able to tell them when they were expecting him again.

In the third week of July, on a bright, sunny morning, they walked up the slope. First through the experimental farm, on which Marthinus delivered a walking commentary. Here the singing of children was once again audible at a distance. People were working in the garden. The vegetable beds seemed well established. Everything created a peaceful, orderly impression.

'Look,' said Marthinus, 'as I've told you before, the farm used to be a kind of farm-cum-installation art work. People who used to hang out here, friends of the founder, maintained that at the time it was often also something of an interpersonal battlefield, with several clans and factions embroiled in vehement internecine strife. That was the situation when the founding father was still in charge of things here. However pure his original intentions for the place, over the years it degenerated into something dangerous and explosive, quite apart from the precarious sanitary situation. There were rumours of child neglect, animal abuse. The whole yuppie neighbourhood was quite rightly in-dignant, because the chaos spilt over into the vicinity, as could have been foreseen. Children defecating on pavements, packs of stray dogs, feral pigs – it was all a scourge for the owners of tidy, suburban gardens. Torches and alarms at night, rumours of riot and even murder – at any rate murderous intent – were an ordeal for the inhabitants of the surrounding middle-class neighbourhood. A complaint was lodged with the Department of Public Works. Several complaints, which be-came progressively more insistent with time. The farm was deemed to constitute a security and health risk.

'The founder too, as I mentioned, presumably had had his fill of the Department and the yuppies breathing down his neck. And probably also of the persistent chaos and warring factions in his back yard. For whatever reason, one day he packed up and left. From one day to the next just handed over the whole caboodle lock, stock and barrel to someone else. I told you about that. But apparently not before telling the Department, without mincing his words, exactly what he thought of them. An outspoken man, according to all reports. Outspoken and bellicose. I met him once or twice by chance, and he struck me as the kind of guy who could cross the Alps like Hannibal with a whole army and a troop of elephants. Indomitable.

'Enter Jurgen Wesseker. You'll meet the man yet. We'll make a plan. The mind-set of a reformer. He turned up at the city council and the Department of Public Works with a neatly worked-out twelve-point plan. He made a good impression. He kicked off with a mammoth cleaning-up operation. I told you about it. He presented the warring parties and clans with an ultimatum: behave yourselves, subject yourselves to certain regulations, or pack up and clear out. Apparently he inspired enough respect to get the people to buckle down and submit to the regulations. A fair number of the former residents, however, were sent packing.

'Jurgen Wesseker was told he had a year to get the situation up and running. If not, the buildings would be razed, and man, woman and pig be driven from the land.

'It's now almost a year later, and things seem to be on the up and up. You can see for yourself. Everything in beautiful order. The children well cared for, there is preschool provision for them, the residents are put to work in the gardens and in the kitchen, the gardens themselves a pleasure to behold. Beautifully laid out. You can see for yourself.' (Marthinus stopped walking and with a sweeping gesture indicated the whole area – as Adam might have signified the paradisiac nature and extent of the Garden.) 'The animals in cages. Each according to its nature. Pig with pig and rabbit with rabbit. No sign any more of the packs of stray dogs. The buildings well maintained – properly cleaned, fixed up, painted. It wouldn't surprise me one bit if everything here proceeded according to a carefully worked-out timetable.'

And indeed, as Nick saw, everything was clean, orderly. In any case absolutely no sign of any health risk. As a matter of fact, there was the pleasant smell of freshly turned soil, of grass and leaves, and the enticing aroma of freshly baked bread.

'But,' said Marthinus, 'whether it will remain like that, whether Jurgen Wesseker will succeed in turning the place into the model community that he envisages – in the first place whether he will succeed and in the second place whether it's sustainable – that remains to be seen.

'As I've said, there are powerful and chaotic forces at work under the surface. Even if Jurgen takes them into account, that's not to say he'll be able to control them. The informal settlement is right next to the farm, and there's a constant influx of people trying to find a safe haven there. And then there are the evicted factions who are probably planning revenge initiatives.'

Marthinus came to a sudden halt. 'Can you also feel,' he said, 'the menacing powers stirring beneath the surface?'

Nick felt nothing. The ground under his feet felt very solid.

'I can sense it,' said Marthinus. 'A tremendous force threatening to derail everything, just below the surface. It feels as if everything here that is orderly and under control is balancing very precariously on the surface. I reckon Menasse would be very sensitive to the vibrations and emanations here. He's bound to know exactly from which sphere trouble and worse are to be expected. I'll bring him here soon, together with Jurgen Wesseker. It can only be to Jurgen's advantage to be prepared.'

Nick could just picture it: Menasse picking up the emanations here like a diviner indicating water with a dowsing rod. And then, once he'd determined where the menacing forces were hiding under the surface – what would they do to safeguard themselves?

They walked on. Nick was grateful that it was no longer high summer. Lovely the surroundings – all bush-covered slopes and kloofs. To him the surroundings seemed peaceful, but he evidently lacked the receptivity to emanations of Marthinus or Menasse.

Once again they slipped through the fence much higher up. (Nick thought the wire looked slacker and less well camouflaged with every visit.) Before them stretched the settlement, also apparently peaceable in the morning sun. Bigger, Nick fancied. More shelters of all kinds of material – mainly plastic and branches – spiralling wisps of smoke, a few children playing among the temporary tents and shelters. Big muddy puddles of water everywhere after the recent rains. The mud couldn't be very hygienic. Even a dog or a chicken or two. Here and there clusters of young men in hoodies in coldish huddles regarding them distrustfully.

When they reached Tarquin's corrugated iron shack, the door was closed. Marthinus knocked. No response. After a long while one little curtain was tweaked open. The young girl with the large earrings who had poured them whisky on their previous visit opened the door a chink.

'Isn't Tarquin here?' he asked her.

'No,' she said.

'When is a good time to come and see him?' asked Marthinus.

The girl hesitated.

'Tarquin's not coming back again,' she said.

'Is he staying somewhere else now?' asked Marthinus.

Again the girl hesitated. 'No,' she said, 'he's not staying nowhere else. Tarquin's dead. They shot him.'

'Oh Lord,' exclaimed Martinus, 'who shot him? When?!'

'We dunno who it was,' said the girl.

Nick suddenly had a crystal-clear image of Tarquin as he sat here before, like a Mafia Buddha in the sun, with the golden neck chain and earrings, the diminutive chin, fleshy neck and small, resolute mouth, the slightly oily curly hair, cut short against the skull. But especially his emanation suddenly manifested itself clearly to Nick's vision – an emanation of total entitlement, of being absolutely one hundred per cent in charge. The world at his feet, triumphant with a glass of Johnnie Walker Blue in his hand.

He and Marthinus moved downhill quickly, through the wire fence, through the farm, where the children were now playing under the trees and hailing them with shrill voices. A few even pursued them, yelling, but were promptly recalled by their minder. Out through the gate (guarded by the Xhosa-speaking man).

'Who would have done that?' asked Nick.

'It could have been anyone,' said Marthinus. 'It could have been gangs. It could have been the police. It could have been someone with a grudge against him. So do you see what I mean,' he said, 'there are forces at work here constantly. Nothing here is ever static; everything is perpetually in motion. There are constant regroupings, a never-ending battle for control. Chaotic forces, seldom benign.'

'Yes,' said Nick, 'I can see that.' But all that he could *actually* see was Jan Botha pushing the dead Tarquin into the Salt River mortuary on a gurney.

*

One evening when they were once again sitting at Marthinus' place, Nick asked Menasse to expatiate on the Kabbalah's vision of good and evil. (Anselmo Balla was there too. They were sitting in the sitting room by the fire. Balla was staring morosely into the fire with his large, melancholy, Romanesque eyes. The flickering of the flames played on his broad, egg-shaped head. He wasn't talkative this evening. Apart from the fact that his body spasmed at regular intervals, he sat completely still.) Very complex, said Menasse. If he could summarise it briefly: The tendency to evil, the yetzer ha'ra, or animal instinct, is inherent in all people, as is the yetzer ha'tov, the tendency to good. Look, said Menasse, evil manifests itself in ever more subtle forms, and for that reason every thought, emotion and habit must be scrutinised with care. Our existence, like that of Adam – who, with Eve, was responsible for the disequilibrium between good and evil – is closely linked to the earth, to the body, to the material sphere, and our Adamic nature is inclined to evil. The tendency to good, the desire to do good, must be constantly cultivated through sustained effort and through zealous dedication and watchfulness.

After Menasse and Balla had departed, both of them into the black night (in the taxi that Marthinus had as always ordered and paid for), Marthinus said to Nick that he suspected that Anselmo Balla suffered from the same condition as Samuel Johnson, namely Tourette's syndrome. In fact, he saw him as a kind of incarnation of Samuel Johnson. Perhaps not quite such a distinguished man of letters, but with a similarly robust erudition and loquacity.

Nick said to Marthinus that he felt, in the light of what Menasse had said tonight, like Adam – heavy, earthbound, freshly created from clay – clay into which just a tiny bit of life had been breathed, just enough to allow him to function at a very primitive level.

*

The end of the break arrived. Nick had to go back to the art school. Apart from Jan Botha, three new students were assigned to him. This time he was alert to any deviant interest (satanism and the like), but all three girls' proposals struck him as woefully conventional. But he'd learnt his lesson. The more innocuous their projects, the better. Even if they wanted to do petit point, he'd be damned if he'd resist them. Only one of them, a braying redhead, said she'd really liked what Liesa Appelgryn did. She also wanted to implement that toxic emotional soil as fertiliser in her work. Oh dear Lord, thought Nick, but if that was the way she wanted to go, so be it, as far as he was concerned. Tits and forests of pubic hair were probably wholeheartedly wholesome, all things considered. The kid he thought he should watch was a thin, bluish-pale little blonde, with dark rings under her eyes, who couldn't quite decide what she wanted to do.

Albrecht Bester was still in hand-wringing mode. He'd decided that he didn't want the accused students back at the art school. They were out on bail, but he didn't think that their presence could have a good influence on the school and the other students, he told Nick.

Nick heard nothing from the woman. (He realised it was better like that, although he still longed for her fragrant hair and eager body.) He avoided the town, because he was scared he might bump into her there. Even in the city he kept himself small, as if expecting the husband to send a revenge posse after him.

Back at the art school, thoughts of Karlien impinged on his consciousness again. He'd once asked her whether she listened to music. Yes, she said. 'To what?' he asked. She hesitated. In retrospect he thought that she might have censored herself, because she replied: As in Miley Cyrus and suchlike. He'd told her to go and listen to Black Sabbath – to any of the death metal groups, there had to be lots of them. The church invaders and other anarchists. To Diamanda Galás (the *Plague Mass*). To anything that went against the grain, he told her. He'd thought he had to shock her out of her comfort zone, out of the middle-class torpor of privilege preventing her from breaking through to something cruder, something more confrontational – something that would give her satanism project more substance than the insipid photo and the sensational little magazine article. He remembered that she'd been close to tears that day. He'd thought that was because she didn't understand what he wanted from her. Now he thought that it was probably because she'd been panic-stricken about her situation. Black Sabbath, death metal – she'd probably thought: Oh puh-lease, been there, got the T-shirt. (As well as, of course, the black candles, the desiccated frog, the cat skeleton, all the accessories, equipment, everything requisite for the dumb kids to execute their senseless deed.) He'd never know.

It upset him every time he looked at Jan Botha's clean-shaven head. He missed that rich, fragrant head of hair. (Into which he'd felt an urge to push his face.) He didn't know if he was imagining things, but it was as if Jan's work had lost something of its power. Jan now also worked more on his own, came in less frequently. When Nick asked him how things were at the Salt River mortuary, he said he was bailing out for a while, for the time being he wasn't working there any more. It had suddenly started getting to him – the carnage without end.

Nick told Marthinus that he hoped Jan Botha would grow his hair again and wear eye make-up when he felt he'd done enough penance. He hoped it would happen soon, because Jan Botha's work was losing its cutting edge.

*

Early one morning I once again have a vision. It comes to me with great clarity while I'm still lying in my bed between sleeping and waking, the horizon gradually changing colour, but without my being aware of it.

I see three spheres. The top one is the biggest by far and it contains the other two. It is the sphere of the whole universe, the extensive Nothing, with all galaxies and dark matter whirling, churning, exploding and expanding within it.

Then there is the middle sphere. Compared with the first sphere it is minuscule. In the great cosmic array it registers as less than a mote of dust, but I can see it clearly. It is positioned immediately above the third sphere – a thin disc, fragile as ice, thin as one of the rings of Saturn. In this sphere, or disc, is contained everything that has ever happened on earth – all history, and everything that has ever been produced and imagined and contrived – all cultural artefacts.

The third sphere is the terrestrial sphere. It is like a well, a morass of primeval slime and mud. In this all living forms are present – everything that ever came into being and everything that ever died out, all evolutionary phases, but in no chronological order. In this sphere I find myself. I cannot see myself, I have no inkling of the nature of my incarnation. I am not necessarily human – I could also be fish, or amphibian, or early terrestrial animal. I am only one of the trillions of forms that plod around uncomprehendingly in this primeval mass. I don't know from what kind of eye I'm seeing – it could be a simple light-sensitive surface, it could be a composite or a single eye. I don't know if I've died out yet, or am still evolving. I am merely something registering at a very basic level, without comprehension of self – a primitive, unstructured neural process, a light-sensitive *something*, a minuscule splintering off from the cosmos.

When the vision has passed, I get up out of bed, put on my dressing gown, make myself some tea, and watch the sunrise.

Thirty-four

Sometimes in the late afternoon I walk in the vineyard with my good friend Willem Wepener. The vines are leafless, only the bare shoots in neat rows, and the posts supporting them. In the pathways between the vines there are pools of water. Everywhere along the way there are hollowed-out tunnels. I don't know what lives in these, but I like the tunnels. They evoke another life, a subterranean life. I ask Willem how he would describe the colour of the landscape. (He is attuned to colour like a dog to smell.) Van Dyck brown, he says, and ultramarine, mixed with white. The colour of the mountains on the horizon he describes as a milky blue. In one spot, in the vicinity of a few pine trees, there are often signs of human habitation. A man's trousers, a mud-stained fleece top. Even a hair curler one day, pink. Signs of fires. I wonder who lives here. There was a report in the newspaper that part of a vineyard had been chopped out for firewood.

As we walk back, the landscape has already darkened considerably. Table Mountain is visible, only the uppermost edge of it is still distinguishable, near-translucent against the blanching evening sky, partly swathed in mist. The vineyard is suddenly much darker, almost not visible in the fading light, sharply delineated against the tender, rosily glowing evening sky. But I smell the piquant aroma of khaki weed growing among the vines, and the damp smell of soil. Somewhere in the distance a plover calls, and a hadedah flies past, high up, skirling, on its way to its nest.

*

Nick became aware of resenting Jan Botha for cutting his hair. Jan seemed diminished to him. Nick had liked Jan's sturdy bodily presence, there'd been something reassuring about it. And then of course the fragrant hair. He'd liked the smell of Jan's hair. He'd even liked the faint undertone of some other smell, something that he'd associated with the Salt River mortuary. He was also seeing quite a bit less of Jan Botha these days, and more of the three students assigned to him. Another reason why he couldn't wait to get away from the art school. Once his contract expired, they'd never see him again.

*

Nick told Marthinus that it might be groundless, but he felt responsible for what had happened to Charelle. He still had a notion that somebody had avenged himself on her for staying with him. Somebody could have got to know in some way that they often had supper together. He was worried that the guy who'd stalked her thought that they had a relationship, or something. He couldn't think that she'd been targeted just because she happened to be in the vicinity of the perpetrators. It was terrible enough that it had happened to her, he said, but if he had to know that his presence had in any way – in *any* way – been conducive to it … well, then he didn't know. He didn't know how to deal with these feelings.

These were difficult things, said Marthinus. He himself wouldn't know how to cope with feelings of guilt, of accountability. With tricky moral questions like these, said Marthinus, he was inclined to look to the sages – he didn't set much store by philosophy and psychology. He was more inclined to turn to someone like Mr K. Or Prince Gautama Buddha. Or to throw the I Ching yarrow stalks. The Bible he had always found engrossing, even inspiring. Especially the prophets. As he'd said, he was now reading Ezekiel again. It gripped him exceedingly. God telling the prophet: Eat the scroll. Then there were the Kabbalah and Jewish mysticism – something that Menasse could help Nick with; and then there was the Koran. Anselmo would know about the Christian mystics. Even though he denied it, he was steeped in Catholicism. He was himself, said Marthinus, very much attracted to people like St John of the Cross. Definitely something there. There was something in each of these options that appealed to him.

'And loss,' said Nick, 'how does one deal with feelings of loss?'

'Oh Lord,' said Marthinus, 'that I really don't know. But I find it helpful to look after my pigs, and to read Ezekiel.'

*

A day later the agent phoned and said the offer on Nick's house had been withdrawn. The prospective buyers were no longer interested.

In fact, said the agent, the buyers had suddenly disappeared without a trace. She couldn't reach them anywhere. She was sorry about that.

Nick was relieved. He thought, well, so that left him without any other option.

Thirty-five

One morning at the end of July I read a small news item in the paper. By chance I had once again gone to have coffee in town. Ever alert and on my guard. I wouldn't have read the report if my eye hadn't fallen on the phrase 'high-security psychiatric institution'. That, after all, was one of the destinations on the agenda of the stalker – didn't he want to go and visit his poor disturbed cousin there? A head-on collision, all four passengers killed instantaneously. The identity of the driver is not known, but the three passengers were all inmates of the high-security psychiatric institution just outside Moorreesburg. The car was en route from Moorreesburg to Stellenbosch. The superintendent of the institution declined to comment. The names of the deceased will be released once their next of kin have been informed.

Without needing any further confirmation, I just *know* that the driver is the man, the hollow-cheeked disturber of the peace. I know it for a fact and without a doubt.

What could it mean? Had he abducted his cousin and two other patients, or simply taken them on an outing? (As if that man could do something as dead ordinary as taking three severely disturbed people on an outing.) If the superintendent doesn't want to comment, it suggests that the people had left without her permission. He must definitely have been hatching some plot. Now nobody will ever know. En route to Stellenbosch. Well did you ever. The hollow-cheeked stalker and the old father both suddenly out of circulation.

*

Nick read the same report in the paper. Sock me with a soggy fish, he thought. Victor Schoeman? Hadn't Marthinus earlier that year thought that Victor had had something to do with inmates of the same place? Which eventually turned out not to be the case. And Jan Botha had reported that Victor – who else would pose as Vincenzo Anastagi? – would drop in as soon as he was back in town from Moorreesburg. For the time being he would say nothing about this to Marthinus. He wanted to suss things out for himself first.

For a week or two after reading the report Nick bought the paper every morning. He found no report on the identity of the people who'd died in the accident. When after a fortnight he'd still not found anything, he phoned the high-security psychiatric institution to enquire whether the identity of the three patients had been made known yet, but the superintendent said that no information was being provided to members of the public. When would it be made known, he asked her. The family of the deceased had been informed, she said. And the identity of the driver? She could unfortunately not be of assistance to him on that matter. (Fascist whore.) She couldn't perhaps divulge what his connection with the patients had been? No, she was sorry, she thought she'd made it quite clear that she could not provide any information.

In an older paper he did though by chance come across a small item to the effect that Tarquin Molteno had been shot and killed on the Cape Flats in a gang-related shooting incident. Molteno had been a notorious figure on the Cape Flats, the report said, involved over the years in any number of skirmishes with police as well as with gangs. (Marthinus had been right, Tarquin, with the diminutive mouth and gold neck chain, had known no loyalty other than to himself, because he'd collaborated with whatever faction had been most advantageous to him.) Nick wondered if the body of Tarquin had ended up with all the other fatalities in the Salt River mortuary. He'd have to ask Jan Botha, perhaps it had even happened on his shift. (He'd told Nick that he'd started working there again.) Perhaps he'd even been responsible for fetching the body, loading it on the stretcher, and transporting it to the mortuary.

When Victor Schoeman did not turn up on his front stoep after all – as he'd feared – other matters obtruded themselves upon Nick's attention. (Charelle was evidently not prepared to talk to him again.) But he'd like to know whether it had really been Victor, and if he'd started imagining things (spurred on by Marthinus), but since there was apparently no way of finding out, he gradually let it go. He let the whole Victor business go. Although, he had to admit to himself, it would have given him a great deal of pleasure to know for sure that it had indeed been Victor who had so spectacularly expired in a head-on collision.

*

The four fellow students who'd been involved in the satanism event and had been arraigned on charges of drug dealing and assault, had had their case postponed to early in the next year. Albrecht Bester said he couldn't forgive them for what they'd done to the image of the school. But he was working on it, he told Nick, because he knew himself as the forgiving type. He was *seriously* working on himself.

The braying redhead was painting her own variations on tits and pubic shrubbery. She certainly did lavishly implement emotional soil as fertiliser for her creations. Nick let her be. After Karlien he was grateful to have a student who could muck on with abandon and without a qualm. The joke was, he had to admit, that he found her work quite strong – confident, and with a brutal energy. It was the anaemic little blonde who worried him – he didn't like the way she vacillated and couldn't reach a decision on what she wanted to do. It reminded him too much of Karlien.

Jan Botha's hair was growing, Nick noted, and one day he was sporting eye make-up again. A gladdening sign. (His work also imme-diately seemed more edgy, more gutsy to Nick.) That meant that his period of penance was elapsing. Nick would dearly have loved to know what he was doing penance for (perhaps get a tip or two from him), but he'd learnt that if Jan didn't volunteer information, it was no use interrogating him.

*

At the beginning of August Marthinus let Nick know that a friend of his had died. He was making a bonfire for him. Did Nick want to come by? In the late afternoon Nick found Marthinus in his back garden, stoking an enormous fire. Together they sat watching the flames. Marthinus told Nick about his friend. He'd been a fast runner but a slow swimmer, said Marthinus. He'd suffered from a deep-seated melancholy. He'd never been able to process disappointments in love, and he'd had quite a few of those, because he wasn't an easy person to live with. Set exceptionally high standards for himself and his lovers. Nobody could keep up. Not somebody for the banal daily grind, that too had exhausted people. People wanted distraction, they didn't want to be perpetually confronted with the eternal and the weighty verities, especially not at the outset of a love affair.

The fire was burning well. Marthinus was satisfied. 'Look,' he said, 'how merrily old Arnie's memorial pyre is blazing. A good sign. It portends an unhindered voyage to the underworld. That, in any case, is what Menasse would say.'

The memorial fire was indeed burning vigorously.

Only now did Nick tell Marthinus about the newspaper report. Marthinus reacted surprisingly laconically. It wouldn't surprise him at all, he said. It would be gloriously characteristic of Victor to meet his end in a car with three insane passengers. It was one hundred per cent down his alley. In tune with his modus operandi. Victor was the kind of person who'd decide that if he had to go, he'd take three or more people with him. That it had been three mentally disturbed people perhaps counted in his favour as an act of humanity. They should watch an appropriate video that evening to commemorate also his passing.

Nick laughed incredulously. 'But I have no idea or confirmation that it was in fact Victor!' he exclaimed.

'If it wasn't him,' said Marthinus, 'it's close enough to him. It's actually not even important whether it was really him or not.'

Nick glanced at him quickly to see whether he was joking, but Marthinus was gazing in front of him quite solemnly.

'And if Victor really is dead,' said Marthinus, 'then the smoke twirling so vigorously can be a favourable portent for him as well. I suppose we can, in spite of all his nonsense, not begrudge him an unhindered voyage to the underworld.'

At first Nick hesitated, then he said: 'Yes, I suppose not. If in fact he is dead, of course.'

'And if he's not dead,' said Marthinus, heaving another enormous log onto the fire, his large, lively face glowing in the light of the flames, 'then we wish him an unhindered voyage through life. Whether he turns up one day on your front stoep or not.'

'With his sneering mug,' said Nick, wryly.

'With his sneering mug and destructive energy,' said Marthinus. Nick laughed. Marthinus added another log. His face elated in the light of the fire.

'I tell you,' he said, 'just watch this fire burning now. That skein of smoke is drifting straight up to heaven.'

That evening they watched *Faust* by Alexander Sokurov. Marthinus had decided it was an appropriate video to recall Victor – whether dead or not – in spirit, to commemorate him, whatever. Nick found it a highly disturbing film. He found the image of Margaretha distressing. He found in her embodiment of total undefilement the potential for degradation. As if this potential for degradation were worse than the degradation and depravity itself. Like the invisible worm in an apparently healthy apple. He found it a disconcerting valedictory gesture for Victor

Schoeman. How strange, if they didn't even know whether he was one of the dead. The colours of the film also perturbed him – the tonalities of grey, so characteristic of the precise, cold tonalities of Flemish and Dutch painting. He found the image of Faust rooting in the innards of corpses for the origin of the soul disconcerting. But at the same time he found the film a good choice. It accorded with a sombreness in himself, which he could of late not escape. Its colours, mouldy greys – clay-grey, ochre-grey, brown-grey, in combination with black and greenish-black – were the colours of his own state of mind. Grey, he thought, it brought him up against grey once more. Grey that did not stimulate, but was perceptually inert. In this film it signified the inertia of death. He found it a cold, cruel, upsetting film, and he was grateful that he and Marthinus could sit in front of the fire afterwards.

Marthinus said: 'That's why I like Russian novels and Russian film-makers. The Western art world is directed at the body, at sexuality. The issues implicit in it are social issues. Eastern art, and I include Russia in that, concerns itself with spirit and transcendence. All subjects that are taboo in Western art. That's what I like. I like an engagement with spirit and transcendence. That's why I like so much what Menasse says. That's why I find reading Ezekiel so disconcerting. Even in spite of Mr K, a man for whom I have the greatest admiration, saying: Pay unconditional attention, there is only the *now*. With everything else we merely delude ourselves.'

*

On a Saturday morning in mid-August Nick and Marthinus were sitting in Marthinus' back garden. It was a beautiful, clear day. They were drinking tea. (Marthinus was a great tea-drinker, Nick had discovered.) Everything here was as carefully tended as in the front garden. Lawn, shrubs, vegetable beds. In the garden the five pigs were foraging.

Marthinus told Nick about Ezekiel, in whom he was immersing himself at the moment. Nick listened and he watched the pigs.

Marthinus said: 'I'm reading various versions of Ezekiel. I even bought myself the new translation of the Bible. Ezekiel had his vision on the 31st of July 593 BC! So there Ezekiel was standing on the banks of the River Chebar in Babylonia when a gigantic cloud bore down on him. On the banks of the River Chebar, on the 31st of July, just think! Couldn't be clearer than that! Nothing shabby about that vision. And no mean feat to describe that chariot so precisely. Remember, said God to Ezekiel, the children of Israel are a rebellious bunch. A hand is extended and God gives Ezekiel a roll of a book with lamentations and songs of mourning written on it. He must eat it. He must eat it and fill his bowels with it. What an image! Magnificent! Who could think up something like that nowadays? Nobody. Forget it. Not with the aid of any substance you can name. The modern imagination falls short of it.'

They drank tea. Marthinus talked. The pigs foraged tranquilly in the garden. The mountain was there, all rocky face and steep ravine. Awe-inspiring. No wonder Charelle hadn't wanted to look at it when she first arrived in Cape Town. Behind them was the sea. Although it was winter, the day was pleasantly warm.

Nick asked Marthinus how it had come about that he bought this house. Had he always known that he wanted to keep pigs?

Marthinus laughed. 'In the eighties I worked for the trade unions. That I've told you. That's where I met Victor Schoeman. Though he didn't last long there. He's not someone who can be subservient to another person. After that I was overseas for a while, and when I came back, I started working. I made money. I became a fat cat. I became alienated from my principles. I say that and am ashamed of it. I was heading straight for self-destruction. One day I was sitting in the Gardens. I was on the edge of despair. A man was sitting next to me. He turned to me and said "If you'll excuse me, I think you're a soul desperately in need." The man was Menasse. He gave me his card. Real estate. He showed me the house. He approved the emanations, as he called them. I bought it. We became friends. I started reading piles of stuff. I read everything that I'd never got round to before. Or that hadn't appealed to me. I simplified my life drastically. I acquired the pigs. I laid out the garden and now I maintain it on a daily basis. I try to do good where I can. I have enough to live on.'

Nick was taken by surprise by the story. A fat cat – he would never have suspected that of Marthinus.

Marthinus elaborated on the pigs. He said that each had a clearly distinguishable personality of its own. The black potbelly, Aunty, was the matriarch. She was named after the figure of death in one of Marthinus' most beloved novels. She was trouble-free and undeniably dominant. The oldest boar, President Burgers (he who had ended up in Nick's garden one morning some months ago), was a noble animal, said Marthinus. A ponderous personality. If he'd believed in reincarnation, which was not the case, then he'd have believed that this animal had been a noble ruler, somebody like Kubla Khan. The black-and-white sow, Bathsheba (for Nick the most interesting of the pigs), was headstrong – very contrary, a strong will. She did not let herself be dictated to or hemmed in. Very assertive. The young boar was Joseph, he was very eager to please, still very impressionable. And the youngest sow, Dolly, was a bit uncertain, but she was still young, she had yet to find her feet among this self-assured crowd.

Marthinus said he found it a valuable spiritual exercise to watch the pigs. A form of meditation. He'd often calmed down in their presence.

'The River Chebar is in Syria,' said Marthinus. 'Seven days on end Ezekiel sat dismayed and astonished among the Jewish exiles. Then he had to lie on his left side for 390 days. A day for each year that Israel had sinned. God would tie him down with ropes so that he couldn't turn on his other side. Now God gave him the recipe for the bread he had to eat every day. But Ezekiel put his foot down when God said: Bake the bread on human excrement. God made a concession – something he doesn't often do, believe me – right, Ezekiel can bake the bread on cow dung. On his side Ezekiel had to lie and prophesy. He had to warn Israel what they could expect when the Lord lost his temper and turned against a people. Parents would eat their children, and children their parents, among other treats. Tell Israel, said God, I'm speaking to them in my jealous zeal. Jealous zeal. Trust the God of Israel to come up with such a turn of phrase.

'Then by way of a change I read Mr K,' said Marthinus. 'In his own way as little inclined to countenance a compromise as the wrathful God of Israel. Pay attention! he said. See how thought chases its own tail!

'Now I wonder,' said Marthinus, 'did Ezekiel there on the banks of the River Chebar await God in his glorious manifestation in the same way as the young Jiddu awaited the emissaries of Annie Besant on a rock next to a different river?'

Nick did not know. He envied Marthinus his openness of mind.

Thirty-six

Liesa Appelgryn, in town, visited Nick in his studio. She looked at his work and said they were birds of a feather – bottom feeders – and she could see he also thoroughly implemented that toxic soil for his work. Bottom feeders, no less. His association was with the mud-coloured barbels with spiky stubble-beard that somebody once caught in the muddy water of some dam. He and Liesa drank a lot of whisky and had sex on the sofa where he had last spent the night in drunkenness, after Charelle's visit. Tits and pubic bush quite as rampant as in her paintings. She was enthusiastic, she was loud, she was appreciative of every kink and loop of the sexual act. He thought poor woman, who is contented with so little, or then at least pretends to be, because enthusiastic and appreciative of her sexual charms he most certainly was not. At half past two that morning she took a taxi back to her hotel. He slept on restlessly and dreamt of intricately stacked squares.

Marthinus asked him the following evening if he felt like watching Sokurov's *Faust* again. Initially Nick hesitated, but then consented anyway, and found the film even more upsetting than the previous time. He found the innocence of Margaretha as depicted bordering on the perverse. He struggled to find words for it when he was discussing it with Marthinus. Marthinus thought it was to do with the context in which Margaretha was represented – with the unearthly light falling on her face, with the dark leafy backgrounds against which she was delineated, and with the whole atmosphere of corruption and moral decay in the film.

A few days later Nick was sitting in the coffee shop where Buks Verhoef had been shot and where he'd seen Victor Schoeman a while ago. Something compelled him back to the place. Perhaps to convince himself that Victor was indeed permanently off the scene. Perished in the presence of three mentally disturbed people. He'd hardly sat down when his ex-student, Karlien, and her mother, the woman with whom he'd frolicked so joyously at Oesterklip, came into the coffee shop. By the time they saw each other, turning back was not an option. Mignon brought the child on her arm to his table. He leapt up clumsily and enquired after Karlien's physical welfare. Was she in better health? (She was wearing a scarf that was probably supposed to camouflage the scar artfully.) She looked pale and listless. The mother, by contrast, had a fetching (sexual) flush to her cheek. Over the child's head they caught and held each other's gaze for a few moments. Karlien was taking the rest of the year off, explained the mother (slightly breathlessly), and she was planning to do a course at a beauty academy in town the following year. Nick met Karlien's eyes briefly after this announcement from her mother. Cynical, with something provocative in it – an expression he'd never seen in her eyes in all the months that she'd sat passively and indecisively in his office. It caught him on the wrong foot. When they said goodbye, his and the mother's eyes met again for a few moments. Shortly afterwards he left, his coffee barely drunk.

At the end of August he said to Marthinus, look, as far as the sale of the house was concerned, he was going to hang on now and see who would come up next with an offer to convert his house into an art brothel. Sometime soon some crook was sure to present himself. A shortage of crooks there had never been. In the meantime he could probably start emptying out the polluted rooms – the rooms in which, according to Menasse, the energy had been disrupted – and chuck out everything that he didn't need. He had a lot of rubbish in there, clutter that he'd schlepped around for years. Look, he said, he knew it would be a good idea to get Menasse to show him the ropes. Instead of moping around in his house thinking all sorts of unproductive thoughts, as was his wont, he might as well sit in those rooms and think of the Good. But he'd thought about it long and hard, he said, he couldn't do it. As he'd said before, it wasn't his scene. He'd be violating himself – and his own integrity – if he were to force himself to do something like that. If there were such a thing as negative energy in his house, if Menasse were right – if there was a cloud of regret and melancholy hanging over his house, as Menasse had clearly sensed – then he'd have to find some other way of living with it, or of driving it out. He felt like a prick having to admit it, but he was saying it now in any case. Furthermore he could probably also ask Jan Botha whether it would be possible to do volunteer work at the Salt River mortuary on Saturday mornings, but he didn't feel up to that either.

Marthinus said: Oh Lord, he understood completely. If it wasn't Nick's scene, it wasn't his scene. But if he were ever to change his mind, he was perfectly prepared to tackle room by room with Nick. He wasn't all that sure himself what the Good was, but he didn't think it really mattered much. Just sitting still and focusing on melancholy and regret was probably good enough.

Nick thanked him. In all these months, he said to Marthinus, he'd been in all respects a reliable and supportive friend.

Marthinus said don't even mention it. Done with pleasure. Meanwhile he'd organised them a whole series of Pasolini DVDs: *Oedipus Rex*, *Medea* and *The Gospel According to St Matthew*.

Nick said he was glad, he liked Pasolini's work.

'Oh Lord,' exclaimed Marthinus, 'just think – Oedipus! Medea! The St Matthew gospel! The little cluster of women and the apostles in fluttering robes advancing towards the cross through the rippling grass, looking as if they're standing still in one spot! Mary Magdalene stumbling and falling, stumbling and falling, supported by the women in black robes. Everything in black and white. The little cluster that seems not to be making any progress, but that carries on moving, stumbling, against the wind, with the fluttering robes, and the waving grass! Brilliant!'

Towards the end of their trip, Isabel had one day, sitting across from him in the museum cafeteria, suddenly interrupted her bitter diatribe and said: Console me. It was so unexpected that he didn't know whether he'd heard her aright. Console me, she said again. He was caught unawares. They looked at each other. He didn't know what to say. She looked down. She'd seen his incapacity. There were tears in her eyes. She got up. He hurried to the Oriental rooms, to the depictions of bucolic bliss – where the locust moves its leg in the fifth month, and shakes its wing in the sixth month, on a paper scroll from the eleventh century.

In the afternoons she usually read, but she didn't discuss with him what she'd read. Only once she told him about something she'd read that had made a deep impression on her. It was in a novel based on the true story of the experiences of a young boy who'd been separated from his parents during the Second Sudanese Civil War. She told him that the boy told about another boy who along the way had found a deep hole and had climbed into it. The hole had been formed by a bomb. His friends had said goodbye to him because they were used to boys leaving the group in various ways or dying. The boy remained in the hole for three days. He didn't move; he enjoyed the silence inside the hole. He dug himself a small cave on the one side of the bomb crater and with straw from a half-burnt hut fashioned a small door to cover the entrance. In this way he could also hide from animals. Nobody visited him or sniffed him out, neither man nor beast. Nobody knew he was there. When he got hungry the first day he crawled out of the hole to the deserted village, to a hut where he scrabbled a bone out of the ash. On the blackened bone there were only about three mouthfuls of goat's meat, but it kept him satisfied for a whole day. He drank from puddles of water and crawled back to his hole, where he stayed day and night. On the third day he decided to die, because it was warm in the hole and there were no sounds inside. And he did die on that day, because he was ready. Not one of the boys who'd walked with him saw him die in that hole, but they all knew that the story was true. This tale, Isabel said, had moved her deeply, because she also had a need to climb into a deep hole like that and to stay there day and night. For an indeterminate time. She also had the desire to die, she said, but she was probably not ready yet, because she was still alive.

Thirty-seven

It's icy cold. It's the end of August. In a short while the first freezing spring showers will start falling. By day the mountains are swathed in swirling clouds of mist. Sometimes they are completely veiled by these. The rain falls in soaking flurries. Five pied crows are starkly etched against the misty landscape. I watch them. At night the wind keens around the corners of the house. My Neanderthal skull of wire and white beads stands on my bedside table. Its eye sockets are enormous.

I am alone. That I have always been. I have my friend Willem Wepener, for whom colour is a guiding principle. I have you. We share the memory of Jacobus, in life, in death. Willem and I saw him in the small back room with the green Mr Price curtain. In death his once mobile face was calm, monumental. I have the pleasure of the Olivier brothers' lovely, tantalising, at times obscene videos. Willem has Arikha. I have the memory of the salty, stinking sea, of the transformation of silkworms, of the narrow head of the noble black greyhound bitch. I have the image of Ricardo Reis, the alter ego of Fernando Pessoa, keeping vigil in Ricardo's room at the foot of his bed. I have a prospect of the mountains, of the horizon, where mountain and sky meet, where the sun rises every morning, with more splendour than I can ever find words or tears to express.

*

In the early hours, the hour before it gets light, I hear somebody say my name. A man's voice – deep, imperative, but quite tinny, with a slight echo.

I wait to hear what else will be said. Nothing. Nothing else. I lie and wait. The voice was distinct. With an echo. But it leaves no after-echo. I lie and wait to hear if the voice repeats my name. But it doesn't happen. I lie and wait and listen until I hear the birds singing outside.

*

The café where we met at the beginning of the year, after we hadn't seen each other for a long time, the day when it rained so hard, no longer exists. It either burnt down or was converted into an art gallery. Anything is possible. I hear from you sometimes, a short email, or a postcard, even. You are restless, you stay on the move. I must ask you, someday, what purpose it serves.

Like you, I experience the town as a treacherous place, where one could perish in obscurity, even though the moon here is more glorious than anywhere else. At night when the moon is full I open my mouth. The wind blows through it as if through a grotto. It feels as if I am eating the wind, and am fulfilled by it.

Ingrid Winterbach's novels have won numerous awards, including the M-Net Prize, the Hertzog Prize and the University of Johannesburg Prize. Her work has also been published in the Netherlands, France and the USA. Winterbach is also a visual artist. She lives in Stellenbosch.